GUILTY
SIN

ALFA INVESTIGATIONS

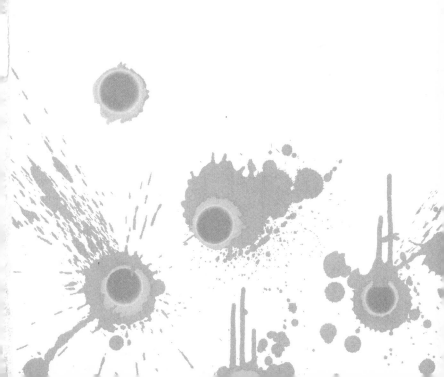

Published by Bliss Ink
Editor Silently Correcting Your Grammar
Proofread by Julie Deaton and Rosa Sharon
Cover Design © Lori Jackson Designs
Formatted by Allusion Graphics

GUILTY
SIN

ALFA INVESTIGATIONS

CHELLE BLISS

Hey there ALFA lover,

Welcome back! Sorry for the long lag between *Wicked Impulse* and *Guilty Sin*. I know many of you were worried about Ret, but you shouldn't. He's pretty badass and knows how to throw a punch.

So, here's *Guilty Sin*. Ret's story.

But... this one comes with a WARNING.

Guilty Sin is about LOVE. Unconditional, uncontrollable, fall-to-your-knees-can't-live-without-the-person LOVE. But it's also about LUST, passion, and pleasures of the flesh.

There's MENAGE ahead. If it's too much sexiness for you, you can skip the spicy bits and still have a kickass story to read.

I hope you love *Guilty Sin* as much as I do. Sometimes the words come out and I have no control over where the story goes. That's how *Guilty Sin* happened.

Enjoy,
Chelle, xoxo

CHAPTER ONE

RET

Dropping my bag to the floor, I collapsed backward onto the mattress. I focused on the stain on the ceiling, wondering how in the hell anything got up there.

"Dude, I thought you were smarter than this," James pleaded on the other end of the phone, unhappy because I took off without bringing someone as backup.

"I've been after this guy for far too long. I know his kind, and I can't risk someone fucking things up."

"When do *we* ever fuck things up?"

"We don't, but Solease is far too dangerous. I don't want anyone else getting hurt."

Martin Solease had been on the FBI's most wanted list for over twenty years, and in the last five, he'd climbed to the number one spot. He'd skipped bail while awaiting trial for murdering his entire family, and then he'd racked up a handful more deaths while eluding the authorities over the last two decades.

"But it's okay if you do?"

He had a point. Being in harm's way wasn't anything new to me. I'd spent my life tracking down assholes, first for the military and then as a bounty hunter. It's what I did. All I knew. The one thing I couldn't get used to was putting those around me, people I cared for, in danger too.

"If I get killed, it's no big deal, man. I don't have kids to worry about like the rest of you."

"Dumb fuck," he hissed. "Alese will have my balls if you die. You know that, right?"

"True that." I laughed, picturing her marching into ALFA and grabbing James by the nuts. "I'll check in with you tomorrow. I'm going to get some shut-eye before I head out tomorrow."

"Bear's coming after you."

"Call him off."

Damn. My father was the last person I wanted hot on my trail and swooping in to save the day like he always tried to do. He wasn't smooth or stealthy like he thought he was; he came in basically announcing himself like a wrecking ball.

"Nope. This one's off the books and doesn't fall under my jurisdiction. Bear's your problem, not mine."

I narrowed my gaze on the stain. "That's bullshit, James."

"I have to run. Keep in contact, and let me know when you're headed back."

"Yeah, yeah."

I let my phone drop to the mattress as soon as the call disconnected and closed my eyes. Bear might have been headed my way, but that didn't mean he'd catch me before I was on the move again. I was sure, at this point, Fran and Alese were climbing the walls, coming up with crazy ways to punish me for my foolish behavior.

When I finally opened my eyes five hours later, I had ten text messages and two missed calls. James was the two calls, probably to bitch me out again, and all the text messages were from Alese.

"I know you are dead set on going after Solease, but I need you to make a quick pit stop in Atlanta first. Details are in your email. I'll call back in a few hours," James said on my voice mail.

Groaning, I pushed myself upright and blinked away the last bit of haze from my eyes before I attempted to read James's lengthy email waiting in my inbox.

The subject line read *Personal Favor – Important and For Your Eyes Only.* I figured it was a ploy, something to stop me from going after Solease, but as I scanned the details of the file along with James's notes, I knew I was wrong.

Nya Halstead was a twenty-five-year-old woman who'd cut off all communication with her family two months ago. Her mother, a Tampa resident and trustee of a local charity foundation, had contacted ALFA to assist in locating her daughter without law enforcement involvement.

The last known location for Nya was in Atlanta, as she'd graduated from Georgia State University just before her disappearance. Mrs. Halstead believed her daughter had fallen for the wrong man and was being held against her will, unable to contact her family. The Halsteads were willing to pay ALFA one hundred thousand dollars for the safe return of their daughter.

Included with the email was a photo of Nya, smiling with her diploma in one hand and her graduation cap in the other. Her long, wavy, brown hair flowed out to the side, carried by the wind, glistening in the sun. Her big brown eyes twinkled as the apples of her cheeks almost kissed the bottom. Her wide smile was infectious,

3

framed by full lips and perfectly straight, white teeth. She reminded me of a young Mandy Moore, a natural beauty.

As I zoomed in to get a better look, the shiny silver collar with a diamond encrusted lock that she wore around her neck caught my eye.

The design wasn't something that could be found at a department store or worn purely for decoration. I'd seen the style before, the handiwork of the only well-known BDSM jeweler below the Mason-Dixon line.

James's notes included information he'd uncovered through our contacts in the Atlanta area. Nya had been a member at Charmed, an exclusive BDSM club, catering to the filthy rich socialites with too much cash and a thirst for the dark side. She hadn't been seen at the club since she disappeared, but she had been a submissive to a Diego Lopez for a year before she vanished.

James had been able to confirm that Nya was last seen with Diego and that Diego would be at Charmed tonight, therefore leaving his home unattended, allowing me just enough time for a thorough search of the premises.

I was out of my room in under ten minutes, coffee in hand from the lobby, and headed toward my car.

Just when I thought things couldn't get any more fucked up, my father was leaning against his car with his arms folded, working a toothpick between his lips. "Morning, sunshine."

Tightening my grip on my bag, I stalked toward the car and cracked my neck. "What are you doing here? Go home, Pop."

He pulled the toothpick from his mouth and smiled. "I'm happy to see you too."

I popped the trunk as he pushed off his car and walked toward me. I practically threw my bag inside the back before slamming the lid. "How did you find me?"

"GPS." He shrugged like it was the most logical answer in the world and I was an idiot for asking.

"You have a tracker up my ass?"

"Nope." He gave me a big, toothy grin, thoroughly impressed with himself. "Tracked you through the company cell phone, wiseass."

I made a quick mental note to ditch the ALFA cell phone as soon as I got back so shit like that didn't happen again. "Fuckin' James." Crossing my arms over my chest, I turned to face him and stared him down. "Go home. Be with Fran."

"Hell, son. Fran sent me here."

I glanced toward the brilliant orange and yellow sky as the sun started to peek over the trees. "For the love of God."

"God ain't got nothing to do with me being here— that's all Fran. I don't want to hear that woman's nonstop pecking about you being in danger while I sit at home, drinking beer and relaxing. I'm going with you, and that's all there's to say about it. You got a problem with it, you call Fran and talk to her."

I cursed under my breath, but I didn't dare call Fran. She wasn't someone I wanted to mess with, and the woman had a tongue more wicked than most men I knew. The last person I needed pissed at me was her.

"I'm not going to Tennessee."

"Where are we headed?"

"Atlanta, but you're still not going."

The man had been absent for almost thirty years of my life, but since the day I agreed to work at ALFA, he'd been practically up my ass, trying to make up for lost time. Sometimes I found his attention palatable, but times like this, where he put his nose where it didn't belong, I wanted to sock him square in the jaw.

He arched an eyebrow, not the least bit shocked at the news. "Halstead girl?"

"Yep."

"Sex club shit?" He held his breath.

"Yep."

He pointed to himself with his thumbs, displaying a cocky grin. "Then I'm your man."

"This isn't really your *thing*," I told him.

"I don't have a *thing*." He put the toothpick back between his lips before rolling it with his tongue.

"Fine," I groaned and finally gave in. I wasn't winning this battle. I knew that much. I wasn't burning time with an argument I had no hope of winning. "Get in the car. We'll figure out a plan on the way."

"Hell yeah! Let's go fuck up some shit."

Dad waited down the street, watching for any sign of Diego while I headed toward the house.

"Coast is still clear," he whispered into the microphone connected to my headset.

"You don't need to whisper. Only I can hear you." I rolled my eyes as I worked the tension wrench and pick in the back door lock.

When the lock finally opened, I moved quickly, searching for any trace of the girl. "First floor's clear," I told Pop. "Moving upstairs."

"You're good to go, champ."

This was probably just another dead-end lead in a missing person's case because families often went after someone or something they couldn't understand. Fetish lifestyles were usually their first target because it wasn't mainstream enough for them to wrap their heads around.

In the last few years, the stigma attached to BDSM had waned, and the lifestyle had grown more mainstream after a popular fiction series had become a pop culture phenomenon. But there were still people who believed the gruesome, overdramatized, and often misguided facts presented by the media about the dangers of sex clubs and their ties to human trafficking.

I made my way through the upstairs, clearing each room except the last. With my gun drawn and flashlight in hand, I pushed open the door, ready for whoever or whatever was on the other side.

All I found was darkness. I spun around, wondering how our intel had been so wrong. This entire thing had been a waste of time. I should've been tracking down Solease, finally putting that bastard behind bars instead of searching a posh mansion on the outskirts of Atlanta. By now, half the bounty hunters in the country were hundreds of miles closer to him, circling like vultures to get their hands on the reward. I'd never be able to make up enough ground to catch up.

I stalked toward the door and holstered my weapon, ready to get the hell out of there before Diego came home and a waste of time turned into a clusterfuck of epic proportions.

Then I heard it. Faint, but my mind wasn't playing tricks on me. I rushed toward the excessively tall bed and fell to my knees, lifting up the bed skirt and exposing a metal cage underneath. A woman huddled near the opposite corner with her knees pulled to her chest, burying her face. She whimpered as I pointed my flashlight at her, and she scurried farther away, pressing her back flush against the other side.

"Ma'am," I said softly, shining the light on myself so she could see my face. "Your mother, Jeanine Halstead, sent me."

"Mom," she whispered with a shaky voice and peered over her knees, shrouded in a pile of brown hair.

Flashing my light on her again, I could finally see the big brown eyes from the photo staring back at me. "Hang tight. I'll have you out of there in a minute."

Nya scurried across the hardwood floor on her knees with tears running down her face. "Help me," she pleaded and wrapped her fingers around the bars until her knuckles turned white.

Diego was lucky he wasn't home. It would've been my pleasure to torture him slowly and watch him die, begging for his life like a little bitch, after the way I'd found her.

I darted my eyes to hers as she stared at me with her face pressed against the bars while I worked the lock. "You're safe now, little one. You're safe," I told her as I pried open the last chamber inside the lock, popping the metal clasp.

Nya crawled out, wearing nothing except the collar from the photograph. She could barely stand as she tried to push herself off the floor. Without a second thought, I wrapped my arms around her before she collapsed, cradling her. She clung to me, her fingers laced tightly around my neck as I jammed everything into my back pockets.

Running down the steps, I was out the front door and heading toward the car with Nya safely in my arms. She rested her head against my chest, still and silent as I stalked down the driveway toward my father. His eyes grew wide as soon as he saw the girl in my arms.

"The fuck. She's naked," he said in a low tone as I motioned for him to open the door so I could get her inside and us the fuck out of there.

"I didn't have time to dress her." I placed Nya in the back seat and grabbed a blanket I'd kept in the back just in case. "You're safe now," I repeated, trying to get her to calm down as I wrapped the blanket around her naked, trembling body.

"Don't go," she said, her voice soft and laced with fear as I backed away, about to close the door.

"This guy's an animal and deserves to be put down," my father said behind me, pacing next to the car like a caged lion. "I'll drive. You look after the girl." He didn't wait for me to answer as he opened the driver's-side door.

I didn't have time to argue, and with one look at Nya's face, I knew I couldn't sit in the front and leave her in the back, trembling and alone. Getting in on the other side, I maintained a safe distance from Nya—for her sake, not mine. After a traumatic experience, I knew human touch and even nearness could be overwhelming to a person. But instead of staying on the other side of the back seat, she crawled in my lap and wrapped her arms around my neck.

My dad's eyes were glued to the rearview mirror, watching in just as much shock as me as she placed her head on my chest. "Go," I told him, ready to get the hell out of Atlanta.

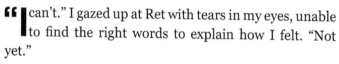

CHAPTER TWO

NYA

"I can't." I gazed up at Ret with tears in my eyes, unable to find the right words to explain how I felt. "Not yet."

I couldn't go home. Not yet, at least. My parents already thought I was a freak, and if they found out what happened, they'd have me committed.

"I promised, Nya," Ret said from the bed next to me.

I chewed my lip and pulled the strings of my hoodie tighter, wishing I could hide. "My parents won't understand."

He rubbed the back of his neck, cursing under his breath. "I don't know if I understand either."

I kicked my feet, knocking the backs of my heels against the box spring and stared down at the dirty carpeting. "Do you know anything about..." I stopped, wondering the best way to approach the topic and to explain BDSM to him.

He nodded with a slight smile, eyes still on me like he could read my thoughts. "I do."

"Oh," I whispered, rolling the strings of the sweatshirt between my fingertips and digging my toes into the carpeting. "Diego was my Dom, and at first, I entered into our relationship willingly."

"Go on," he said softly.

"But after I graduated, I was ready to go to New York. I had a huge job opportunity there, and I thought Diego was coming with me."

"Did he say he was?"

"Not exactly." I closed my eyes and sighed, knowing I was about to sound like a complete idiot. "He said he wouldn't be able to let me go, but I figured he meant he was moving with me even though he never said the words."

"Don't be so hard on yourself. It was an easy mistake to make."

Covering my face with my hands, I laughed into my palms and tried to keep the tears at bay. "Two days before I was supposed to leave, Diego summoned me to his house, and I obeyed, and I never stepped foot outside of his mansion again."

"Your parents understand it's not your fault, Nya. Things like this happen. I wouldn't have a job otherwise."

I turned my head with my hands still covering my face and peeked through the slits between my fingers. "Dumb people like me, huh?" I mumbled.

"I will not allow you to talk about yourself like that, little one." His voice was firm yet kind. "We all make mistakes. Your parents will be happy just to have you home and safe."

I dropped my hands to my lap. "They think I'm a freak." I looked him straight in the eyes. "They'll think I deserved what happened to me and that I'll need Jesus to save me from my sexual deviance."

"There's nothing wrong with enjoying pleasure of any kind as long as it's consensual."

I held in my laughter because he'd clearly never met my parents. They made the Westboro Baptists appear sane. If anything involved pleasure, they were against it...especially sex.

"Your parents can't force you to do anything against your will. If they truly believe you deserved what happened, then you either set them straight, or you need to learn to deal with them from a distance to maintain your identity as well as your self-esteem. You're an adult, and although they're your parents, they're not in charge of your life anymore."

"It's easy to say, Sir, but not so easy to do."

"Ret, please," he corrected me.

"Ret," I replied and paused for a moment. "That man in the other room. He's your father, yeah?"

He sighed heavily and nodded. "Afraid so."

Ret's father, the man with the long beard and weathered face, didn't have an unkind word when he spoke to his son. He was patient, affectionate, and everything humanity should be, especially in regard to family.

"You're lucky to have such an understanding father. Mine is a minister, and sex, especially before marriage, that deviates from the norm is a hard limit for him."

"My father is the furthest thing from understanding, but the man is flawed himself. He can't pass judgment on me when he's messed up so much in his own life."

"At least he doesn't speak the word of God, putting the fear of damnation in you and preach at you every chance he gets."

My father had pounded the Gospel into my head for as long as I could remember. I sat in church every Sunday, the well-behaved daughter, at the side of my perfect mother. My father's sermons were filled with fiery hell and a message of redemption only through true faith and complete submission to the word of God.

Even as I'd sat there, listening to the words, I never believed a word of his speeches. The message of the Bible was forgiveness, generosity, and kindness. We were all supposedly children of God and should be accepted for who we were and not punished for how we were created.

When I'd question my father about faith and the existence of God, in private, of course, he'd go into an hour-long diatribe about my heathen ways and my eventual damnation that no amount of prayers could stop.

Ret's face softened, and he almost smiled. "Oh, he's preached, but his words aren't anything you'd find in the Bible."

I pulled my leg under my bottom and faced Ret. "That's what a good father should do. He shouldn't judge you and damn you to hell."

"True." He finally smiled.

"If I go back, I'll never be the same again," I said, holding back the tears because, even after the hell I'd lived, I didn't want to change into a bible-thumpin' robot. I didn't want to forget who I was, and there was no way in hell I'd become a clone of my parents, even if that meant pushing them out of my life forever.

"You don't know that."

"I do," I told him because I did.

"Maybe the time you spent apart changed them. The worry they felt for the last few months had to wear on them and may have softened their views. I'm sure they'll be more accepting."

I arched an eyebrow, calling bullshit, because I knew my parents better than anyone. "So, when they find out that in order to live out my sexual fantasy, I was a submissive, giving myself fully to a man who locked me up against my will, they'll think what?" I paused, rubbing my palms against the baggy sweat pants Ret had given me, and sucked in a breath. "They'll say 'Hallelujah, at least she's safe'? Come on. We both know better than that."

"Weirder shit has happened." He shrugged.

"Yeah," I muttered and took a deep breath.

I knew people changed, but there was no way my parents' viewpoint had made such a dramatic shift since I disappeared. If Jesus didn't make them nice, my disappearance wouldn't either.

"We better get some sleep. We have a long drive tomorrow," he said before turning off the bedside light.

I crawled under the covers and tried to get comfortable, but I hadn't worn clothing in two months. The feel of it against my skin felt foreign and intrusive.

Most nights, Diego had me in his bed, with my arms secured to the headboard and my ankles shackled to the end of the bed. He'd curl his bare body around my naked flesh, pinning me.

When Diego wasn't home, he locked me in the small, three-foot-tall cage in complete darkness. Those were the times I liked most. I didn't fear the blackness or being alone, because nothing or no one could hurt me. I dreaded his footsteps across the floor, coming to uncage me, only to chain me down again.

Pulling my legs to my chest, I turned to the side and stared at Ret through the darkness. His body covered more than half the bed, and his feet hung off the end, making him look like a giant...godlike, even.

Don't go there. Get your shit together, Nya.
You're free.

CHAPTER THREE

RET

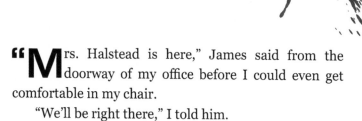

"Mrs. Halstead is here," James said from the doorway of my office before I could even get comfortable in my chair.

"We'll be right there," I told him.

Nya sat across from me, twisting her hands in her lap without an ounce of excitement on her face. I didn't imagine there would be any. Not after everything she'd told me. Her relationship with her parents was complicated, but that was typically how it was when children didn't fit into the pretty little mold that had been laid out before them.

I'd never had such issues. With my father off doing his own thing, my aunts raised my sister and me, but never once did they judge me for anything I did or wanted.

"Are you ready, Nya?" I asked, watching her closely and looking for any signs she'd run.

She swept her hand across her cheek, maybe wiping away a tear or as a nervous tic, but she didn't bring her eyes to mine. "I guess so. I don't have a choice."

"We all have choices."

She stood, eyes downturned toward the carpeting, but she didn't say another word. I'd taken part in a few family reunions, but usually, the air crackled with so much excitement before the big moment that everyone in the office was pumped.

With Nya, that was not the case. From the moment she walked into ALFA, she made it quite clear that her parents were no better than the man who'd held her against her will.

The very idea of that was hard for us to wrap our heads around. Each of us had parents who weren't judgmental. They might have been overbearing and a pain in the ass, but they never tried to force us into something or made us feel like shit about our decisions.

Nya followed James down the hallway as I walked behind them, rubbing a knot out of my shoulders. I was ready to collapse after a restless night's sleep, wearing far too much clothing. All I wanted to do was get home and crawl under the covers with Alese, leaving everything behind.

James entered the conference room first, Nya practically hiding behind him. She glanced back at me as she stepped inside, and my stomach twisted from the pained expression on her face.

James stopped near the end of the conference table with Nya almost glued to his back. "Mr. and Mrs. Halstead."

A woman popped up from her chair as she glanced around. "Where is she?"

The woman exuded money with immaculate clothing, perfect hair, and flashy jewelry that was way too big for her small frame.

Nya stayed behind James for another moment before finally moving to his side, making herself visible to everyone. She lifted her face, brushing her brown hair over her shoulders, and straightened.

"Nya," her mother said, slowly approaching her with her arms outstretched.

Nya hadn't looked up and seemed frozen, almost catatonic, as she stood next to James. There wasn't any happiness about this event that should've been nothing less than joyous. Even when her mother wrapped her arms around Nya, giving her a tight hug, she didn't reciprocate.

Nya's hands were at her sides as she stood perfectly straight with her mother still holding her tightly. She stiffened even more when Mrs. Halstead whispered something in her ear.

"Nya," her father said, not moving from his spot, only giving her a slight and very sterile head dip as Mrs. Halstead finally released her.

"We can't thank you gentlemen enough for finding our little girl. We'll take her off your hands," Mr. Halstead said, motioning for what appeared to be a doctor they'd brought with them.

My hands curled into tight fists, and James's went rigid. We were here for a happy reunion, not for giving Nya over from one type of imprisonment to another.

The man stood, moving toward Nya with a syringe in his hands. She stepped back, moving closer to me and putting as much distance between herself and him as she could.

What the fuck was wrong with these people? They were exactly as Nya had described them and even worse than I could've ever imagined.

"Now, Nya. This is Dr. Faraday. He's here from the Biltmore Institute. He's going to help you get better."

"I'm not sick," she finally spoke, raising her head up to face her father.

James stepped in front of Nya, and I pulled her back to my side, blocking the doctor and her family from her.

"You're not well either, dear. Just let the good doctor give you something to help you settle down."

"We can't let you do that, sir," James told Mr. Halstead.

"Shh," I said to Nya who was practically in tears as she stared up at me with the widest eyes.

She wrapped her hand around my arm, tethering herself to me. "Don't let them take me," she begged.

"Mr. Caldo, we paid you for the safe return of our daughter and nothing more. She's ours."

James didn't back down as he squared his shoulders and stood his ground. "She's not property, sir."

"What's going on here?" my father asked from behind me.

I peered back, giving him a look that said there wasn't a damn thing good happening. As if on instinct, I grabbed Nya's hand and passed her off to Bear. He took her without question, ushering her toward his office as James and I blocked the doctor and Mr. Halstead from advancing.

"You have no right to keep our daughter from us." Mrs. Halstead stalked toward the door, trying her best to get past us, but it wasn't happening.

I stepped to the side, obscuring the entire doorway and stopping anyone in the room from leaving or going after Nya. Bear wouldn't let anyone get their hands on her. He'd protect her with his life, and there wasn't a person at ALFA who would let anything happen to her, including me.

"Mrs. Halstead, your daughter doesn't need to be drugged and institutionalized. She's been through enough. I've spoken to her at length, and she's of sound mind," James said.

"Where did you get your degree, good sir?" the doctor asked, syringe still in his hands.

"My job is to know people. I've worked at the CIA, and I have skills you could only dream of, Dr. Faraday. Unless you have a court order to commit Nya, you will not touch her, and she won't be leaving with you today," James told her father.

"How dare you?" Mr. Halstead stepped up to James, but he didn't so much as flinch.

We'd been confronted by men a hell of a lot meaner and more dangerous than this rich asshole. He wouldn't get far, no matter how much he raised his voice and no matter how much he threatened us. Nya wasn't going anywhere as long as she had the team at ALFA behind her.

"We paid you for her return, Mr. Caldo, and you haven't delivered."

"I refuse to take any more of your money. I will not allow you to force her to be committed, and we won't permit her to leave with you today under any circumstances."

Thomas entered the room, and I took the chance to duck out, letting them handle the Halsteads while I went to find Nya and tell her she had nothing to worry about.

When I entered my father's office, Nya was sitting in the corner, holding her knees, and rocking gently with her face buried. Bear looked at me and shrugged, completely lost on how to handle a situation like this.

I motioned for him to step out, leaving Nya and me alone to talk. Slowly, I lowered myself down to the floor next to her, waiting in silence until the door clicked closed.

"Nya," I said, keeping my voice soft and calming. The last thing she needed was something more to jar her, pushing her deeper inside herself. "You're safe."

She slowed her rocking but kept her face hidden, pressed against her knees. "I told you they were horrible people."

"You did." I wanted to touch her, soothe her in some fashion, but I knew better than that. After everything she'd been through, touch was something that needed to be avoided if possible.

"I'm not sick, Ret."

"I know you're not."

"You should've left me with Diego."

My entire body tensed as anger flooded me. Not toward Nya, but her asshole parents for making her feel as though she was better off with a sick fuck like Diego. "Don't ever say that. It doesn't matter what your parents want, Nya. We won't let them take you."

She lifted her head, and her eyes met mine. She blinked, probably figuring I was full of shit. But I hoped I'd gained a small sliver of her trust in the last twenty-four hours so that she'd have faith in my word. "I don't have to leave with them?"

"You're an adult. They can't force you to do anything, and I won't allow them to lay a hand on you. I didn't save your life for you to lose it again."

She chewed on her bottom lip and stared at me. I let her process my words as I sat a foot away, not moving. "Where am I going to go, Ret?"

I hadn't thought that far ahead. None of us had. We saw a woman in need. No one in the office wanted to hand her over to be placed in a worse situation than she was before. "I have a guest room you can use until you figure out your next move."

She glanced at my finger, catching sight of my ring. "But what about your wife?"

Pressing my thumb against the gold circle, I twisted the thick ring around my finger. "We're not married. She's my partner, my submissive, but not my wife."

"Will she have a problem with it?"

"I'll talk with Alese, but I'm sure she'll be okay. She'll understand."

For the first time since I found her, I saw a smile spread across Nya's face. Alese probably wouldn't be overjoyed by the idea, but that was for me to handle.

"Say that again."

Alese's expression was hard to pin down. I knew her better than anyone in the world, but in that moment, I wasn't certain if she wanted to kick me in the balls or not.

Alese and I met a few years ago. I was a Dom and she was a bit lost, not sure if she was a top, bottom, or switch. I had been about to give up my search for a submissive and move to a new city to start over again, when Alese became something of a pet project. My goal was to help her figure out where exactly she fell in the lifestyle, but after spending time with her, I knew I wanted no one else.

She tried my patience at times. Her road to discovering her inner submissive wasn't an easy one, but it sure as hell was entertaining. I couldn't imagine being with anyone else either. She challenged me in so many ways.

"She needed someplace to go. I thought she could crash here for a bit."

"Is the girl damaged?"

I rubbed my hands together and debated how many of the details I should divulge to Alese. She deserved to know everything, but I didn't want to throw it all in her lap at once. "She doesn't appear so. She needs to be treated with kindness after what she's been through, but her parents don't seem to understand what happened or the lifestyle she was trying to enjoy when her world ended."

"Tell me how she ended up a prisoner."

"She met a Dom, much like you met me, and he made her believe they were going to have a relationship. Before she knew it, she was his captive without any communication with the outside world. What started out as fun led to her being locked in a cage under his bed and his sex slave."

Alese peered around me to look toward the car where Nya sat in the passenger seat, waiting for my sign. "That's just awful."

"It is." I nodded as Alese's body relaxed, and I knew she wasn't about to say no.

"Her parents wanted to commit her?"

"Yep. They had a doctor with them, waiting to drug her."

"I can't imagine. She can stay until she's back on her feet."

"Thank you, *piccola*."

Alese stepped toward me, wrapping her arms around my middle and burying her face in my chest. "You didn't even have to ask, you know. I wouldn't have protested if you told me she was staying."

I wrapped my arms around her and held her tighter than usual. "I'm your Master in the bedroom, but we're partners in life, Alese. I couldn't bring a stranger into our home without you having a say in the situation."

"It'll be nice to have another woman around, even if it's only for a little while. There's way too much testosterone in this place for me sometimes."

I laughed softly and touched her chin, raising her face to mine. "I'm sure you two will get along well."

"I'll help her any way I can."

I placed my lips against hers, kissing her as her boyfriend and not her Dom. Our relationship had changed over the years, leaving our play for the bedroom or the club. Alese, although a complete submissive, wasn't my slave. She had her own life to live, and I embraced everything she wanted to do as long as it didn't take her away from me.

I had no doubt that she would be good with Nya. She'd help her through this time, building her up and helping her transition back into society under her careful eye. Alese had a way with people, softer than I'd ever been and more loving toward everyone.

CHAPTER FOUR

NYA

Sitting in the car, I watched Ret as he spoke to Alese. She kept peering over his shoulder as she stood on the front steps, staring at me through the car window. I couldn't imagine what she thought about him bringing home a strange woman.

The house was three stories, white with gray accents, a stark contrast to the deep, cloudless sky behind the structure. Peeking through the space between Ret's house and the neighbors, the ocean crashed against the sand and sea gulls flew overhead, almost beckoning everyone to follow.

Ret glanced backward and smiled before facing Alese again. Maybe I should've gone with my parents, letting them do whatever they wanted to make me better instead of adding complications to Ret's life since he was the man who saved me. He'd already gone above and beyond his job, making me feel safe when I hadn't even thought that was possible.

Ret and Alese were a perfect pair. His wide shoulders, imposing height, and masculine face were like something straight out of a Hollywood movie. He'd absolutely be one of those badass characters who put down the bad guy with a few kicks and a knockout punch to the face. Alese was the complete opposite. Smaller framed, with delicate features, and totally feminine in every way possible. Her large breasts, tanned by the Florida sun, practically spilled out of her tank top.

I was just about to get out and call the entire thing off when Alese walked toward the car. At first, I wanted to sink down into the seat and disappear, but as she got closer, she smiled.

"Hey, Nya." She stood near the passenger door, not too close, yet close enough that I could see the tiny freckles dotting her chest. "You want to come inside?" she asked.

I twisted my hands in my lap, glancing down for a moment. "I should just leave," I whispered, probably looking like a lunatic sitting in the car carrying on a conversation with myself.

"Come on. Let's get you settled and out of the heat before you melt in there, princess."

The handle jiggled, and I snapped out of whatever moment I was having and looked up as Alese opened the door. "Sorry," I whispered. I didn't know if I was sorry I had ignored her so far or I hadn't bothered to climb out of the car myself, but saying the words made me feel better.

"Don't be silly. There's nothing to be sorry about."

I climbed out, inhaling the salty-humid air for the first time in months.

"Beach lover?" she asked.

"I used to be."

I'd missed the ocean. I'd spent countless days lying on the white sand of Florida when I was younger, listening to the waves roll in, crashing against the shore before rolling back out again. I never really appreciated the beauty and tranquility of living so close to the ocean until I didn't have it anymore. There were nights, more than I could remember or wanted to, where I lay inside that cage, closed my eyes, and dreamed that I was lying under the scorching hot sun, soaking up the rays. That was the only way I kept my sanity for so long in captivity.

"I am. I spend time every day listening to the waves. It's therapeutic and soothing."

"It is." I didn't go into any more detail. Didn't tell her that picturing a place like this was the only way I'd kept myself sane while I was locked in Diego's cage or strapped to his bed.

"How about we head down to the beach before we go inside? Would you like that?"

I glanced at Ret, still standing near the front steps, and he nodded. I wasn't really looking for his permission, but I didn't want to impose more than I already was. "I'd like that a lot."

Alese walked toward the side of the house, and I followed closely behind her. "Ret, can you bring us some wine?"

"Let me make a call, and I'll be right out," he said.

"So, you and Ret are..." I left the statement open because I didn't know how to finish it.

Ret had filled me in on how they'd met...much the same way I'd met Diego. Watching them now, I wouldn't be able to tell that he was her Dom or that she had an ounce of submissiveness in her, but Ret told me they saved that for the bedroom. If I hadn't heard it with my own ears, I never would've believed it.

"I love that man with my whole heart."

I didn't know what to say to that, but I was a little jealous I hadn't experienced love like that yet.

"We met a few years back. I was a switch, and Ret told me I was a submissive instead and challenged me. The rest is history."

We came to the back of the house, and touching the horizon was a virtually endless aqua blue sea. For a moment, I wondered if I was dreaming everything and I was still trapped under Diego's bed. Maybe he'd killed me or I was unconscious after one of his rough moments, and my mind had taken me away to a better place. I didn't realize I'd stopped walking until Alese backed up and softly touched my arm.

"Are you okay? Is this too much?"

I shook my head and kicked off my sandals, digging my toes into the warm, dry sand. "It's just so beautiful."

Alese didn't speak, just stood at my side as I took in the beauty in front of me. For a moment, I felt breathless and dizzy, the sensation of freedom finally crashing over me like the waves rolling up the sand just a few feet away.

Leaving my sandals near the grass, I walked toward the water, unable to take my eyes off the rhythmic waves as they swept across the shore as if calling me forward. I moved slowly, taking in every sound and sight I'd missed and dreamed of since the last time I'd stepped foot in Florida.

When I sat down, Alese moved to my side, sitting just a foot away. I drew my knees up to my chin, staring out at the vastness, in awe of the beauty. I almost became overwhelmed.

"Did you want to be alone?" she asked.

"No," I said quickly. I wasn't ready to be alone again.

"I brought the white," Ret said, coming up behind us before he sat down next to Alese.

"Good choice," she said, but I didn't glance over.

My eyes were too fixed on the horizon and the way the sun danced off the water like glitter dotting the surface. I'd never thought I'd see the Gulf of Mexico again. I'd never really thought I'd see much of anything besides the inside of Diego's mansion until he grew bored of me. Being back on the sand, with the sound of the waves and the relentless sun burning brightly overhead, I knew Diego had not broken me. He might have stolen time from me, but he didn't steal my soul. I'd be okay. It would take time for me to get back to the happy girl I once was, but for the first time in a long while, I felt like it was entirely possible.

"Would you like a glass, Nya?" Alese asked and held a wineglass in front of me.

I turned my face, smiling at the beautiful, kind woman at my side before taking the glass from her hand. "Thank you, Alese."

"Let's toast." She raised her wineglass and held it in front of her, waiting for us to join. I did the same, followed by Ret. "To new beginnings," she said. "We've all needed one at some point, and although it's scary at times, there's nothing more wonderful than possibilities."

We clinked our glasses together, but I didn't reply. Her words were true and profound. I once again had a world of possibilities at my feet, and no one, not even my parents or Diego, could stop me from following my dreams.

I sipped the wine, savoring the flavors as they danced across my tongue. For two months, I'd had nothing to drink except water, but even that was when Diego felt like giving me a sip. I held the delicate glass between my two palms, stared out across the water, and drank the wine as slowly as possible because the taste was just as magnificent as the scene before me.

"Maybe we can watch the sunset later," Alese said.

I remembered going to the beach with my parents, watching the sun as it kissed the horizon and the sky filled with the most brilliant shades of pink and orange. There was nothing more beautiful or awe-inspiring than the moment the sun finally disappeared, illuminating the sky in one final light show before darkness descended across the bay.

"I'd love that," I said.

"Whatever you ladies want, I'll make happen," Ret said easily.

God, Alese was the luckiest girl in the world.

CHAPTER FIVE

RET

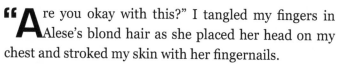

"**A**re you okay with this?" I tangled my fingers in Alese's blond hair as she placed her head on my chest and stroked my skin with her fingernails.

She peered up with her beautiful blue eyes and gave me a small smile. "I am. I wasn't sure at first, but after spending time with her, I can't imagine ever letting her parents get their hands on her."

I turned my head and kissed her forehead, content and happy to have someone as caring and understanding as Alese by my side. "I know. They're not good people."

She curled back into me, stroking my chest again with her hand. "Thank God we don't have to deal with people like that in our lives."

"Sometimes we forget how fortunate we are. I'm sorry I headed out of town without talking about it with you first. I know I promised I wouldn't do that again."

She flattened her palm against my chest and sat up a little, looking me in the eyes. "You were a naughty boy, Mr. North. Maybe I should teach you a lesson." She giggled, sounding just like me when we played.

"Mind your place, woman." I smirked.

"Someone's getting a spanking."

I grabbed her wrist, rolling over and taking her with me, pinning her under my body. "You missed me."

She struggled a little, pretending she wanted to get away. Something she liked to do to make her feel she had some control over the situation, when we both knew she didn't. "I did not miss you." She glanced toward the ceiling, giving me attitude.

"Come on, *piccola*. You missed me...or at least my cock." I smirked, sliding my lower half between her legs. "I bet if I touched your pussy, you'd be dripping for me already."

Her eyes darted to mine for a second, and that was all it took for her to break down and grin. "You locked up all my toys before you went out that night, and then you took off. Do you know how hard it is for me to come using only my fingers?"

Alese had a bad habit of masturbating when I wasn't around. Our agreement was no coming without me, but she hadn't been able to keep her end of the bargain lately. To mess with her a little, I'd lock up every single toy I could find and take the key with me when I left. She always complained, but I made sure she never went to bed without at least one orgasm when I was home.

"Am I supposed to feel bad for you?"

She narrowed her eyes, and any trace of her smile vanished. "You should."

"It was one night. You could've waited."

"You know my sex drive is off the charts lately. Waiting a day is nearly impossible anymore."

"What am I going to do with you?"

She arched an eyebrow, the cocky grin back. "You can fuck me and make me come at least twice."

"At least twice?"

Fucking women. Luckiest sons of bitches on the planet. They could come over and over and over again without a single moment of rest in between. Shit like that didn't happen for men except in fiction and the movies. Our bodies needed time to recover, but not Alese. She could go all night and still beg for more.

She placed her hands on my face and brought my lips down to hers, gazing into my eyes. "Three times is fine. I'm not picky," she said, grinding her pussy against my cock. "I deserve as much."

I wasn't going to argue with her or deny her what she wanted. This wasn't about play or orgasm denial, something I'd found useful with Alese over the years. Sliding my hand down her side, I glided my fingers across her abdomen as I lifted my body and moved to her side.

I lowered my mouth to hers, sealing her moans as my fingers grazed her clit and slipped through her wetness. She let her knees drift to the bed as she spread her legs as far apart as possible, silently begging to be penetrated. Alese loved to be filled. My finger, cock, toys...it didn't matter as long as she was stuffed.

Moving slowly, I pushed my fingers inside, curling them ever so slightly to press on her G-spot. Her nails dug into my skin and held me in place, rocking with my movement. Every time I pushed my fingers deeper, my thumb would skid across her clit and cause her body to quake with anticipation. I loved that about her. Her body was always so responsive to me, always so ready for whatever I gave, and she never seemed to get enough.

My pace quickened, and I pushed my fingers deeper, moving in and out of her faster as our tongues danced together in a frantic and haphazard rhythm. My cock ached to be inside, surrounded by the lush warmth of her pussy, but the first orgasm wasn't about me and never had been.

I pushed a third finger inside, stretching her to the limit, which earned me a strangled cry of passion as her lips fell away from mine. She pressed the back of her head into the pillow, and her mouth fell open as she gasped for air the closer the orgasm came. My strokes became more focused, the pads of my fingers pushing hard on her G-spot with each swipe before thrusting back into her.

She arched her back, thrusting her breasts into the air and closer to my lips. Her skin glowed in the moonlight streaming in through the bedroom window, covered in a fine sheen of sweat and sex.

Leaning forward, I closed my lips around her nipple and flicked the hardened tip with my tongue. Her pussy clamped down, drawing my fingers inward and pulsating as I sucked the puckered flesh.

I moved my hand faster, fingers thrusting harder and deeper as I closed my teeth around her nipple just to the point of pleasurable pain and sent her right over the edge. Her breathing halted, mouth wide open with her eyes closed, and her body convulsed at my side.

Watching a woman come, especially Alese, was the most beautiful thing in the world. Knowing I could do that to her was the biggest head trip in the world. She was mine entirely...mind, body, and soul. Every orgasm she had was because of me, and mine belonged to her.

When I woke in the morning, I rolled to my side to find the bed empty and Alese nowhere in sight. Last night, she'd received her three orgasms, deserving every single one of them. Many women in her shoes would've bitched me out for bringing another woman into our home. But my Alese, she had a heart as big as her libido. I'd move heaven and earth for her if it meant she'd be happy.

I slung my legs over the bed, leaning forward and yawning. The late night wouldn't help me focus today, and I knew the office would be a flurry of activity, especially after the shit that went down with the Halsteads.

A few minutes later, the sound of voices drew me downstairs. When I walked into the kitchen, Nya sat on a stool across the counter from Alese as she danced across the tile floor, singing into a spatula, wearing one of my old T-shirts.

When our eyes locked, she didn't stop her performance either. She swayed her hips to the beat, belting out lyrics about love and staring at me as if she'd written the song just for me. I didn't dare interrupt as I made my way around the counter and kissed her on the cheek before grabbing a coffee cup because it was entirely too early to be that energetic.

As Alese screeched out the final line, holding the very last note longer than necessary, Nya clapped wildly as she rose to her feet, giving Alese a standing ovation. "That was perfect. I'm not sure I've ever heard something so beautiful."

"You need to listen to more music," I said as I poured the coffee into my cup, barely able to see straight.

"Don't listen to him." Alese swatted my ass playfully, earning herself a warning glance. "He's always a little grumpy in the morning."

"I hope I didn't keep you two up too late," Nya said, clearly unaware of the real cause of my sleepiness.

"Nah. We're night owls. Anyway, he'll be fine after he has coffee. It takes him a little while to join the living."

I leaned against the counter and watched them over the rim of the mug. Nya returned to her stool as Alese finally started to stir the hash browns, which were on the verge of becoming cinders because she was more concerned about her performance than their meal.

"So, do you want to go shopping today?" Alese glanced back at Nya.

Nya sighed and sagged against the counter as her brown hair spilled forward. "Yeah, but…"

"There's no buts about it, missy. We need to get you some clothes because my hand-me-downs aren't going to cut it." Alese smacked Nya's ass with her free hand and laughed. "Unless you're going to gain twenty pounds in a hurry."

"If she's eating your cooking, it'll never happen."

Alese turned to me, her blue eyes wide and wild, but we both knew she was a shitty cook. Somehow, she was even worse than Fran, and that crap was hard to pull off. It was like she purposely sabotaged every meal so I'd stop asking her to feed me. Luckily for me, my time in the military had dulled my palate to the point that I could eat sand if it filled my belly.

"I can't believe you just said that." Alese gawked at me as Nya giggled, covering her mouth with her hand.

That was the first time I saw a relaxed Nya, a little carefree and step closer back to the girl she probably had been before Diego got his hands on her. I don't know if it was me or maybe Alese's infectious playfulness that put her at ease, but in that moment, I knew I'd made the right choice. By surrounding herself with happy people, accepting people, she'd have an easier time sliding back into society than in the hands of her judgmental parents, no matter how many antipsychotic drugs they pumped her with.

I glanced at Nya as I slid my coffee cup along the counter. "You'll understand after you have her 'world-famous' hash browns."

"I'm going to stop cooking for you," Alese threatened, bumping me with her hip as she handed Nya a plate of her very well done and totally dry breakfast.

"Baby." I wrapped my arm around Alese's waist and pulled her against me. "Make me that promise again." She smacked me as I laughed. "I'm playing. I love your cooking."

That was the biggest lie I'd ever told in our relationship. Everything else I was truthful with her about, but when it came to her cooking, I just couldn't see the hurt in her eyes. She tried. God, how she tried to cook, but it didn't matter what she made, she fucked it up to the best of her ability.

"Good because I'm making your favorite."

Oh, shit. "My favorite" was really the worst thing in her entire repertoire. It was some sort of dried-out casserole, barely edible, and needed to be choked down with two beers.

"I could help," Nya said quickly. "I used to be a good cook." She pushed her food around the plate, suddenly sad. Maybe it was the *used to* part that made her happiness evaporate, but I saw the change just as Alese did.

"That would be great, but only if you want to. I could always use an extra pair of hands. We'll stop at the grocery store after we go to the mall."

"I'd like to feel that I'm contributing in some way."

I prayed that her version of cooking was better than Alese's. Hell, if it was even just a little better, maybe I could convince Alese to let Nya cook just so she felt useful. Maybe the work would help Nya regain some confidence. I didn't know what I was thinking, but I was willing to try anything to help her find herself again.

CHAPTER SIX

NYA

"Let me see." Alese sat outside the dressing room as I changed into another outfit. She'd picked out easily thirty different items, and I didn't know how to process so many choices or even what was in style anymore.

I wanted a few pieces of comfortable clothes...nothing flashy or expensive. I didn't care to wear anything too revealing or formfitting, but Alese had other plans. She said I had to get at least five outfits and two pairs of shoes before we could leave the mall. I didn't really know how she expected me to pay for anything. I hadn't had a chance to get a new copy of my credit card or any identification since Diego had destroyed mine when he'd decided to keep me.

I stepped out of the dressing room in a pair of skinny jeans and a tank top with a built-in bra for support. I felt a little like my old self again, even if the jeans were tighter than I was used to wearing. After a few months of no clothes, material of any kind felt weird against my skin, almost suffocating, but I couldn't very well walk around naked without having my ass thrown in jail for public nudity.

Alese stared at me, tapping her chin before she motioned with two fingers for me to twirl in a circle. I turned slowly and caught a glimpse of myself in the mirror. When I'd graduated from college, I was a size ten, comfortable with my body and with a rock-hard plump ass I had worked hard to get.

But Diego fed me very little, restricting my food when he felt I didn't behave or react the way he wanted. Which, based on my flat ass and the hip bones peeking out below the hem of my tank top, happened more times than not. He was a sick bastard. I'd known I had to get away. Every day I'd planned my escape, waiting for him to fuck up, but the bastard was too calculating to let that happen.

"I look like an anorexic." I pushed on my hips, wishing I could get my bones to be not quite as visible, but only calories would do that. "I want my body back."

"Honey." Alese walked toward me and came to a stop behind me, her blue eyes finding mine in the mirror. "You're beautiful no matter what size you are. You want to go bigger and better? I'm down with that."

"I just want my old life back." Suddenly, I felt a mix of anger and sadness, unsure which one was more overwhelming. Tears filled my eyes as I stared at the waif in the mirror, all skin and bones with no ass or tits.

Alese slowly moved closer and wrapped her arms around my waist. "Oh, Nya. I'm so sorry, love. I'll do anything to make things better."

Tears filled my eyes because her tenderness was almost as unbearable as my sadness. No one besides Ret had shown me an ounce of compassion or caring in months, and I wasn't sure how to process the emotions that came with it. With Diego, I knew how to handle his

42

anger...how to tap out of reality and let my mind drift to a faraway place, practically bringing on an out-of-body experience. But sweetness was something I forgot how to handle.

"Don't cry, love."

I wiped my cheeks, sniffling back the others that threatened to fall. I was not this girl. I had never been a crier. Rarely did I ever let Diego see me affected by his actions. I cried the first week he held me captive, but I quickly learned my tears were futile. He loved my tears, basically got off on my sadness, and that's when I learned sorrow was a meaningless emotion that only fueled his lust for me.

"Tears are useless," I whispered when she didn't let go of me.

"No, they aren't. Don't ever feel that way. When you're sad, cry. When you're mad, I'll take you to kickboxing so you don't break my shit."

I turned to face her, and she finally released her arms from around my waist. "I don't really get mad, Alese."

"You will, Nya. You're going to go through a process now that you've regained your freedom after what Diego did to you. You're going to be sad, then angry, then maybe you'll want revenge. Your healing will be in stages and not overnight. If you want to cry, cry. I'll get the wine, and we can cry together."

"What do you have to cry about?"

She placed her hands on my shoulders and gazed into my eyes with a sweet, sorrowful smile. "I'll cry with and for you. For your loss of innocence. For your loss of trust. For your loss of time. There's so many reasons I'd cry with you. Imagine all the women still trapped in a situation like you were in, but without anyone who bothered to look for them."

"I'm grateful to my parents for hiring someone to track me down, but I can't be with them. Does that make me a horrible human being?"

"It doesn't."

"Thank God. I have enough baggage to deal with on top of everything."

"Nya." Alese held out her arms like she wanted to hug me, but she didn't step forward. "Can I?"

Alese was one of those people who just threw off good vibes. It was hard not to like her. Hard not to find her energy infectious and her carefree attitude calming when everything around me felt foreign. "You may," I told her, but I moved my arms around her first.

She embraced me, gently at first, again careful not to set off any triggers. I tightened my hold on her, almost tethering myself to her body as I placed my head on her shoulder. For the first time in as long as I could remember, I felt something besides fear when someone touched me. Never had a hug meant so much even when it was such an inconsequential gesture that I wouldn't have thought twice about before.

We stood there holding each other for a few minutes. I almost cried again, but I fought back the tears because I didn't want Alese to think I was upset. I wasn't. I felt joy, comfort, peacefulness as I stood in her arms with my eyes closed.

"Can I help you ladies?" the saleswoman asked, interrupting our moment.

"We're fine. We'll take everything," Alese replied and tightened her hold when I tried to wiggle free.

"Fabulous." The saleswoman was beyond excited to hear the news.

44

"You can't," I said, feeling a little uncomfortable that she was going to foot the bill for all the clothes I had tried on.

"Shh." She gave me a hardened stare. "Everything."

"I'll pay you back," I whispered.

"Cook this week, and we'll call it even."

I gawked at her, confused by the offer. "That's not fair."

"Seriously. I hate to cook. I keep making things worse and worse, hoping Ret will take over, but he never does. He just keeps eating the burned shit like it's the best damn thing he's ever put in his mouth."

I laughed and shook my head. "You do it on purpose?"

She raised an eyebrow, waving her hands in front of her pristine outfit, straight down to her designer pumps. "Do I look domestic?"

"Well." I stepped back, taking in her beauty. Alese was drop-dead gorgeous with lush curves and no sharp edges. Her long blond hair was swept over her shoulder, half pulled back in a braid that looked like something out of a fashion magazine. "You definitely don't look like a boring housewife. I'm super jealous."

Even her makeup was on point, something I'd never been able to pull off. I was a chick, but I sucked at anything girlie. Who knew that was even possible? But somehow, I lacked any skills when it came to makeup and hair. I watched hundreds of online tutorials, which made that shit look easy, but every time, I came out looking more like a train wreck than a runway model.

"I will teach you all my skills. We have the clothes. Now we just need your hair and makeup."

I pulled at the messy braid I'd attempted before we'd walked out the door. Pieces stuck out, making it look like more of a mess than an actual style. Trying on clothes, repeatedly pulling things over my head, didn't help the situation either.

"I'm a disaster," I mumbled as I started to walk back to my dressing room.

"Don't say that. You're a knockout."

My insides warmed with her compliment. It had been too long since I'd heard anything nice said about me. I was never the type of person who needed the affirmation, but after months of listening to Diego tell me I was a worthless piece of trash, hearing the opposite was more than nice... It was exactly what I needed to feel a little more human.

I glanced at her over my shoulder, smiling as she stood near the mirror with her hands resting on her hips. "Thanks, Alese."

She nodded once and shooed me toward the dressing room. "Go get changed. We have a long day ahead of us."

I tossed and turned for the fifth time before I threw off the covers and moved my legs over the side of the bed, unable to sleep for the second night in a row. Spending the day with Alese made me feel more alive than I had in a long time, but it didn't keep the nightmares at bay.

Every time I closed my eyes and started to fall asleep, I'd see Diego's face and startle awake. My heart beat erratically, and I couldn't seem to catch my breath. I stayed awake until I was so exhausted I practically passed out.

I peered around the dimly lit bedroom, thankful for the night-light Alese gave me yesterday. I told her I wasn't sure I could sleep, and she thought it would be the best way to make me feel a little safer instead of lying in the darkness. She was right, it did help, but not enough to make sleep come any easier.

I padded across the floor carefully, turning the handle of the door slowly to avoid waking up Alese or Ret. They'd already done so much for me, and I didn't want to disturb them more than I already had.

I glanced down the hallway, making sure the coast was clear before I stepped outside my room. The guest bedroom was at the end of the hallway, which was lined with doors to an office and the master suite.

The house seemed small yet perfect, compared to the compound Diego owned. I remembered the first time I walked into his mansion before he decided to keep me. I thought he lived like royalty, and I couldn't imagine what it would feel like to have that much money.

I grew up a privileged child. My parents had more money in the bank than they knew what to do with, but they didn't spend it on palatial mansions, opting to hoard as much as possible for God knows what. There was a difference between being wealthy and being rich. My parents were wealthy, but Diego was filthy rich. A man with his bank account didn't have to be bothered with anything, including the law, and I knew that firsthand.

A tiny beam of light shone from the doorway of their bedroom. At first, I scurried past the cracked door, but I backed up a step when I heard Alese's voice.

Curiosity got the better of me as I peered in through the small opening. Ret sat on the foot of the bed with Alese across his lap, naked and with her hands bound. Ret held the rope between his fingers, stopping Alese from falling over, while his other hand glided across the bare skin of her ass.

I touched the handle, ready to rush in to save her, until she lifted her face and a smile played on her lips.

"What did I tell you about that, *piccola*?" Ret asked, his hand still sweeping across her skin in circles. "Have you learned your lesson yet?"

"I'm sorry, Sir."

He raised his hand, and I held my breath. "You didn't answer my question, little one."

She bucked wildly as his hand came down against her ass, raising her head as her feet kicked in the air. I gasped, shocked to see Ret be so harsh with her after everything I'd witnessed the last two days.

I couldn't move. It was like my feet were glued to the floor. I knew I shouldn't be watching. I knew I should've run back to my room and sealed myself inside, but I couldn't, no matter how many times I told myself to go.

"I learned. I learned," she called out, closing her eyes as his hand went back to her ass, but this time to soothe the skin he'd just battered.

He stared down at her and loosened his grip on the ropes around her wrists for a moment, but I couldn't see his eyes. "You love to be spanked, don't you?"

She nodded, and he jerked the ropes. "Yes, Sir. I love when you spank me."

I gasped for air, forgetting that I hadn't been breathing because I'd been so engrossed in the scene playing out before me.

"Are you wet, my sweet?"

"I'm always wet for you, Master."

His hand drifted between her legs as a low hum came from his throat, and Alese stilled in his lap. She moaned as his hand disappeared. My insides convulsed, a small piece of the sexuality I once felt returning.

Before everything went sideways, when I was just a clubgoer, I loved to be finger-fucked. It was the number one thing that got me off. There was something more demanding about it, more pleasurable than a cock. Or maybe it was the fact that a majority of the dicks I'd had inside me were never big enough to get me off.

"Greedy little cunt," he grunted, working his fingers into her faster, harder.

She mewed, pushing her ass against his hand, wanting more, like I'd asked for a hundred times myself. I stepped back, feeling like an asshole for watching them, but I forgot to remove my hand from the doorknob because I'd been so engrossed.

The door creaked softly, and my eyes widened, panic setting deep in my bones. Ret's head snapped up, but his hands never left Alese. He peered toward the doorway and narrowed his eyes, but he didn't stop. I held my breath again, staying stock-still and praying he'd think it was just the wind or maybe something else. I wanted him to think it was anything except for me watching from the hallway.

When he didn't come charging toward the door and returned his full attention to a very naked Alese, I tiptoed back to my room and locked myself inside.

I crawled under the covers, and I felt something I hadn't in a long time. I slipped my hands under the sheet and into my shorts, closing my eyes as I replayed Ret and Alese over and over again until my muscles tightened and an orgasm unlike any I'd felt in a long time ripped through my system. I gasped for air, rocking in the aftermath until sleep pulled me under.

GUILTY SIN

CHAPTER SEVEN

RET

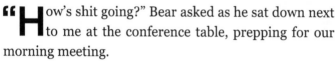

"How's shit going?" Bear asked as he sat down next to me at the conference table, prepping for our morning meeting.

"Good." I didn't know what the man wanted to hear. He must've thought I was going to bring home a woman who had basically been a sex slave for two months and that we'd have wild orgies.

"You have two women under the same roof, and all you can say is good?"

Bingo. The man never ceased to amaze me. He always had sex on the brain, and I almost felt sorry for Fran. Almost. She was just as much of a spitfire as my father and just as much of a troublemaker.

"Nya isn't mine, Pop. Remember?"

He nodded slowly, pursing his lips. "I know, but come on."

"You saw how she was when we found her? What did you think was going to happen with the three of us?"

He glanced toward the ceiling like he was dreaming up every scenario possible, stroking the hair on his chin. "I dunno, but something."

I shuffled the paperwork in my hands, organizing it in priority order for later. "The girls went shopping yesterday."

"Sounds exciting," he mumbled and rolled his eyes.

As if on cue, the rest of the ALFA team filed into the conference room, looking just as tired as I felt. I hadn't planned to stay up so late last night, but I couldn't get my fill of Alese, and she seemed insatiable. Afterward, I kept thinking about Nya and seeing her outside our door, watching us. I wondered what she thought, how she felt, and if it bothered her in any way.

I didn't let it stop what I was doing. I didn't ease up on Alese because Nya saw something she shouldn't. The fact that I found her fast asleep in her bedroom this morning instead of rocking in the corner was a step in the right direction.

"First off," James said, standing at the head of the conference table and leaning on his knuckles. "I want to talk about Nya Halstead and what has transpired since we didn't release her to her family."

The chatter around the table died down, and everyone turned their attention to James. I was waiting for this talk, wondering if we were going to be sued for some bullshit reason because rich assholes like the Halsteads could make just about anything happen if they threw enough cash at it.

"Last night we received a letter from their attorney for breach of contract. I feel like it's the first step in their offensive to try to regain control of their daughter," James told us.

They were grasping at straws, but I was sure with enough time and resources, they'd find something else to hurl at ALFA to make us pay.

"Ret, I need you to take Nya for a mental evaluation. We need to know if she's of sound mind or if she is any way sick and in need of therapy," James said.

"I'll get that done as soon as possible." I gave him a chin lift before jotting myself a note. It would be the first thing I'd do today and probably the most important.

"Her health and safety are our first priority. We've never experienced this with a case before. As you know, we always return the missing family member, especially children, but the Halsteads and Nya are a special case," James continued.

The rest of the ALFA team sat quietly, listening to James and scribbling on their legal pads. I glanced down at my dad's paper, and he was drawing a stick figure of a woman with very large breasts. The man would never grow up. But then, he wouldn't be the same if he ever did.

"If we know she's of sound mind and can make her own decisions, we'll be able to fight the Halsteads without any issue. If she's in need of help, we'll have to make it happen or else we could find ourselves in even deeper legal trouble. I've put in a call to a doctor and an attorney at my club, and we'll be enlisting them in our fight," James finished.

"Ret." Thomas set his phone down and gazed down the table as James sat down next to him. "Why don't you call Alese and have her bring Nya here? We'll have an appointment scheduled with the doctor this afternoon and get the ball rolling."

"On it."

"Now, let's talk about some of our other cases. Sam, where are you at with the Connor case?" Thomas asked.

"I'm meeting with Mrs. Connor today. I've been able to track all the money her ex-husband stole from her. It wasn't easy, but I have a long enough paper trail for her to bring it to a judge and seize his assets."

While the guys talked about the Connors, I grabbed my phone, shooting Alese a quick message. I knew she wasn't a fast mover, especially in the morning. If I didn't know better, I'd swear the girl had molasses in her veins.

Me: Alese, swing by the office in a few hours with Nya, and I'll take you both to lunch.

Alese: But it was makeup day... Can we do lunch another day?

Makeup day? I didn't even want to know what kind of girl shit that involved, but I was pretty sure it would result in a substantial charge on Alese's credit card. I didn't understand why she bothered with all that crap. She was a knockout without a drop of makeup on her face.

Me: It's more than lunch. She needs to be seen by our physician, and I thought I'd treat you two to lunch as a bonus.

I needed to speak with Nya to get a feel for her mental health after what she saw last night. If it affected her in any way, the meeting with the doctor could be an absolute mess. I only hoped that what she saw didn't bother her and that it didn't set her back or remind her of the time she spent with Diego.

Alese: You got it! We'll be there at eleven, 'kay?

Me: Perfect.

Nya and Alese came barreling through the door of ALFA three minutes late in a fit of laughter. If I hadn't witnessed it myself, I wouldn't have believed Nya was ever a victim, let alone captive for over two months. Everything I learned in the military about imprisonment and the toll it could take on someone's psyche didn't seem to apply to her.

Maybe it was the fact that some part of her enjoyed the treatment Diego gave her. The BDSM lifestyle was complicated, and sometimes the mindfuck it offered served the different needs and fetishes of certain people.

She seemed at peace around Alese. I was sure some of that had to do with the fact that they were both women and that Nya's captor was a man. She probably wouldn't be as happy if it were only her and me without Alese present.

Angel raised an eyebrow, looking just as surprised as I was by their laughter. "You two having a good day?"

Alese leaned over Angel's desk, resting on her elbow as Nya eyed me from behind her. "The best. How about you, sweetheart?"

"You know...as well as I can with these guys."

I rounded the corner from the hallway and glanced at Angel, giving her a playful smirk. "I heard that."

"Not you, Ret. You're the easiest one here. The other guys..." She paused and glanced around. "They're a pain sometimes. Anyway, where are you headed?"

"Lunch," I said and wrapped my arms around Alese's waist, pulling her against me.

"Quickie?" Angel asked.

I peered over Alese's shoulder, staring at Nya, who was doing everything possible to avoid my gaze. "No, doll. Today, we're really having lunch."

Alese held me tightly, burying her face in my neck as I laughed. "It's a pity."

James walked into the room and cleared his throat, looming large as he always did. "Hello, Nya."

She lifted her head with no expression on her face. "Hello, Sir."

"Are you well?" He kept his distance, careful not to move too close to her because none of us really knew if she had any triggers.

I should've thought more about that before I brought her home. My need to rescue her from her parents outweighed my common sense. As a Dom, I should've been more cognizant of what she'd been through and spent a little more time getting to know her before I left her alone, especially with Alese. But it didn't even occur to me because she seemed calm and unafraid when we sat on the beach together.

"Yes. I'm well."

"She's great, James." Alese stepped away from me, peering up James's tall frame, and smiled. "We were supposed to have a makeup day, but Ret called us in."

His eyebrows drew downward, but he didn't ask. James had enough women in his life to know better than to ask. "I'm sure you can do makeup tomorrow."

"We can. Maybe I'll call Izzy."

James finally cracked a smile. "She'd probably like that."

"That girl is on point with her eyeliner."

I glanced upward before rubbing my forehead. "Let's get going, ladies. We have to be back at one." I held my arms out, ushering them both toward the door before I had to hear anything else about makeup.

"Have fun," Angel called out, always the chipper one in the office. I was thankful to have her around. There were far too many men around, and we needed a little softness, especially when clients came in.

"We will. Bye, James." Alese gave him a playful smile over her shoulder, which earned her a warning glance from me. "Don't be so serious all the time, baby."

"We'll talk about this later," I told her, tightening my grip on her hip. I wasn't really serious or pissed, but I knew Alese did shit just to get a rise out of me.

"You going to spank me again?" She grinned as Nya's eyes widened.

I raised an eyebrow, following her lead, but keeping my eyes on Nya, who was blushing. "If you deserve it."

"I always deserve it."

I leaned forward, brushing my lips against hers. "You mean you always want it."

"Can't blame a girl for going after what she wants."

She was relentless too. Alese wasn't one to shy away from a situation, especially if she could use it to her advantage. We didn't fight. There was no yelling. Any issue we had, we worked out in the bedroom. It seemed to keep the peace and made for the least complicated relationship of my entire life. The "Make Love Not War" slogan worked for us, and there was no way in hell I was messing that up.

CHAPTER EIGHT

NYA

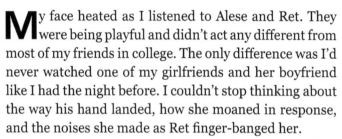

My face heated as I listened to Alese and Ret. They were being playful and didn't act any different from most of my friends in college. The only difference was I'd never watched one of my girlfriends and her boyfriend like I had the night before. I couldn't stop thinking about the way his hand landed, how she moaned in response, and the noises she made as Ret finger-banged her.

I remembered Diego being with me like that, some kindness and playfulness, when we'd meet at the club and do a scene together. It didn't change until he convinced me to move in with him. I foolishly thought our relationship would stay the same, but I learned quickly that the public persona he displayed was nothing like the monster he became behind closed doors.

"God, everything looks so good. I'm famished." Alese studied the menu at the little diner Ret suggested around the corner from his office. "What are you in the mood for, Nya?"

I glanced down at the three-page menu and didn't even know where to start. Everything sounded delicious, and if I'd had a stomach big enough, I would've had more than one dish. "Maybe a burger."

Ret smiled at me from across the table. "That's their specialty."

I still couldn't bring myself to look at him. Part of it was guilt for seeing something I shouldn't, and the other part... That was more complicated. Something about Ret turned me on, but I knew I shouldn't feel that way after everything I'd been through—and for the simple fact that he was Alese's man.

"That's what I'll order, then."

"I have to go to the ladies' room. Order me a BLT and sweet tea if she comes by," Alese said as she slid out of the booth.

Ret nodded, and I stared at her like a deer caught in headlights. "Want me to come?"

She stood next to me with her hand on my shoulder, squeezing it lightly. "Don't be silly. Stay and talk to Ret. I promise he doesn't bite."

The blush that had started to wane was fully back in place as I laughed off her statement, but my insides twisted into knots. I watched as Alese walked across the restaurant, rubbing my hands together in my lap and avoiding looking at Ret.

My biggest worry was that he saw me last night and was upset about it. Maybe he'd toss me out on my ass, or worse yet, lock me in my room. I didn't know what to think about anything anymore. Diego had robbed me of my ability to read people.

"Nya." Ret's voice was strong but not harsh. "Look at me."

I closed my eyes for a moment as the knot in my stomach grew to what felt like the size of a basketball. As I slowly opened my eyes, I let my gaze flicker to Ret's, and I held my breath.

"We need to talk about last night."

Damn it. He did see me.

"I know you were outside our door last night."

I squeezed my eyes closed again, tighter than before, and gritted my teeth, waiting for him to tell me it was time for me to find some other place to live.

"Nya..." He paused.

I opened my eyes again because I knew I couldn't avoid what was coming next. Not even closing my eyes could save me from my own stupidity.

"It's okay, Nya," Ret said softly.

My eyes snapped to his, the words he spoke surprising the hell out of me. "It is?"

"I hope what you saw didn't scare you. I know you've been through so much, and I'm not sure if it triggered any bad memories. But I want you to know that I love Alese very much, and I'd never do anything to hurt her."

I swallowed, my tongue practically sticking to the roof of my mouth as I blinked at him in confusion. How could he think he scared me? I guess it would be a natural thought after the way he found me, but nothing about what I witnessed made me think Alese was in danger.

"I'm sorry," I said again, at a loss for any other words.

"Did it scare you?"

I felt his penetrating gaze across the table even when I glanced down at my hands still twisting in my lap. "No, Sir. You didn't scare me."

"Did you have a nightmare afterward?"

"No."

"Does Alese know?"

I lifted my head, widening my eyes. "No way. I haven't said a thing."

"It's okay, Nya. We're open about our life, and that includes sex. Alese isn't shy, but I also didn't tell her that you watched us. That isn't my secret to share."

"I didn't mean to watch. I couldn't sleep and was going to get a glass of water. When I heard a slap, I couldn't stop myself from looking inside to make sure she was okay." I wasn't being totally truthful, but I was too embarrassed to say anything else.

"It's understandable, and your reaction was natural."

I gawked at him, shocked that he was so level-headed about everything. I thought he'd chastise me for invading their privacy even though that hadn't been my intent.

"It was?"

"I never want you to feel frightened or ashamed again, Nya. You've been through far too much to ever feel that way again. Right now, we'll keep it our little secret. If you ever want to talk to Alese about our relationship, she's very open and will probably talk your ear off, but her heart's in the right place."

"Thank you," I said just as the waitress walked up to the table, tapping her pencil against her tiny pad of paper.

Alese slid back into the booth, smiling at me before grabbing Ret's hand and intertwining her fingers with his. The tenseness I'd felt about what I saw and how Ret would react had vanished, but I still would never admit that what I saw turned me on. The emotions I felt about the entire situation and had started to feel about both Alese and Ret weren't right, and I knew it. Even after Diego fucked with my head, I could still tell the difference between right and wrong...even if my body couldn't.

I stared at Dr. Valentine, fiddling with the hem of my dress as he spoke. We'd already been talking for an hour, and he didn't show any signs of stopping anytime soon. He did most of the talking, asking me about my experience and how I felt about everything. He questioned me about my sleep patterns, my appetite, and if anything had caused me a massive amount of stress since Ret rescued me.

"No, sir."

"Our meeting is confidential, Ms. Halstead. Anything we discuss will not be shared with anyone, including your parents or the employees here at ALFA."

I nodded, unsure if I could trust his words, but I knew, as a doctor, he wasn't legally allowed to share my information unless I gave him permission. But I'd seen my parents bully doctors into telling them things I didn't want them to know. Dr. Valentine wasn't my first shrink, after all. My parents had always tried to control me and usually enlisted a doctor to do it. That was why I went to college so far away; I needed to break free of their overprotective insanity.

"I know," I said softly, smoothing out my dress near my knees with my fingertips.

He scribbled something on the notepad before bringing his eyes to mine again. "Do you blame yourself for what happened?"

I shook my head, but I wasn't one hundred percent truthful. I played a role in my captivity. Diego didn't kidnap me off the street. I went willingly, giving myself to him, but I never thought he'd keep me from my family and society by locking me away in his bedroom.

"Do you feel like harming yourself?"

"No." My response was swift. In no way had I ever thought of harming myself. Life had always been precious to me. Even at the worst moments, the ones where I let my mind drift away, I never wished for my life to end.

He wrote something down, and it took everything in me to keep my ass planted in the seat and not rip the notebook clean out of his hand. I wondered if he was making a case to have me committed, or if all the answers I was giving him were wrong. "Am I broken?"

"You're much better than most who lived through the same experience. Although you've been through a horrific event, you don't seem to have a fear of others or a distrust that many victims feel afterward."

"Doctor..." I paused, swallowing roughly and squeezing my hands into tight fists. "There's only one man I fear, and he's hundreds of miles away. I can't imagine he'd come after me. He wouldn't risk the possibility of being arrested. In Atlanta, he had the police on his payroll, but in Tampa, he has no pull. When we drove across the state line, I knew I was safe and that Diego could never hurt me again."

"Mr. North has never frightened you?"

"Ret?" I gawked at the doctor because the question was laughable. "He saved my life, sir. Why would I be scared of him?"

Ret was the person I trust most in the world. Maybe I was being naïve, but him and Alese had been nothing short of amazing to me. The way they treated each other was filled with respect and love. Something I wished I found with Diego.

"There's no right or wrong way to respond, Ms. Halstead. Fear is a powerful thing, and even in the best circumstances, it's a very natural response after a traumatic event."

"Do you know about my lifestyle?" I asked, wondering if he was the right man to talk to me.

Often the men my parents would hire to be my doctor didn't have the slightest clue about the BDSM lifestyle, and they would judge me from the moment I walked in the room. I could never explain why being a submissive was a massive high or get them to understand about subspace.

"I do. I've been in the lifestyle with my wife for the last twenty years."

I lifted my eyebrows, completely taken aback by that information. It shouldn't have been surprising, but somehow it was.

"So, I understand the level of trust involved in and out of the lifestyle."

I nodded. "I've been sitting here, trying to figure out a way to explain my feelings about what happened with Diego. I know I should be rocking in a corner somewhere, crying about the time I lost, but I don't feel that way."

"There's no one way to feel or respond in a situation like this."

"I know. The months I spent with Diego, I kept lying to myself, repeating over and over again that he was just playing out an extremely long and sometimes cruel scene. When he became rough, I'd let my mind drift and escape whatever he was doing to my body to keep myself sane. I knew it wouldn't last forever. My parents have always stuck their noses where they didn't belong, and I knew it was only a matter of time before they'd come looking for me."

"Did you find pleasure with Diego?"

"Sometimes. But other times, when he was cruel, my body would respond even though I didn't want it to."

"We can't stop a natural response, Ms. Halstead."

"When I met Diego and we'd do scenes with each other at Charmed, he knew I loved pain just as much as pleasure. I think that's why he picked me. He didn't kidnap me from my house. I willingly moved in with him. In a way, I feel responsible for what happened to me."

"No matter how much you love pain or pleasure, no one has the right to hold you captive and keep you from those you love."

"Yes, sir. I know that. I knew that. Maybe if I were a normal girl who loved softness and had no concept of what BDSM was, I'd feel differently about the situation... Maybe I'd be committed at this point. But for the first time since I graduated from college, I feel like anything is possible, and I don't plan to waste another moment of my life living in fear."

I refused to be a victim. There was no way I would let Diego steal any more of my life after the hell he put me through. Maybe I was insane for not feeling the right emotions after everything I'd been through. I knew I didn't deserve what happened to me. No person, boyfriend, or Dom, had the right to steal my life because I loved to be spanked. Diego may have stolen some time, but he sure as hell wasn't going to steal my life.

CHAPTER NINE

RET

Nya's results were probably surprising to the others, but based on just the short amount of time I'd spent with her, I wasn't shocked. Even after everything she'd been through, she didn't seem afraid or fearful of me in any way, and I hadn't found her in the fetal position covered in tears. The doctor wanted to see her for weekly sessions to check up on her for the next month, but he didn't find her delusional or suffering from a psychotic break.

"What should we watch?" Alese asked, scrolling through the on-demand video selection and passing half the things I wanted to watch.

"That one," I said as she scrolled over the latest action movie I'd been dying to see.

She turned to me, raising an eyebrow, because she'd made it quite clear it was ladies' night. "What do you want to watch, Nya?" she asked, ignoring me.

"I've missed so many movies. You pick."

"Romantic or funny?"

"Um," Nya mumbled and twirled a strand of her brown hair around her finger. "I don't care as long as it's happy."

"Romantic it is, then." Alese smiled and clicked on the only one I prayed she wouldn't pick.

The movie already looked sappy, with a couple almost embracing in the picture on the guide, and I knew the next two hours wouldn't go by any faster than the rest of my day. Alese climbed onto the couch, placing herself between us, and made herself comfortable.

"I heard this one is amazing. The guy..." Alese started.

"Alese, don't ruin this one," I told her.

She grunted, but she didn't finish her sentence.

Nya laughed at her side and hooked her arm with Alese's like they'd been best friends for years. Alese rested her head on my shoulder and laced her fingers with mine. I placed my feet on the coffee table, sinking down into the couch and preparing for a long two hours, but it seemed to make the ladies happy. I couldn't ask for anything more than a little peace and quiet.

But as I sat there, watching the horror show on screen, I knew I was going to be in trouble. The cover lied, selling the movie as a happy story about love. The guy, who was in a horrible accident, then had to use a wheelchair, and the girl, who was his employee, had become attached to him.

The girls were already sniffling, and I knew the worst was yet to come. The same thing happened when Alese made me watch that walking movie where the girl died of cancer at the end. She was a blubbering mess, and I'd caught her watching it again more than once because, I swear, the woman loves to torture herself.

Nya gripped Alese tighter as the woman on screen pleaded with the man about his life after she fell in love with him. "How could he do that to her? What a selfish prick."

I understood the guy's thinking. I mean, who wanted to live a life in pain, suffering and remembering what you had but could never have again. As a man, I totally understood and would've probably made the same decision. The guy had his mind made up before he ever knew she existed. He wasn't being selfish, he was being realistic, and he knew what lay ahead for him if he didn't do this.

"I'd fucking rip off your balls," Alese said, squeezing the skin near my knee so tightly, her fingernails almost broke the skin. "I'd straight up tear those fuckers off."

I didn't speak because I wasn't stupid. I was outnumbered and didn't have a death wish. Right on cue, they both began to cry, finally letting their tears flow as the woman in the movie started to yell at the man about his choice.

Tonight was supposed to be relaxing and fun, but by the way the two of them were wailing, I knew I was completely fucked. The entire night they'd be talking about this movie, half in tears and angry as hell. Maybe I'd go for a walk on the beach while they ranted about the choice the man made for his own happiness even if it meant he'd die.

The woman stormed away, but when she came to her senses and the man went away to end his life, the girls cried harder.

"I can't believe he's really going to go through with this," Nya wailed and wiped away her tears that hadn't stopped falling since they'd both realized where this story was going.

"He's an asshole." Alese was pissed, but she'd picked this movie without bothering to find out what happened. "A selfish, greedy asshole."

"I understand him."

Alese turned to me, face covered in tears and full on glared at me with red eyes as she untangled her fingers from my grip. "The fuck you say?"

I motioned toward the screen. "He doesn't want to live that way or trap the girl either. He's doing the least selfish thing in his mind."

"Fuckin' men. He could live a lot longer, but he's choosing to die."

"He's choosing his own destiny...there's a difference."

"Oh my God. I can't watch." Nya covered her face, leaving space between her fingers to see the screen.

Alese interlaced her hand with Nya's and returned her attention toward the television. I slung my arm around the back of the couch, settling in for a long-ass night with two emotional women because I sensed the next part of the movie would completely wreck them both.

"Maybe he won't go through with it," Nya said.

"Yeah. Maybe she'll convince him to stay for her. I mean, love can make people do weird things."

I rolled my eyes, but I kept the words I had on the tip of my tongue bottled inside. I'd already gotten myself in enough trouble. The last thing I needed was to add more gasoline to their tear-fueled fire.

As the man died, they cried harder. I squeezed Alese's shoulder, trying to comfort her as I handed them both tissues.

"That was so..." Nya's voice trailed off as she blew her nose.

"Beautiful," Alese said, finishing Nya's sentence like they were on the same wavelength.

What I'd hoped would be an evening with some laughs and maybe drinks down on the beach turned into an emotionally charged evening with half a box of tissues being demolished and the girls with such stuffy noses they couldn't pronounce anything correctly.

Alese pushed herself off the couch, clutching the used tissues in her fists. "I need wine. Lots of wine."

"'Cause that always helps you stop crying." I couldn't stop myself from saying it. I knew I should've kept my mouth shut, but sometimes I couldn't help myself.

She placed her hands on her hips, staring down at me with puffy, angry eyes. "I cried once when I drank wine. Once."

I jumped up from the couch, needing a drink myself. "I'll get the drinks and meet you on the beach."

Alese wasn't in the mood for any type of humor, and having her tipsy-sad was better than pissed off. By the time I got down to the beach, Alese and Nya had spread out a blanket and lit a few candles near the waterline.

"Thank God." Alese plucked the bottle and wineglasses from my hands and placed them on the blanket in front of her, filling them quickly. "I need this. I've been wound so tightly lately, and that movie did nothing to help."

Nya took a wineglass and dropped her gaze. "Is it my fault?"

"Sweetheart," Alese said and placed her hand on Nya's leg, "it's not your fault."

"I showed up, and now you're stressed out."

Alese lifted Nya's glass to her mouth, nudging it toward her lips. "Drink your wine."

I stayed silent, sipping my whiskey, and watched them. I felt like they needed to discuss whatever was going on, and maybe Alese would have an easier time opening up to Nya and vice versa.

Nya stared over the rim of her glass as Alese continued talking. "Sometimes I need a really good session to get out of my head. Ret and I haven't been to our club for a while, and I think I'm due for a good old-fashioned ass-whupping."

"Baby, I'm ready when you are," I teased with a playful grin.

There was nothing I liked more in the world than playing with my girl. If she wanted her ass spanked, I wasn't going to tell her no. I'd do anything she wanted, fulfilling her every fantasy and meeting every sexual desire she could dream up.

"Oh. I used to be like that. Well, before..."

"I'm sorry," Alese said, frowning. "That was insensitive of me."

"No. No." Nya shook her head and tried to pull off a smile. "I totally understand. I looked forward to going to the club. Sometimes I'd just watch, especially before I met *him*."

Catching her watching us through the door totally made sense now. She was a voyeur. I think everyone in the world had a little voyeur in them, but some people got off on watching more than others.

Alese's face lit up. "Oh my God. I love watching too. There's something so erotic about seeing two people fucking. Jesus." She fanned her face with her hand. "You should totally come with us if you want. You know, if it wouldn't give you nightmares. I'm sure Ret could get you a temporary membership."

"I don't know," Nya said, glancing at me with red cheeks.

"I can make it happen, but only if Nya wants to go and you're one hundred percent okay with inviting another person with us."

"She's not just another person, Ret. Nya can stay with us all night, even," Alese told her.

I raised my eyebrows, shocked that Alese would allow someone to watch us have a session. We'd never had anything but a private room and never invited another person in to watch. "You sure about that?" I asked.

"It's Nya. Of course I'm sure. If she wants to stay in the common area and watch other people, she can, but if she's too afraid, she can come into our room too."

I grunted before I took a sip of whiskey.

"I don't have to," Nya said quickly.

Alese gave me a look like I was fucking shit up and needed to set things straight. "We'd love for you to come, Nya. I'm just surprised at Alese's openness. It has nothing to do with you. I used to scene only in public before I met her. I'm not afraid of you seeing what we do."

"Well..." Nya licked her lips and looked at Alese. "I have to be honest with you, Alese."

Alese's eyebrows drew down as she tilted her head, waiting for whatever Nya had to confess. "Okay."

"So, the other night..."

"Yeah?"

Nya twisted the wineglass in her hands and took a deep breath. "I was walking by your bedroom. I heard noises, and I may have looked inside and saw you two having..." Nya dropped her voice "...sex."

"You watched us?"

"Yeah." Nya nodded slowly.

"For how long?"

"Just a few minutes," she said and grimaced.

"Well, then why are we even talking about this? You've seen me naked, so going to the club is no big deal."

"Well, if you don't..."

Alese touched Nya's arm and glanced over at me. "We'd love for you to come with us if you're up to going."

"I'm up for anything as long as I'm with you two." Nya smiled, but this time, it was genuine.

I polished off my drink and was about to say something I never thought I would from the day I'd met Alese. "Then it's settled. I'll call ahead and reserve a room for the three of us."

I knew this was opening a proverbial can of worms, but if Alese wanted it and Nya was into it, I was down for anything.

CHAPTER TEN

NYA

My stomach fluttered as we walked toward their bedroom. Alese held my hand, peering at me over her shoulder every few steps to help calm my fears.

I asked for this. I wanted what was about to happen, but that didn't make the entire thing any less scary.

After seeing Alese and Ret together and the kiss on the beach, I wanted to remember what it felt like to be touched by someone other than Diego. Ret and Alese offered something different, something gentle and sweet. I may have only known them for a few days, but touching them...kissing them, was no different than meeting someone at a club and spending the evening with them.

No. That wasn't entirely true.

They weren't complete strangers to me. I'd watched them closely since I stepped foot in their home and saw nothing but love and respect between them. Both Alese, for all her craziness, and Ret, with his macho bravado, had a side that called to me.

I'd thought Diego would be that for me. I thought he was the one who would sweep me off my feet and shower me with so much love, all while feeding my *sexual needs, that I'd never be with another person. I couldn't have been more wrong.*

But I needed to move forward. I wanted to forget the past and go into the future with new memories, amazing experiences, and never take another moment for granted.

"I've never done this before," I said, laying my heart out there because I was worried I'd do something wrong.

Even though I was a kinkster and frequented the club in Atlanta to explore my sexuality, I'd never been with two people before. I didn't know the first thing about what to do, where to put my hands, or even how to start.

Alese turned me around to face them as we stood at the end of their bed. My gaze flickered to Ret, taking in his masculinity and size. He towered over me, covered in muscles, tanned skin, and dark hair. He watched me as he stood next to Alese. I swallowed down my nervousness, knowing I was in good hands even after I'd seen him spank her.

The man rescued me, for God's sake. I couldn't imagine he'd hurt me, especially not with Alese here.

She touched my face, forcing me to look at her. Her smile almost kissed the corners of her ice-blue eyes, causing her high cheekbones to protrude a little more than usual, and somehow making her more beautiful than ever. "We'll only do what you want. If you ever want us to stop, just say pickle."

"Pickle?" I held back my nervous laughter because I didn't want either of them to back out.

"Yes. Pickle. Do you just want Ret to watch, or do you want him to touch you too?" she asked with her hands resting on my shoulders.

"Nya," a voice said as my body rocked. "Nya, wake up." My eyes flew open to find Alese sitting next to me with her hair in curlers. "It's time to get up. You have to get ready, or we're going to be late."

My heart pounded as my dream came back to me. I had been about to have sex with Ret and Alese, and every bit of the vision felt so real.

"You okay?" she asked and moved her face closer. "You look flushed."

I jumped up from the couch in a panic as if she could read my thoughts. "I'm fine. I was just, um, I must be hot from sleeping."

Alese tilted her head, eyeing me. "If you're not feeling up to it, you don't have to come."

I glanced down at the floor, unable to look her in the eye. "No. I'm fine. I just need a shower and to get ready. I don't even know what to wear tonight. I don't have any of my old club clothes."

"Wear the black skirt and the hot strapless bustier we bought the other day. They're sexy enough for the club, and you won't feel overly exposed in front of new people. You were a knockout in that outfit."

I blushed again, loving her compliment more than I probably should. "Thanks, Alese. You're a lifesaver."

"Now go." She shooed me toward my bedroom. "We're leaving in an hour."

"Oh God," I squealed and ran forward, filled with more excitement than I'd felt in a very long time.

"Whoa!" I rocked backward and my jaw dropped as we stood on the top of the stairway leading down into the club.

The common area at this club was beyond amazing and more ornate than the club I'd frequented in Atlanta. The overhead lighting was muted toward the middle of the space and more dramatic near the walls, showing off their deep red color. The public areas were along the walls, fully visible and totally packed with participants and onlookers.

In the center of the room was a bar, lined with people in all forms of dress and undress, including submissives kneeling on the floor near their Masters' feet.

To the right was a section with couches and chairs, and not a single one was empty as people chatted. Some were even making out for everyone in the club to see.

Alese nudged my shoulder with hers. "It's pretty kick-ass, isn't it?"

I was transfixed as I took in every square foot. This was a voyeur's ultimate fantasy come true. I nodded, unable to say anything else because I was still trying to process all that I was witnessing.

The club in Atlanta was small, and not much happened in the public areas of the club. People didn't seem to be as open about their sexuality as they were here.

"How about a drink first?" Ret said, but I barely heard him over the beat of the music.

"We'd love one," Alese answered for both of us when I didn't speak.

I barely blinked as I gawked at the people below. "This is crazy," I said, finally dragging my eyes to Alese.

"Come on. It's more fun to watch up close."

I followed behind her and Ret, careful not to fall down the dark staircase in my new heels. I kept my head downcast, trying to avoid the eyes I knew were on me. I was fresh meat, ripe for the picking, and I'd been in clubs long enough to know that every available Dom had their eyes on me from the moment I walked inside.

When we reached the bottom of the staircase, Ret pulled me close and leaned in, placing his mouth near my ear. "Stay close. Don't wander away without telling us where you're going."

I shook my head, twisting my hands together in front of me. "I won't."

There was no way in hell I was going to wander off anywhere without Ret or Alese at my side. I'd already gotten myself in enough trouble not to want to repeat that mistake again.

"Wine, or something stronger?" Alese asked as she slid into one of the empty seats at the bar.

"Stronger," I told her and looked down at the woman on the floor, hanging on to the leg of a pretty well-built man.

My knees hurt just looking at her, but she didn't move a muscle with her hands folded in her lap, head bowed, and completely at the will of her Master.

"Alese doesn't kneel," Ret told me like he'd read my mind again. "Not unless I make her."

Alese glanced at me and winked. "We have an understanding. If Ret wants me to kneel, I will, but tonight isn't about that."

"Oh," I said, raising my eyebrows. "What's it about?"

Alese reached out and grabbed my hand, lacing her fingers with mine. "It's about you, silly."

"Me?" I squeaked.

"Yes. Well, it's about me, really, but you too."

My gaze moved to Ret, who was leaning over the bar, talking with the bartender and oblivious to our conversation. "Are you sure about this, Alese? I can just wait out here while you guys..." I waggled my eyebrows.

"Don't be silly. It'll be hot. I haven't had anyone watch in a long time, but I remember it was exciting."

"What if I can't?" I swallowed hard, almost choking on the word. "What if I freak?"

She squeezed my hand gently. "If you need to step out of the room, you can. We don't want to upset you. Did you like what you saw the other night? Did it turn you on?"

I couldn't just come out and say it was so damn hot I had to go back to my room and touch myself, reliving everything as if I were her. Even if that was the truth, it wasn't something I was comfortable admitting just yet. "It didn't upset me."

Alese smiled. "Did it turn you on?"

"Yes," I admitted and bit my lip, stopping myself from saying anything else.

"Drinks," Ret said, holding out the two glasses of whatever he ordered us on the rocks.

I gulped down two mouthfuls and winced. The burn at the back of my throat was something I hadn't prepared for, thinking it was something other than tequila. I had a checkered past with that liquor, and most of the time, things ended with me not remembering too much.

"It's good, no?" Alese licked her lips like she was savoring the flavor.

"It's good," I lied. Even if it tasted god-awful, I needed the liquor to help ease my fears about what was going to happen.

I'd never watched people I actually knew. They were always people at the club in Atlanta with whom I never had any real contact or connection, but this time was going to be something totally different.

CHAPTER ELEVEN

RET

"**O**n your knees," I said the words to Alese as soon as we entered the private room. She gaped at me for a moment, but as soon as I crossed my arms over my chest, she kneeled without saying a word. "Nya, if something becomes too overwhelming, you can step into the hallway, but don't go anywhere else."

"Yes, Sir." Nya nodded as she sat, keeping her eyes trained on us. Alese smiled, staring across the room and seeming to enjoy this more than I would've imagined.

"I brought something for you, sweetheart." I fished a blindfold out of my back pocket and dangled the black material in front of Alese's face, knowing how much she was about to hate me.

"No," she growled.

I raised an eyebrow. If she wanted to argue with me, I'd make sure to hold off her orgasm until she was practically bursting at the seams.

"Yes, Sir."

Placing my fingers under her chin, I lifted her eyes to mine. "If you're a good girl, I'll let you look. But until I think you're ready, you're not allowed to watch."

"It's so..." She grimaced.

"It's so what?" I baited her to finish the statement, but she didn't.

Alese's tongue poked out and swept across her bottom lip as I ran my finger across the top of her corset and over the swell of her breasts. I ached to be inside her, burying myself so deep not even an inch separated our bodies, but this wasn't about me. It was about us and Nya.

I tied the blindfold tightly, making sure Alese couldn't sneak a peek during the scene even though I knew she'd try. I moved behind her, giving Nya a full view of Alese as she kneeled on the floor. I dipped my fingers inside the back of Alese's corset, about to pull the strings, when I glanced toward the couch, seeing Nya scooting forward and touching her lips.

Bending down, I placed my ear next to Alese's and inhaled the sweet perfume she'd worn especially for tonight. "Do you like being watched?"

Goose bumps broke out across her skin as she nodded. "Yes, Sir." Her tongue poked back out again, driving me half insane, but I was sure that was part of her plan.

Her body jerked backward as I pulled the strings of her corset loose. Alese's breath caught as the material fell away from her body, exposing her breasts. Her nipples pebbled immediately as the cool air rushed across her chest.

"So beautiful." I traced the swell of her breasts with my fingers, slowly moving across her skin.

Alese tilted her head back, and she moaned as my hand moved lower and I raked the tips of my fingers across her nipple. Her lips parted, and she swayed backward, giving me a magnificent view of her breasts and better access.

I bent down on one knee, cupping her heavy breasts in my hands and using my thumbs to toy with her nipples. She gasped as I pinched and pulled on her nipples, knowing how much she loved rough breast play.

My gaze moved to Nya as she slowly stroked the tops of her own breasts and leaned forward with most of her body hanging over the floor as her eyes zeroed in on my hands.

"Do you like this?" I asked, running the rough pad of my thumb over Alese's hard nipples, but I kept my eyes locked on Nya.

"Yes," Alese moaned and swayed, gravitating toward my touch.

Nya parted her lips, tongue sweeping out just like I'd seen Alese do a hundred times. Her eyes flickered upward, catching me staring at her as I played with Alese's breasts. Nya pulled the corner of her bottom lip inside her mouth and bit down, looking completely innocent and beautiful.

I slid my hand down Alese's front and between her legs, slipping under her skirt. She was wet, practically dripping with desire, and we had barely started. She opened, pushing her knees apart as my fingers glided against her slick pussy. She shivered and inhaled sharply as my thumb swept across her clit.

"Open your legs wider," I told her, swatting at her inner thighs with my hand.

My dick was as hard as granite as she tilted her head back and rested it against my chest while she pushed her knees farther apart. This was a slow form of sensual torture for me. The entire experience would be an exercise in patience and restraint for Alese as well as me.

I pushed two fingers inside her greedy pussy and curled them upward, pressing against her G-spot. My other hand pinched her nipple, keeping pressure on the sensitive bud as I pulled my fingers out and thrust them in deeper this time. Her breathing became erratic as her insides clamped down around my fingers, sucking them back inside.

Nya watched us, stroking her inner thigh with one hand and groping her breast in the other, completely transfixed and in the moment. The hunger in her eyes made me harder almost to the point of pain.

I slid my fingers out of Alese's beautiful cunt, leaving a trail of her wetness up the middle of her body before circling her breast. "Up," I told her, needing to have better access—complete access—to her entire body.

She complied, stretching out her arms as I swept my hands over her tender skin. I undid the zipper at the back of her skirt, letting the material fall to the floor near her feet. Taking her hand, I helped her step out completely naked for the first time in front of someone other than me. Nya swept her gaze across Alese's body, lingering on her perky breasts before dipping to her pussy.

Taking Alese by the hand, I led her to the punishment bench. The name was a total lie. Strapping her into it was the furthest thing from punishment. She loved every minute of being on full display with each hole ready and willing to be filled. I guided her onto the bench, helping her get on without hurting herself. There was a flash of a smile on her face as I buckled her wrists.

"Are you excited?" I asked, tightening the leather straps so she couldn't move.

"Yes, Sir."

My hand traced the curve of her back before circling her ass. "You love this, don't you?"

She shuddered as my finger slid between her cheeks, running over her asshole. "Yes." There was thirst in her voice.

"You want all your holes stuffed?"

"I'm yours to do with what you want, Sir."

I smiled and sucked in a breath. There was so much I wanted to do with her, and her willingness to please me always sent shivers down my spine. I fastened the straps around her ankles, and she pulled against them, testing their tightness.

"You can't move, my love." My back was to Nya as I dipped my fingers into Alese's wet pussy and groaned. My balls throbbed, and my cock strained against my jeans, begging for some relief.

I thrust my fingers deeper, pummeling her cunt over and over again as she tried to squirm but couldn't. She gasped when I pulled my fingers out, leaving her empty and wanting. I walked to the bag I'd left near the door, digging inside and peering over at Nya for a brief moment.

Her knees were farther apart as she leaned back into the couch with her eyes moving between Alese and me. Her hand stilled under her skirt, watching me closely as I dug into the bottom of the bag to retrieve Alese's favorite anal plug and the bottle of lube.

Nya's eyes widened at the size, but anal play was Alese's specialty. When I'd met her, the girl had an arsenal of anal toys but swore she wasn't into ass play. Testing the waters, I'd quickly learned her statement was a complete lie.

I smiled at Nya and mouthed, "Don't worry," trying to calm any fears she had about what was about to happen as I walked back toward the bench. Lifting the bottle in the air, I drizzled the lube down Alese's ass, letting the liquid slide over her pussy and form a puddle on the floor.

Using my fingers, I spread out the lube before slipping the plug through the wetness, coating every inch completely. Alese moaned, knowing what was coming, practically panting as the tip pushed against her asshole.

"You love having your ass stuffed, don't you, *piccola*?" I said, twisting the tip inside her opening.

"Yes," she panted, pushing her ass toward me and trying to force the plug deeper, quicker.

"All your holes are greedy."

"Only for you, Sir," she said and gasped as the widest part of the plug slid past her opening.

My eyes practically rolled back as the need building inside me grew along with my cock. Movement across the room caught my attention as I pulled on the plug and had Alese shaking.

Nya had lifted her skirt, giving me the full view of her beautiful pussy as her fingers dipped inside, disappearing. I sucked in a breath, overcome with more lust and need than I ever thought possible. Nya's eyes were locked on mine, watching me carefully as I licked my lips and pulled my gaze away and back to my girlfriend.

I bent my body over Alese, letting my cock push on her plug, driving it deeper as I placed my mouth near her ear. "Nya's enjoying herself," I whispered. "She's watching you get filled and fingering herself."

Alese groaned, probably wanting to punch me because she couldn't see. I grabbed the bulb hanging from the plug, giving it a quick squeeze. This wasn't just any anal plug, but an expandable one, making her feel even more stuffed than she already did. Her head dropped forward, and her back arched in pleasure.

Fuck, I didn't know how much more of this I could take. I'd probably blow my load like a teenager at this rate if I weren't careful and didn't restrain myself.

Nya hadn't run out of the room, but besides the anal plug, I'd been gentle on my Alese. This wasn't about scaring Nya, instead about bringing pleasure to everyone involved and letting Nya explore her own body, remembering the pleasure of touch.

This wasn't about me. I kept repeating those words, trying to keep my shit together long enough to give Alese, and maybe Nya too, more than one orgasm.

I straightened, pushing against Alese's plug with one hand while I unzipped my jeans with the other. Nya's eyes were on me, no longer watching Alese as she writhed against the bench, her greedy cunt looking to be filled and pleasured.

"Tell me you want my cock," I said, inching my jeans down my thighs.

"I want your cock."

My hand came down hard against Alese's ass, reminding her of her forgotten word.

"Sir, yes, Sir," she bit out quickly, earning her the palm of my hand against her reddened flesh.

Nya gasped and rocked into her fingers, eating up every minute of this just like me.

CHAPTER TWELVE

NYA

Fuck me. I'd forgotten how hot and erotic it was to watch two people bound by passion in a delicate dance of push and pull. I couldn't take my eyes off them as Ret pushed down his pants, exposing his massive cock.

My heart raced, pounding in my chest faster than before as my eyes swept across his body while he pulled off his shirt and threw it to the floor. *Dear God.* The man had everything and so much of it too. His long body was covered with tight muscles and perfectly sun-kissed skin. A small patch of dark hair had fallen over his forehead, almost covering his blue, intense eyes and making him look younger and somehow less intimidating. The muscles in his arms moved under his skin, flexing as he rubbed a hand over Alese's ass slowly and methodically, following the swell of her cheeks.

There was a playful smirk on his lips when I lifted my gaze to his face. I plunged my fingers deeper, pretending I was the girl strapped to the bench about to be fucked and pleasured until I was begging for him to stop.

My eyes dropped to Alese as she panted, mouth open and wanting to be filled every bit as much as I did. He reached for the bulb on the anal plug, and my eyes widened as my asshole constricted, imagining that thing inside me, stretching me.

I was so turned on my fingers glided through my wetness with no resistance, slipping into my cunt like they were always meant to be there. I licked my lips and swallowed, my mouth dry and thirsty for something more, but not daring to move from my spot.

My breath faltered as he pushed his cock inside, grunting as he slipped past the plug and her body writhed in front of him. I squirmed and plunged a third finger inside, needing the feeling of fullness Alese was no doubt experiencing. Her breasts jiggled, bouncing forward with each thrust of Ret's powerful hips against her body.

I felt each stroke, matching my rhythm with his as Alese's hands wrapped around the bench and she moaned. I was so turned on, more than I'd been in months as I watched Ret fuck Alese silly. She gasped and so did I as he swiveled his hips, touching every bit of her pussy from the inside.

His grunts became louder and more punctuated. I thought he was about to come, following me over the cliff of ecstasy as I squeezed my eyes shut, too overcome with sensation to keep them open. My muscles seized and my breathing halted as the waves crashed over me again and again until I gasped for air, completely spent.

I opened my eyes, and they instantly widened as they fixed on Ret, still buried deep inside Alese and pumping into her like he was more of a machine than a human being.

"Damn," I whispered under my breath, seriously impressed with his skill and stamina.

The only sounds in the room were skin slapping against skin, Alese's moans of pleasure, Ret's grunts, and my harsh breathing, working together to create the most beautiful symphony of ecstasy.

Ret tightened his grip on Alese's hips and buried his other hand in her hair, tipping her head back and giving him more leverage. I watched, completely consumed by the scene playing out before me. Alese's mouth fell open as she gasped for air. Ret's hand loosened in her hair, but she didn't let her head fall forward as he moved his fingers to the material tied around her face.

The blindfold dropped to the floor, and Alese opened her eyes, blinking away the haze and pinning me with her gaze. Lust built inside me, faster than it had ever happened before. My fingers slid against my wet flesh, my eyes locked on Alese and hers solely on me.

She grunted, matching Ret, as he slammed into her body, slapping her ass every few strokes. Her eyes watered as she bucked and begged for relief. I thrust my fingers deeper, watching her eyes follow my movements as I followed Ret's lead and kept perfect pace. My wrist ached at the speed, but I couldn't stop; I wouldn't stop.

I widened my legs, feeling emboldened by the look of lust and want on Alese's face as she watched me pleasure myself while being fucked relentlessly by Ret. I stuck my hand in my strapless top and pulled out my breasts, needing something more to push me over the edge a second time.

I bent my neck, pulled my breast to my lips, and closed my mouth around my hard and aching nipple. Pleasure shot through me, splintering inside my body until my toes curled.

I flickered my eyes to Alese, finding her still staring at me, scorching me with her gaze as I sucked on my nipple and thrust my fingers between my legs. Alese's hands tightened around the bench as her eyes rolled back. Ret moaned, calling her name as he reached underneath the bench and slapped her pussy with a thud.

I gasped, my eyes widening as she tossed her head back and wailed, shaking against the restraints. Her moans came out on a crescendo, echoing off the walls of the tiny space as I followed her over the edge, unable to breathe.

I held Alese's gaze as the orgasm rolled through me stronger than the first—and longer. Alese moaned as Ret slammed into her, drawing her orgasm out longer than I thought humanly possible as he followed.

I lay there, legs open, gasping for air, with my fingers still deep inside me, watching them as the aftershocks had both their bodies quaking. Sweat beaded across their flesh, glistening like a thousand points of light. I wasn't sure how long we stayed like that... Me staring, Alese gasping, and Ret's shaking legs showing he was, in fact, human after all, but it was intense and the single most erotic moment of my life.

No one had laid a hand on me, yet I came as if someone had flipped a switch, reawakening my hunger for sins of the flesh. I glanced toward the floor, slipping my fingers from between my legs and closing my knees, suddenly feeling overexposed. I didn't know what had come over me as I let the lust and passion take control and all reason escaped me.

I kept my eyes on the floor, covered my breasts with my top, and wondered how the rest of the night would go. I'd never watched anyone I knew and didn't know what proper protocol was for something like that. I mean, did I talk about it? Compliment them on their performance, even? I had no clue if we were supposed to pretend like the entire thing hadn't happened even when it did.

These two people, the man who saved me and my new best friend, showed me their bodies, letting me into their intimate life, and I didn't want to say anything to ruin the amazing thing we had going. If they threw me out, where would I go?

I sat in silence, hearing the rustle of their clothes, and closed my eyes, praying I hadn't fucked up. *Just breathe.* I kept reminding myself there was nothing to fear. This was Alese and Ret, two of the nicest people I'd ever met.

The couch dipped on either side of me. "Nya." Ret's deep voice sent a shiver down my spine. "Open your eyes," he said.

Slowly, I brought my gaze to his, swallowing the fear that had settled in the back of my throat. He touched my chin, lifting my face higher to fully meet his stare. "Are you okay?"

"Yes, Sir," I responded quickly and blew out a shaky breath.

"Do you regret being here?" Alese asked as she placed her hand gently on my leg.

I shook my head, turning to face her with a smile. "No, ma'am. I enjoyed myself."

She grinned and waggled her eyebrows. "Me too."

"We both enjoyed having you here. We know it was a big step for you." Ret smiled, but he kept his hands to himself as he wiped away the sweat that had formed on his forehead with a towel. "I don't remember the last time she lasted that long."

"What about you, tiger?" Alese chuckled and made a noise more like a baby lion, but it was cute anyway.

"I couldn't give in so easily. I wanted to draw it out, but I'm not sure I'll be able to walk tomorrow."

He laughed and I cracked a smile, sitting between the two of them as they teased each other. It should've felt odd, but it didn't. I should've been uncomfortable, but I wasn't. There was a peacefulness inside my soul that I hadn't felt in a long time, and it was present because of Ret and Alese.

Ret climbed to his feet and held out his hands. "I could use a drink. How about you ladies?" I slid my hand into his, just like Alese did, and let him pull me from the couch. My legs wobbled as my knees started to give out, but Ret wrapped an arm around my back, steadying me. "Maybe just a soda for you." He grinned.

"No way, buddy. I want booze."

"Three waters and three drinks, it is, but no more," Ret said as he opened the door for us to walk out before him.

I went first, walking like I knew where the hell I was going, when I didn't have a clue. I followed the deep thump of the bass toward the common room, hoping the music wasn't leading me astray.

"You really went easy on me, Ret. Getting soft in your old age?"

I laughed, keeping my face forward as Alese spoke to Ret.

"Baby, I didn't want to scare the girl. This was about each of us having pleasure, not just you," he told her, and I could hear the playfulness in his voice.

"Sometimes I need a good spanking."

"Your ass says you got it."

"Don't go all soft on me. I won't even have a bruise tomorrow the way you were swatting me," she told him. "Man up."

"Watch it," he warned, dropping his voice so low I barely heard him say, "We still have time."

Fucking hell.

CHAPTER THIRTEEN

RET

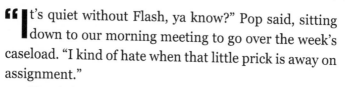

"It's quiet without Flash, ya know?" Pop said, sitting down to our morning meeting to go over the week's caseload. "I kind of hate when that little prick is away on assignment."

"Don't be an asshole. He's not loud," Morgan told Pop as he straightened the pile of files he had in front of him. "Not like you, at least. If you weren't here, we'd probably finally enjoy some peace and quiet."

Pop touched his moustache, running his fingers through the hair that was longer than usual as he stared at Morgan. "You'd miss my beautiful face."

Morgan rolled his eyes. "Don't push your luck."

"Who's your daddy?" Pop teased, elbowing him in the arm.

Morgan grumbled under his breath, hating being reminded that Bear was, in fact, his stepfather. It still felt odd to think I had a stepbrother, but I rolled with it. Even Janice seemed to take it better than I did, buddy-ing up with our new brother easy. Legally, we were an insta-family, but that didn't make family dinner any less weird.

Thomas walked into the conference room a little more dressed up than usual, and everyone noticed. "Hot date?" Frisco teased him before he had a chance to sit.

"It's my anniversary, and I'm taking my girl out to dinner after work today."

"An expensive dinner," Angel said from the doorway. "I'm only working a half day today, boys, so you're going to be on your own this afternoon."

"We got this." Pop winked, always trying to be the slick one.

"Does anyone need anything before I seal you inside?"

"We're good, baby. Thanks." Thomas slid the folders down the table like he always did to start every meeting. "Let's start with Matías. Where are we with him?"

Matías was a wanted criminal, specializing in human trafficking. So far, the FBI, Interpol, and other legal entities hadn't been able to catch him before he moved on to his new destination with a fresh crop of victims. I'd been tracking him, working with my contacts in the BDSM community to try to get a jump on his location before even the authorities got a whiff of his whereabouts.

I leaned back in my chair and tapped my pen against the folder, happy with the response I'd received from the BDSM community. No one wanted a guy like Matías on the streets. We had enough bullshit to deal with without a man like him kidnapping people and selling them into the sex-slave industry. "I have feelers out to all my community contacts. I expect to hear from them today. We should be able to move soon."

"Let us know as soon as you hear something," James told me.

"I will, boss."

"Next order of business. What cases are we closing out this week?"

"I have a hell of one that I can finally say is over. Cheating husband and shit got ugly." Pop gave him a big, toothy grin.

My phone started vibrating and dancing across the table, catching my attention. "I have to take this," I said before heading toward the door to take Connor's call.

Connor was the owner of Forbidden in Jacksonville and a longtime friend since we'd crossed paths in our younger days. If the man had intel, I'd jump on it because he was a man of his word and wouldn't yank my chain with bullshit information.

"What's up?"

"I did some asking around. Matías has been here on and off the last few weekends. If you want him, you better get your ass up here before he takes off again."

"We'll be there. Thanks, man."

"If you don't show, I'll handle him myself."

"I said we'll be there. End of conversation."

"Noted."

I walked back into the conference room with a huge, shit-eating grin because we'd finally gotten a solid lead on Matías's whereabouts. "Found the fucker."

"Where is he?" James asked.

"He's been frequenting a club in Jacksonville called Forbidden a few nights a week and has been there the last two weekends."

Thomas leaned back in his chair, swiveling from side to side. "I can't believe he's still in Florida."

James nodded as did everybody else because no one could believe that a criminal mastermind like Matías could be so stupid. "He must not have heard about my trip to Taboo. When should we head out?"

Forbidden was only open on the weekend, and knowing Matías, he'd gone underground already, waiting for the weekend to snag another victim. "Let's get our ladies and head up there Friday. We may have to be gone a few days until he shows up. Is that okay, Thomas?"

"Wait." Thomas straightened, and his face grew serious. "You're going to take Izzy again?"

James shrugged like it was the most logical thing in the world and Thomas was crazy for even questioning him. "Yeah. We need the ladies with us to maintain our cover."

Thomas scrubbed his hand down his face. "I don't like it."

"Have I ever let anything happen to her?"

"I trust you. Just be careful. If there's any sign of trouble, get the fuck out."

"I'll be there with them, Thomas. Nothing will happen. I know the owner of the club, and we'll be in good hands," I told him because I'd protect anyone in that room, including their wives, with my own life.

I just had to break the news to Alese and Nya. I needed Alese by my side just as much as James needed Izzy. Nya would have to stay behind because I didn't dare put her life in danger or put her through undue stress. I just hoped she could cope with being alone for a few days while we caught someone who deserved to be behind bars.

"When do we have to leave?" Alese rubbed her temples, not exactly ecstatic about our upcoming trip. Nya had gone back to her bedroom to grab one of my old sweatshirts I'd given to her as Alese prepped dinner.

"Friday morning."

"What about Nya?"

That was the same thing I'd been thinking all day. We hadn't left her alone yet, not for any extended period of time, at least, and I wasn't sure I felt right doing it now. "Maybe my pop and Fran could stay with her while we're gone."

"Oy," Alese groaned and dragged her hands down her face. "If they're our only option."

"She'll be safe with them." I knew my pop would do everything possible to keep Nya safe and calm while Fran cooked her food that was even more inedible than Alese's dishes.

"I'll break the news to her."

"You make it sound like we're getting rid of her."

"That's the last thing I want her to think. I just want to make sure she's okay with it."

"We'll talk to her together. We owe her as much."

Nya strolled back into the kitchen and froze. She glanced between us, knowing the vibe was off. "Why did you stop talking?"

"We didn't." Alese gave me the side-eye before she grabbed the wine I'd set out for dinner.

"We were just talking about this weekend."

"That's all?" Nya moved toward the counter, but she walked slowly, her eyes still moving between us.

Alese smiled nervously. "Let's sit. Dinner's ready, and I made Ret's favorite."

I scratched my head because I didn't really have a favorite. I preferred something that wasn't burned and dried-out, which she did with just about everything. But tonight was pasta, and it was probably the one thing she didn't make like sandpaper, even if it resembled mush.

"Alese and I have to go away this weekend," I said before everyone had a chance to sit down. There was no reason to delay it and end up ruining anyone's appetite. If Nya was going to freak out, it was better to get it out of the way as quickly as possible.

"Oh." Nya frowned, but she didn't have a meltdown. "All weekend?"

"I have a case in Jacksonville, and I need Alese's help. We won't be gone all weekend. Hopefully, we'll be home late Saturday or early Sunday."

Nya pulled out her chair and grabbed her napkin as she sat down, seemingly unaffected. "That's okay. Really. Don't worry about me."

Alese sat next to her and placed her hand over Nya's as she rested it on the table. "We don't want you to be alone in this big house all weekend. We had an idea."

"I don't need a babysitter, Alese."

"They wouldn't babysit you, Nya." Alese leaned forward and grabbed the giant bowl of pasta that would probably be dinner for the week. "They're Ret's dad and stepmom. I thought you might enjoy spending some time with them. Maybe they can just check on you or something. Fran always likes to feel useful." When Alese got nervous, she got chatty, and she was rambling.

I rolled my eyes. That was the understatement of the century. Fran was up everyone's ass and deep into their business, but she was the reason I was here. If she hadn't called me, I probably never would've reconnected with my father. She was nosy, but her heart was always in the right place.

Nya smiled in my direction as she took the plate Alese had filled with so much pasta Nya would be there for an hour even if she didn't come up for air. "I like your dad. He's such a sweet man."

"That's one way to describe him."

"You're hard on your dad. He could be a total asshole like mine."

She had a point, but Bear wasn't the same man he was years ago. He wasn't always the Father of the Year, but she didn't need to know our past. "He's a good guy underneath his bullshit."

"And what about his wife? Your stepmom?"

"Fran is... I don't know how to describe her."

"She is a riot. She puts that big mountain of a man right in his place. She's kinda scary like that."

"I'm okay with them stopping by just so you two don't worry, but otherwise, I could use a few days by myself."

"Understood." I nodded. I knew the feeling. I tried to avoid looking at my plate because Alese had loaded mine up too. Nya hadn't had a minute to breathe on her own for so long that I was sure she could use a little time to collect her thoughts.

We'd given her very little time alone since she'd walked through the front door. I wasn't sure what the protocol was for something like what she'd been through, and I didn't want her to have a complete meltdown either. But after the doctor gave her a clean bill of health, including her mental health, I was sure we could give her a reprieve.

"I'll give you their cell phone numbers, and they'll have yours."

"I don't have one," Nya said.

"We'll get you one tomorrow. Don't worry." Alese smiled. The woman loved to shop, even if it was for electronics. Set her loose in any store and she was happy as could be. "We'll have our makeup day."

"Great," I mumbled as I jammed the first forkful of overly cooked pasta into my mouth. I didn't care they were spending money, but I wished they knew how beautiful they were without all the shit on their faces. "I don't know why you two need makeup. You're perfect as is."

They both stopped moving, gawking at me like I had two heads. I thought I was being nice, but they didn't see it that way. I'd thought things were rough sometimes with just Alese, but I could already see the two of them were going to try to gang up on me. It was time to show Alese who was in charge again.

CHAPTER FOURTEEN

NYA

I opened the front door wearing a new outfit Alese had picked out, feeling like a million dollars and a little like my old self again.

Fran whistled. "Look at her," she said, glancing over her shoulder at Bear, who leaned against the car with his hands crossed over his extra-wide chest. Fran was just how I imagined her after Alese and Ret gave me the heads-up about her. She was an older woman, about the age of my mother, but she carried herself differently.

"Very nice," he muttered, adjusting the toothpick between his lips. "We drinkin' or having a fashion show?"

I closed the door as Fran made her way down the stairs, hiding my smile with my back turned to Bear. There was something about the man that I'd liked instantly.

When Fran called and asked if I wanted to go to their favorite bar to dance and drink, I jumped at the chance. I loved the quiet and serenity of being at Ret's place, but I could use an evening of fun like the old days.

"Don't mind him. He's grumpy tonight."

"Why?" I asked as I tossed the keys into the small black purse Alese had sworn I needed because it matched my shoes.

Fran rolled her eyes and shook her head. "He's upset the guys didn't take him with them."

"Poor thing."

Bear opened the door for me, and I slid across the back seat after pulling my legs inside. He smiled, giving me a quick wink with a smile before closing me inside.

"We ready?" he asked as he settled into the driver's seat next to his wife and started the engine.

Fran shot him a warning glance, and I muffled my laughter because the last thing I wanted was for either of them to regret taking me out tonight. "We're ready."

Bear's eyes found mine in the rearview mirror as he drove. "You settlin' in okay, kid?"

"Yes."

"My kid treating you right?"

"Always. He's a great guy."

"Just like his pop." He grinned.

"Oh lordy," Fran groaned. "The man's already got a big head. Don't make it any bigger."

"Babe," Bear said, glancing in Fran's direction and grabbing her hand.

"What?"

"You love me."

"Yeah. Well..."

"You love my big..."

She narrowed her eyes. "Don't say it."

Bear laughed before bringing her hand to his mouth and placing a light kiss against the top. She snatched her hand away and turned up the radio, blasting some country tune I'd never heard before.

"This song is amazing. Maybe we'll dance to it tonight."

"You know I hate to dance."

"Baby?"

"Yeah?"

"If I wanna dance, we're gonna dance."

"Right," he said quickly, his head bobbing in agreement.

I couldn't control my laughter any longer, placing the back of my hand against my mouth. I muffled the sound. Ret was the luckiest guy in the world to have these two people as parents. I wasn't so lucky. My parents cared, but they also tried to control my entire life. That was the reason I'd ended up in Atlanta to begin with...I wanted my freedom.

Kind of funny that I ended up with the exact opposite after everything was said and done, but I wasn't about to repeat the mistakes of my past nor let them guide my future.

When we pulled into the Neon Cowboy, Fran shifted in her seat to face me. "Don't be scared of any of the guys. They'd lay down their life for you in a minute. The crowd can get rowdy sometimes, but I promise you'll have a good time."

"Okay." I smiled, but my stomach was twisted as the nerves started to take hold. I followed them toward the door and fidgeted with the strap of my purse, all while trying to maintain my balance on the damn high heels

"If anyone gets handsy, let me know, and I'll kick their ass."

"Got it."

Bear held the door open for us. Fran walked in first, me behind her, and him following close on my heels.

The bar was dimly lit and filled with so many people, I couldn't imagine we'd ever find a table. The floor was covered in peanut shells or sawdust. It was hard to tell with the lighting and the number of feet, but the crunch underneath my shoes was hard to ignore.

Fran parted the crowd and sauntered through the sea of people like she owned the place. In the distance, there was a table with three open seats where a group of men was sipping beer. Fran stopped in front of the table, her eyes skimming the group. "Guys. This is Nya."

A few of the faces looked familiar. I'd seen them at ALFA, but I hadn't spoken to them. "Hi," I said, feeling like a kid on the first day of school, filled with fear and excitement.

A man nodded his head, looking a little like Keanu Reeves, but hotter. "Hey, Nya. It's nice to see you again. I'm Frisco, and this is Morgan, Fran and Bear's kid."

"I'm not Bear's kid. Wipe that shit right out of your mind." He leaned forward, holding out his hand to me. "I'm Fran's son, and we've met before."

He was a hunk. In another place and time, I probably would've flirted with him and tried to catch his eye. That was, until I saw his wedding band glimmer under the overhead light.

"It's nice to see you both again."

"Take a seat," Fran said, pulling out the chairs. "Bear will get us drinks. Beer?"

"Anything cold and wet."

"Ahh." A man sitting toward the center of the group, older than everyone else but still handsome, laughed. "She likes her drinks like I like my ladies."

"You really are a strange bastard, Tank," Frisco told him, slapping him on the chest.

"Never claimed to be normal. I'm Tank, doll. Bear's oldest friend."

"Older than dirt," Bear muttered next to me before motioning for me to take a seat next to Fran.

Slowly, I lowered myself into the chair, unable to take my eyes off the group and wondering if Fran and Bear hung around anyone who wasn't tall, dark, and handsome.

"We were just debating."

"About what?" Fran asked Morgan as she leaned back in her chair, and he took a slug of his beer.

"About Ret and James."

The mention of Ret from Morgan got my full attention.

"What about them, son?"

"You think the ladies ever get to spank them, or is it a one-way street?"

The table erupted in laughter and I grinned, but it wasn't an easy, carefree grin. I wasn't sure if they were making fun of them and being assholes, or if this was the type of trash talk they always engaged in.

"I'm sure they tried." Fran smiled and grabbed the beer Bear set down in front of her, having returned in record time. "I can imagine Izzy isn't always compliant."

"Hell, I'd let either one of those girls beat my ass," Tank said and smiled.

"Tank, you'd let anyone beat your ass if it meant you'd get a piece."

"Damn straight. I ain't picky."

Morgan waved off Tank. "No. Seriously. We were talking about Matías and if they'd finally catch the sick bastard."

"Who's Matías?" I asked as I turned my cold beer in my hands.

"The bad guy they're trying to nab this weekend. He's a human trafficker. Sells people into the sex-slave industry. He's a bad motherfucker."

I gasped and covered my mouth. Ret and Alese didn't tell me they were going after someone dangerous.

I'd read a lot about human trafficking before I joined Charmed. It was my biggest fear when I'd become a member and started to find my footing in the community. I wasn't lucky when I ended up with Diego, but I could've been sold and shipped to a foreign country, never to be heard from again. The very thought sent a chill down my spine.

Bear spoke quickly, probably sensing my unease because I was shit at hiding my emotions. "They'll catch him. It's James and Ret, after all. Nobody's getting away from them. I just wish I were there with them."

"You can't go on every assignment, ya greedy bastard," Frisco told Bear. "And let's face it, if you walked into a sex club, you'd probably die from overstimulation."

"Son," Bear laughed. "I was in sex clubs when you were still sucking on your mother's tit. I may be older, but I've lived a hell of a lot more experiences than your tiny little brain will ever comprehend."

I took a sip of my beer, watching them over the rim of my glass. I couldn't get the thought of Alese and Ret being at a sex club, trying to find a human trafficker and stop him, out of my head.

What if something went wrong?

What if they got hurt?

I wasn't worried about myself or where that would leave me. I wanted them in my life, and even in the short amount of time I'd known them, I knew I couldn't imagine life without them.

CHAPTER FIFTEEN

RET

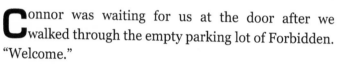

Connor was waiting for us at the door after we walked through the empty parking lot of Forbidden. "Welcome."

I shook his hand, always happy to see an old friend. It had been years since I'd laid eyes on him, and although time had been kind to me, it hadn't been so forgiving to Connor. "Thanks for doing this."

Connor had a partner in the business, a former Navy SEAL named Trent Newsome, who was interested in helping us nab Matías. "Welcome," Trent said with a curt head nod as we entered the lobby. The man looked like stereotypical, hard-core, military special forces personnel. Strong jaw, big muscles, perfect posture, and lacking any type of emotional facial expression as he stared at James and me.

Then his gaze slid to our girls. "It's a pleasure to meet you, ladies."

"I'm Alese." She bowed like she was halfway tame.

"Izzy." Being Izzy, she didn't bow her head, but she looked him straight in the eye, defiant to the core.

"Welcome to Forbidden."

"Thanks for helping us, Trent." I pulled Alese close to my side, staking my claim. James did the same because we both knew there was something not quite right with Trent. It wasn't that he'd try anything, but something was off with him. Maybe he'd seen too much in the military, but I wasn't going to stick around long enough to find out. If Connor trusted him, I'd give the guy a pass because Connor didn't play games.

"The last thing we need is a human trafficker lurking around our club. I'll do anything to help put his ass behind bars."

Connor stepped in front of Trent. "Let's get inside, and I'll give you a tour before you can spend a few hours wandering around on your own."

"Sounds great," I told him.

Connor opened the door, and we walked inside the common area with Trent close behind us. "Matías spends about an hour in this part of the club until he convinces someone to join him in a private room," Connor said as soon as the door closed behind us.

Forbidden was an upscale club with modern touches, having received a complete overhaul after Connor purchased it. A black marble floor and blood-red walls matched the leather furniture that was in the center of the room. On the far right was a viewing platform with a St. Andrew's Cross, one of my favorite apparatuses, and shackles hanging from the ceiling just a few feet away.

"We have a lot of members who are into voyeurism. We make sure to have plenty of areas for them to live out that fantasy."

To the left was the bar, lining the entire wall of the club, with built-in stools and a sleek cement top. Behind the bar was a wall-to-wall mirror that could give any drinker the full view of the action going on behind them, followed by cages and stockades.

"Ah, our area for public humiliation." Connor came to stand next to James. "It's become quite popular lately."

Izzy gripped James's arm, pressing her body flush against him. "Um, fuck that."

"Let me show you the private rooms, and then we'll let you be to do whatever you want."

From the outside, the club didn't look large. But it extended into an endless maze of private rooms and smaller public play areas. Each spot had its own theme or purpose, and everything was top-notch. No cheap, shitty BDSM furniture that looked overused. The amount of furniture and apparatus in the club was mind-boggling. Cages, benches, vacbeds, and bondage chairs were everywhere, along with beds and exam tables in too many rooms to count. This was a playland for anyone in the lifestyle.

"Any questions?" Connor asked after we walked into the last small play area tucked away at the end of the hallway.

We stood around the circular bed that could probably fit ten people easily and must have made for quite a scene.

"How do you monitor everything?" James asked.

Connor crossed his arms in front of his chest and glanced upward. "All public areas have closed-circuit television monitoring, and the private rooms have cameras on the doorways with a two-way intercom in case there's an emergency. We have designated Masters who walk the hallways and public areas at all times to stop anything from getting out of hand."

I stared up at the camera, thankful Connor had enough sense to install equipment in the rooms because the fresh waves of douchebags trying to join the lifestyle were mind-boggling and dangerous. "Can you show us the surveillance room?"

"Sure. We don't keep tapes of anything to protect the security and anonymity of our members, but they're monitored every moment the club is open for business," Connor said, motioning for us to follow him back toward the public area where we'd started our tour.

James whispered to Izzy as Alese clutched my hand, staying close to me as we followed Connor.

"It'll be fine," I told her. "I promise."

She never liked new clubs. She wasn't comfortable around new people and preferred sticking with our own crowd over being more adventurous. I knew tomorrow she'd be fine. She'd slide into her role as a submissive, but tonight she'd let the fear take over.

"Let's hope we catch the bastard tonight, and then we can have one day to play," Izzy told James as we stood outside the nondescript door.

"In here is where we have twenty monitors, along with the intercom system. It's really an amazing thing, and I don't know of a club within three hundred miles that has this kind of setup."

James glanced around the room, taking in the sleek flat-screen televisions lining the one wall. "You've done an amazing job with the club, Connor."

"It's my pride and joy." He smiled brightly. "Now if you'll excuse me, Trent and I have a few things to discuss. We'll let you be, and feel free to holler if you have any questions."

"Thank you," I said, looking between the two men before they walked out.

"Should we set up camp in here?"

James rubbed his face. "I think it's best if one of us is on the floor while someone is in here surveying the entire club."

"We'll be in the club," Izzy said quickly, a little too overeager but completely in step with her personality.

"Works for me. Let's walk through it a few more times until we have the layout memorized, and then we can leave for a few hours. They don't open until eight."

"Just enough time to get ready." Izzy laughed.

James peered down at her and gripped her ass roughly in his hand. "Woman, it better not take you seven hours to prepare."

"Baby," she said, running her fingernail down his bicep. "Not all prep is bad."

He grinned. "Whatever you want, doll."

"Let's do this," Izzy said, walking out of the room before the rest of us.

"You ready for this, Alese? Are you going to be okay?" I squeezed her hand as she stared at the screens.

"I'm fine. I can do this."

"We'll use Izzy as bait. If you'd rather stay here in the control room..."

She held up her hand, silencing me. "I want to do this."

"This place is no joke," Alese said, pointing at the screen where no fewer than ten people were gangbanging a woman as another man watched. "I mean, our club is nothing like this."

"Love, we don't know what's happening behind closed doors at our club."

"Well, damn. It's kind of hot and frightening all at the same time."

I laughed and squeezed her leg right above her knee as my eyes scanned the screens, bouncing back to Izzy and James every few seconds so I didn't miss anything.

Based on the fact that James had tugged on her chain more than once, I'd say she was being mouthy, but that was all part of the plan. Men like Matías didn't want an easy mark. Sometimes, unruly slaves fetched a higher price because men always enjoyed breaking a female.

"Izzy's my spirit animal," Alese said as James pulled on her chain again and she glared at him, sassing something back at him.

Moments later, a very well-dressed man stepped in front of Izzy and James and paused, staring down at her as if he were studying an animal in the wild.

James had already swiveled around on the stool, and Matías motioned toward Izzy with his hand. There was an exchange of words before Connor entered the conversation, standing near Izzy, keeping a watchful eye.

James stepped forward, moving closer to Matías, and spoke again before hooking his hand around Izzy's arm and pulling her to her feet. Everything we'd planned was going off without a hitch, and so far, Matías was taking the bait.

They followed behind Matías, James's hand not leaving Izzy's body as they walked down the hallway toward the private rooms. I was sure Izzy wanted to have James's balls on a silver platter in that moment, but she forged on because the girl was fearless.

Matías pushed open a door, waiting in the hallway for them to enter first. Izzy glanced up at the security camera, and I could see the fear in her eyes.

We were putting her life at risk to catch someone who deserved to be off the streets and to spend eternity behind bars. I wasn't sure I could've done the same with Alese. For as much bravado as she displayed, I didn't think she could've walked into that room on her own knowing what kind of man was following her in.

Izzy froze as soon as she walked inside.

"If shit goes south, call the cops. You hear me, Alese?"

"Got it. Now go," Alese said as I stood near the doorway of the security room.

I ran down the labyrinth of hallways, weaving in and out of people on their way to their own private parties. I didn't have time to fuck around. I had one job, and that was to make it to the room before shit went down and someone got hurt.

I drew my gun before I pushed open the door, pointing it at the spot Matías had stood when I'd last seen him on camera. Matías spun around with Izzy in his arms.

"I'll snap her neck," Matías snarled.

"Fucker," Izzy said and glanced over at James, who was already advancing toward them.

"One more step and it's over." Matías's grip tightened.

I narrowed my gaze, and my finger ticked against the trigger. I wasn't afraid to shoot. My aim was always dead on. My years of military experience had never failed me. I'd been in situations like this before, but never with someone I knew and loved standing at the other end of the barrel, in the arms of the perpetrator.

Izzy didn't wait for me to take the shot; she brought her knee up and smashed her six-inch heel straight down on the top of his foot. He lurched forward just enough for her to break free of his hold and run into James's arms.

"Keep him alive," James told me.

"Can I shoot him at least?" The guy deserved at least one bullet. Not in any place that would end his life. We needed the information only he had in order to even hope to retrieve the thousands of people he'd sold into slavery.

Matías straightened, and his eyes grew colder. "You might as well kill me. I won't talk."

"Orders are to bring him in unharmed unless there are extenuating circumstances."

"This is extenuating." I smirked.

"Just let him shoot the fucker," Izzy said to James.

James grabbed Izzy's arms, untangling her from his body. "Stay here and don't move."

James gave me a look and I knew we were moving on Matías, and I wouldn't be lucky enough to shoot his ass today. We moved fast, overpowering him quickly and closing the shackles around his limbs. Matías screamed, struggling the entire time, but no one outside of our room could hear him.

"Izzy," James said as he stalked toward her.

"Yeah?" she whispered.

"You and Alese go back to the hotel, and we'll be back there as soon as they come to pick him up."

"Okay," she said, nodding slowly and robotically.

He wrapped his arms around her, embracing her. "Are you okay, doll?"

"I'm okay," she said to him and buried her face in his shirt. "I'll be okay. Just a little shell-shocked."

"We would've never let anything happen to you," he said in a soft, deep voice.

"I know. Can we wait here for you? I'd rather have a drink and wait in the common area than walk back to the hotel without you."

He swept his hand across her back. "That's fine." He leaned forward and kissed the top of her hair. "Go wait out there. Alese, if you can hear me, meet Izzy at the bar, please."

"Thanks." Izzy hugged him tighter before breaking the embrace.

She took one look at Matías and stalked forward, her heels clicking against the cement floor. James turned and stared at her, but he didn't say a word. I watched her, my mouth hanging open because her fearlessness never ceased to amaze me.

She raised a hand and slapped Matías as hard as she could, the sound of the impact echoing in the small space. Her fingernails grazed his skin as they swept across his face, leaving a red mark and drops of blood oozing from his cheek.

James looked just as shocked as me, but neither of us said anything as she spun around on her heels and marched out of the room. The satisfied look on her face said everything. I wasn't about to stop her from laying her hands on Matías. He'd done worse to people, and if it made Izzy feel better to slap him or more, I was good with it. I wanted to shoot the bastard, but I knew that wouldn't help any of his victims.

"FBI is on the way," Connor said from the doorway before he jammed his phone back into his pocket. "I'll let them in the back so the customers don't freak out."

"We'll wait with him," James told Connor.

When Connor left the room again, Matías started to beg. "What's your price? I'll double it."

"Shut the fuck up," I barked, wishing I'd put a bullet right between his eyes.

"Ten million. I can have it wired to your account in under two minutes."

James stalked toward him and punched him right in the face, knocking him clean out. "Fucker talked too much."

CHAPTER SIXTEEN

NYA

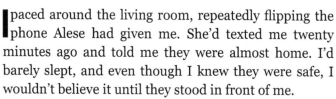

I paced around the living room, repeatedly flipping the phone Alese had given me. She'd texted me twenty minutes ago and told me they were almost home. I'd barely slept, and even though I knew they were safe, I wouldn't believe it until they stood in front of me.

Peeking through the front window at an empty driveway, I grunted my frustration. The last forty-eight hours had dragged by. Each minute felt more like an hour as I stared at the clock, waiting for word about their safety.

When their truck pulled into the driveway, I pulled open the front door and ran down the stairs, almost running toward them. I wasn't sure I'd ever been so happy to see someone as I was to see them in that moment.

Alese waved from the passenger seat before jumping out of the truck. Ret watched through the window, a smile dancing on his lips as I embraced Alese.

"God, I've been so worried about you two," I whispered in her ear, burying my face in her hair.

"We're fine. Ret kept me safe, and I was never in any danger."

I stepped back with my hands gripping her arms so I could get a better look at her. "That's what you say."

"He made me stay in the security room. They used Izzy as bait."

I couldn't imagine how Izzy had felt knowingly being used to lure a psychopath. I didn't know her, but I didn't think I could willingly put myself in harm's way in the same situation, even to catch someone as bad as Matías. After what I went through with Diego, I couldn't put my life and freedom at risk again.

"Miss us?" Ret said as he walked toward us.

"Yes." I smiled and released Alese before moving toward him. "I've been worried."

Worried might have been an understatement. I wasn't going to tell them I was practically manic with anxiety as I paced the house all night. During the day, I'd kept myself busy, cleaning every inch of the house in hopes that time would pass quicker.

I wrapped my arms around Ret's middle and pressed my body flush against his. The gesture wasn't sexual, and it wasn't meant to be. I was thankful to have him. Thankful he was safe just as much as I was to have Alese back.

"I'm happy you're okay."

Ret laughed softly, his body hardening underneath mine with the slight movement. For a moment, I hugged him without his returning the gesture, but then he did it. He slid his arms around my back and pulled me against him. Not too hard, but with the perfect amount of pressure.

"We had to come back," he said as his hands splayed across my shirt, practically covering every square inch of my back. "We couldn't leave you alone."

"Thank God. I don't think I could've taken another day alone. I was about to clean the house for the third time."

"Oh, honey. You need an outlet for all that anxiety," Alese told me as we walked toward the house. "It's not good to stress."

"Have you slept?" Ret asked.

I frowned and felt embarrassed. "Not much," I admitted.

I hated to seem weak. I hated that I depended on them and felt like such a needy person when they weren't around. Maybe I needed to find my own place and break away from them, letting them get back to the life they had before I arrived.

They said if you really loved someone you should set them free. There were no two people who walked the earth that I loved and felt more thankful for than Ret and Alese. Ret saved me, and the two of them helped make me feel human again.

"Maybe we should..." Alese's voice trailed off as she came to stand next to me, and Ret raised an eyebrow. "Sometimes I sleep better after an amazing orgasm."

"I dunno," I said, but the thought sounded great.

Although I'd watched them, we'd never gone any further. I craved what I witnessed through the cracked doorway of their bedroom. I wanted to feel the rush of excitement, kneeling at a man's feet, awaiting my pleasure and his. It had been so long since I'd felt that way, but Ret and Alese made me want things I never thought I'd want again.

She touched Ret's shoulder, grazing his neck with her fingernails. "I could use some cock, handsome. I'm wound so fucking tight after this weekend. You game?"

she asked, staring him straight in the eye and dead serious.

"Baby, I'm always game," he said, winking at her.

Alese turned her attention toward me as I twisted my hands together, unsure if I should say yes, but wanting to more than anything. "You?"

"Yes," I said as my voice trembled.

"You need to get out of your head for a while. Maybe, instead of just watching, you'll let Ret command you tonight. You need a little subspace and to surrender."

I nodded at Alese, knowing full well what she meant, and I couldn't disagree. I'd been wrapped in fear for so long I hadn't given myself time to process a damn thing or given myself a reprieve from anything I'd experienced. Rest hadn't come easily since I'd left Diego's mansion, except after that night at the club.

Ret lifted his chin toward the door behind us. "Let's go inside."

Alese practically squealed with delight as she took off toward the house, leaving us behind. "Y'all coming or what?" she yelled from the front steps of the house.

I moved quickly, following Alese as Ret walked behind me. I wasn't scared as we made our way down the hallway toward their bedroom. I wasn't frightened that either of them would hurt me. They'd already seen my body, and I'd seen theirs. I'd already lived the worst hell imaginable, and I'd never let myself be a victim again.

I wanted what Alese and Ret had. I wanted the love, kindness, and respect they showed each other. Ret adored Alese. He showered her with affection, always making sure she knew he loved her. I wanted someone to worship me the same way. Someone who would lay down their life for me.

In a way, I had that. Ret had saved me, pulling me from Diego's cage before he ushered me away from my parents. He'd saved me twice, and Alese brought me back to life. I never believed in instant love, the kind that swept a person off their feet and made them do foolish things, but with Ret and Alese, I felt it. I understood it, and I knew I wanted more.

"How are we going to do this?" I asked as we walked into their bedroom, stopping just inside the doorway.

"Do you want to keep your clothes on?" Alese asked as she started to pull down the straps of her sundress. "You can, you know, if you're more comfortable."

I smiled as my stomach fluttered. "No. You've already seen me." I glanced down at the floor and blew out a shaky breath. "I've always been comfortable with my nudity anyway."

"Thank God." She laughed, stepping out of the dress and kicking the material to the side. "I was really getting sick of wearing so many clothes all the time."

I peered over at Ret, who stood there with a wicked smile. "I have no issue with you two walking around naked all the time, but don't expect me not to be affected."

"Be affected," Alese said as she groped his crotch. "Be very affected." She smiled and brushed her lips against his as he wrapped an arm around her bare back and pulled her closer.

"Careful what you wish for, love."

"Nya." Alese peeked over her shoulder at me. "Why don't you lie on the bed with us instead of sitting across the room?"

"Oh." A surge of excitement coursed through me. I liked the thought of that...probably more than I should.

I met Ret's gaze, searching for his approval. "We talked in the car about the three of us. We're good with you being as near as you want. You can touch too or be touched if that's what you want," he said with a smile.

My skin tingled and my belly fluttered again as Alese walked toward me and took my hand. "We just want you to know there's nothing you can do that's wrong. Just follow what feels right and natural." She swept my hair behind my shoulder before resting her hand against my skin. "We're not jealous types. If you want to be touched or want to touch, do it."

"But..." I swallowed hard and moved my eyes between her and Ret, confused and turned on. "You guys are in a committed relationship, and I'm just... Just..."

"You're part of us now for as long as you want to be." She smiled, putting my mind at ease. "Ret and I are committed to each other, and nothing that happens between the three of us will do anything to destroy that. Do you understand?"

"I do." I nodded and finally smiled.

I couldn't imagine letting another man touch me. Ret was different. He rescued me and kept me safe. There wasn't another person I trusted more than him besides Alese.

"Now get undressed and get that pretty little ass of yours on the bed," she said as she walked by and swatted my ass playfully.

All the air rushed out of my lungs, and my heart started to race. Not in a bad way, but in an oh-my-God-this-is-going-to-be-amazing manner. Ret walked past me, shrugging like I should listen to Alese and stop stalling.

Alese sat on the edge of the bed, patting the spot next to her as I walked toward her, dropping my clothes to the floor. She swept her eyes across my body as she licked her lips.

Ret leaned forward, placing his fingers under her chin and forcing her eyes upward. "Undress me," he said.

I crawled onto the mattress, resting just behind Alese, observing as she undid the button and unzipped his jeans. He smiled down at her, watching carefully with his fingers still pressed against her chin.

She yanked at the side of his jeans, pulling them down his legs and freeing his cock. I licked my lips, getting the first real view of his size and shape in the bright lighting of their bedroom.

Alese wrapped her fingers around his shaft, slowly stroking up and down and rubbing her thumb along the underside. His body jerked each time, moving closer and into her touch.

He lifted his shirt over his head, throwing it to the floor behind him as she worked his cock in her palm. "Open your mouth," he told her, and she did without hesitation.

I curled my legs to my side and propped myself up, sweeping my hand across the swell of my breast. I watched in awe as she slid his length against her tongue and closed her lips around the base without gagging.

I'd never been able to take a man that size that deep without some sort of gag reflex kicking in and tears streaming down my face. Her lips slid back and forth, her hand still wrapped tightly around him and pressed against her lips, keeping contact with his entire cock with every stroke.

He closed his eyes as he swayed backward and tangled his fingers in her hair, not letting her forget who was really in control.

I wondered what he tasted like and if his cock felt as velvety smooth as it looked. Alese moaned around his shaft with a hint of a smile like she knew exactly what she was doing and what would happen next.

Ret shivered as he glanced down, and he drew in a sharp breath. "Lie back," he told her, releasing his grip on her scalp.

Alese crawled backward with her legs spread, never turning her back on Ret. The hunger in his eyes deepened, and his cock bobbed and weaved, hanging freely from his body with no mouth or hands to support its weight as he moved.

I kept my hands to myself, but I was dying to touch one of them. I'd missed contact, soft and gentle sweeps across the skin that sent goose bumps scattering in all directions. It had been so long since I'd had that type of touch, and I craved it just as much as I wanted to kneel at someone's feet.

I stayed where I was as Alese lay back on the bed and Ret crawled between her legs, nudging her thighs farther apart with his knees.

He glanced at me, and I blushed when his eyes lingered on my breasts longer than I expected. "Touch your nipples."

I looked up, my eyes wide as he gazed at me. "Me?" I asked like a complete idiot.

He nodded with a slight grin. "Yes, you, Nya. Unless you're not comfortable with me..."

I didn't let him finish the statement as I slid my hand to my breasts, sweeping my fingers across my nipples and showing him I was completely comfortable.

"Pinch them lightly," he said.

I sucked in a breath, knowing my nipples had always been sensitive. I closed the tips of my fingers around the bud and applied some pressure. I closed my eyes as I dropped my head back, loving the tingling sensation that cascaded over my skin.

"Touch only your breasts until I say otherwise."

My eyes flew open, growing wide. Don't touch myself in any other way? That was torture, and soon, with the gentle pull of my fingers, I'd be dripping with need with no relief in sight unless he gave his approval.

"Ret, please," I whimpered and pouted.

"Do as I say, and you'll be rewarded," he promised, keeping his eyes trained on my hands as he made himself comfortable between Alese's legs. "You're so wet already, baby." He flickered his eyes up her body as he skidded his fingers across her core.

"There's something so hot about this," she said, finishing on a moan as his fingers drifted across her clit.

I watched his hand as he coated his fingers with her need, moving so slowly it verged on pleasurable torture. But at least Alese was being touched, stroked in all the right places, while I teased my own nipples, wanting to dip my fingers between my legs but didn't dare.

I sat up, tucking my feet underneath me and needing more as I watched Ret push two fingers inside Alese, slowly filling her. My pussy constricted and ached, wishing to feel the same fullness Alese was enjoying while I rocked back and forth on my knees. Using both hands, I pinched my nipples, yanking on them lightly and rolling the tips between my fingertips, alternating the pressure and sensation to stop myself from going mad with lust.

Alese lifted her ass off the bed, offering her pussy to Ret as he thrust his fingers deeper. "You want to come?" he asked her, and I had to bite my lip to stop myself from yelling yes.

"Come on, baby. Gimme your mouth," she pleaded. "I was a good girl." She turned her head and peered over at me with a sinful smirk.

She was good. Their relationship was equal parts push and pull, both of them using every tool in their arsenal to get what they wanted, while keeping the other person happy too.

Ret followed her eyes, glancing at me as I toyed with my nipples and tried to control my ragged breathing. "Spread your legs. Let Alese see how beautiful you are."

Oh God. In the dim lighting of the club's private room, this was easier...less personal and up close. But in the bedroom, only a few feet away with every light shining overhead, it gave everyone a perfect view.

I gave my nipple another tug, feeling the wetness between my legs and knowing they were about to see how turned on I was. I held my breath and spread my knees, giving them both a full view of my pussy.

"She's breathtaking," Alese said, making my face heat.

Their eyes were on me as Ret's fingers continued to fill her pussy, moving in slower, longer strokes than before. "Look how wet she is," Ret said and dragged his tongue across his bottom lip.

I squirmed and sucked in a breath, wishing his tongue were dragging across my clit, lapping up my wetness.

"Keep your legs open, and keep playing with your breasts," he told me before bringing his mouth down on Alese's clit, closing his lips around it as he pushed his fingers deeper inside her.

I felt my eyes roll back as she moaned. The sensations and need that had been building inside me intensified. I felt like I was ready to pop as my body trembled, and I wasn't sure if I could take much more.

He licked her pussy, not missing a single inch of her flesh as he drove her closer to the edge, thrusting his fingers hard and faster. Her fingers curled into the comforter, fisting the material in her palms. "Fuck," she gasped when he pulled away, leaving her empty and panting.

"You want some?" Ret asked as I almost fell forward, gasping right along with her.

I hadn't noticed I'd started to lean forward, drawn to the sights and sounds of her ecstasy. "Me?" I asked, stilling my hands, but continuing to hold my nipples tightly.

"You can stay there, or you can move closer if you trust me enough to touch you."

God, I trusted him. I trusted them both. I was so out of my mind with lust that I didn't hesitate another second as I scooted closer, unsure what else to do.

"Lie down next to Alese," he said as he sat up, positioning his legs underneath his body like I had done.

His cock was hard, sticking straight up, and I wanted so badly to feel the velvety hardness against my skin. But I was turned on, and I was going to do whatever he asked if it meant the throbbing between my legs would go away.

I glanced at Alese, letting a moment of fear flash through my mind until I lay back and she laced her fingers with mine. "Don't worry, Nya. This is his specialty."

"What is?" I asked as my heart started to pound faster, louder than before.

"Finger-fucking." I formed a perfect O with my lips as she smiled. "He's a master at it."

"If you need me to stop, just say 'Red.'"

I nodded, swallowing down the fear that hid just beneath the surface of my lust. Slowly he lowered his hand to my knee and waited for me to adjust to being touched by someone else and naked.

No one had touched me since Diego, and more than anything, I wanted to rid myself of every memory of him. When I closed my eyes, I didn't want to see his face. I wanted new memories, new sensations, new orgasms to wipe away every remnant of him.

"Good?" Ret asked as Alese squeezed my fingers.

"Yes," I said without my voice cracking.

Ret smiled, and my insides warmed. "Close your eyes if you want. Just enjoy this, and don't hesitate to stop me."

"Yes, Sir, but I'd like to watch," I told him. "And I'm okay."

He gave me a quick nod before looking at Alese. "Same goes for you too, baby. Play with those beautiful tits."

I smiled, loving that I wasn't the only one touching myself. His hand moved, and I sucked in a breath, waiting for the moment when he put his hands between my legs.

The pressure of his grip increased the higher up my thigh his hand moved. Gently he pushed against my inner thigh, telling me to open to him. I'd been so wrapped up in my nipples and the anticipation, I'd almost forgotten to give him access to the one part of my body I wanted him to touch the most.

"Jesus, you're both so wet for me," he said as I bent my knees, touching Alese's.

I licked my lips, dying to feel the roughness of his hands against my skin. Slowly, he moved his hand higher, and just when I thought he was never going to touch me there, he glided his fingertips through my wetness.

I gasped at the softness and the warmth of his skin as he raked his fingers across me. I widened my legs in a silent plea for him to keep touching me. I tightened my fingers around Alese's, and I lifted my bottom off the bed as he skated his finger across my clit, sending shockwaves through my system.

There was hesitancy in his touch. Maybe he was as scared as I was, unsure if this was the right thing to do but unable to stop at the same time. The lust outweighed any anxiety I felt about taking this step. I wanted Ret, needing his hands on me to quench the achy desire between my legs.

The thick muscles of his arms flexed as he moved his hands against my body and Alese's simultaneously. I kept my eyes locked on him, moving across his beautiful bare chest, impressive arms, and handsome face. He was watching me, studying my every movement and trying to find subtle cues that I was panicking, but I wasn't. With Alese, he was doing the opposite. His fingers were buried deep inside her, rocking in and out of her body in a steady rhythm.

"Touch me," I said, giving him full permission. "I want this. I want you. I want what you're giving her."

His eyes darkened, burning with as much lust as I felt coursing through my system. Those must've been the words he needed to hear because his soft touches became firmer and more confident.

I closed my eyes and just let myself be in the moment, enjoying the feel of his hands against me. He flattened his fingers, sliding them against my wetness and coating them in my arousal. My stomach tightened as a new wave of excitement washed over me when the tips of his fingers explored my middle.

I sucked in a breath, keeping my eyes closed as he pushed a single finger inside. The pace was agonizingly slow, but delicious too. His thumb brushed against my clit, and I squirmed, wanting more. He pulled his finger out, and I was about to complain when a second prodded my opening. I exhaled, tipping my hips upward, inviting him to plunge his fingers inside me.

My pussy ached to be filled, stretched by someone who wanted to bring me nothing but pleasure. The painful throb disappeared as soon as he pushed two thick fingers inside, stretching me.

I moaned as my pussy contracted around his fingers, loving every minute of his touch and wanting more. Slowly, he moved his fingers, curling them upward and stroking my G-spot.

Every fear I had fell away, replaced by the urgency to come, chasing the orgasm I wanted and needed more than air. I opened my eyes, making myself remember this was Ret and not Diego. I had to keep myself in the moment and firmly in reality. Ret's touch alone should've been enough. Diego never touched me so gently, but I opened my eyes anyway.

"Alese, get up and get on your knees," Ret said as his fingers slipped out of her but remained deep inside me.

Alese moved quickly, planting the side of her head against the comforter and facing me. She presented him her ass, smiling and staring at me as I turned to face her. We stared at each other for a second, but I glanced back at Ret just as he pressed the tip of his cock between her legs and thrust into her.

I bit my lip and moaned as he filled her and pushed his fingers deeper inside me too. He rocked against her body, finger-fucking me too, in the same fast-paced rhythm. He curled his fingers inside me, stroking my insides and massaging my G-spot, driving me closer to the edge of bliss.

"Yes!" I chanted as my toes curled and my body tightened. "Yes!"

He sped up his hips, pummeling her pussy over and over again as his fingers rocked against my insides, bringing me more pleasure than I ever knew possible.

Two swipes of his thumb over my clit had my back arching off the bed as the orgasm slammed into me. I gasped for air as colors exploded behind my eyes and every nerve in my body sprang to life, rocking me to the core. Aftershocks rattled through me as his fingers slowed, eventually stilling, but never leaving my body.

On his knees before me with Alese still facedown on the bed, Ret smacked her ass so hard her body lurched forward. It was enough to send her over the edge in a howling orgasm, which he followed. I watched as their expressions morphed, the pull of pleasure too intense to keep a straight face. They were at their most vulnerable, riding the waves of pleasure at my side.

I watched, mesmerized by the scene before me, listening to Ret moan her name before his body stilled. I whimpered when his fingers left my body and he rolled to his side with Alese between us.

I smiled as I stared up at the ceiling, my heart sputtering in my chest and my muscles too weak to move. I'd let another man touch me, and I didn't freak out. But that wasn't hard with Ret.

"Yeah, that was..." Alese said, sucking in a breath and swallowing. "Yeah."

"I know," I whispered, knowing exactly what she meant when she really didn't say anything at all.

For the first time in months, I felt nothing but joy, contentment, and serenity.

CHAPTER SEVENTEEN

RET

"I think I fucked up," I told James, sitting across from him inside his office the next afternoon.

He leaned back, blowing out a long, drawn-out breath because I wasn't the first person to utter those words to him. "What happened?"

"Nya."

He pulled his hand down his face, letting out a strangled groan. "What about her?"

"So." I hunched over with my elbows resting on my knees and stared at the floor. "We may have slept with her." I closed my eyes and grimaced, waiting for James to jump over the desk and knock me on my ass.

The wheels on his chair squeaked against the plastic carpet protector. "We?"

"Yeah." I lifted my head just enough to see he was still seated, which was a good sign. So far, James and I didn't have to come to blows over something I did inside my bedroom.

James and I had an understanding about sex. As members of the same club, often seeing each other and the other's woman in very little clothing, we never talked about sex at work. What happened at the club, stayed at the club. We were different people there. The two lives never crossed, and so far, we'd been good at maintaining the separation.

"The three of us," I said and finally brought my eyes to his. I wasn't scared of James. Not of his power, at least, but he was my boss, and I didn't want to put the business in jeopardy.

"Oh," he said, sounding more shocked than pissed.

"I'm sorry." My facial expression wasn't a frown, but I wasn't smiling either. I didn't know what the fuck to say or how to look because I'd never done something as stupid as that in my entire life. Business and pleasure never mixed in my line of work, but then, I'd never rescued someone either.

"Did she want it?"

"Well, yeah."

"Interesting." His eyebrows shot up as his head jerked back. "She's full of surprises."

"That's one way of putting it."

He laced his fingers together before resting them on the desk. "What happens in your house is your business. The doctor gave her the all clear. We are no longer employed by the Halsteads, and Nya isn't our client either. She is willingly staying with you, and you didn't force yourself on her, right?"

"That's a laughable statement. You know me better than that."

"I know, man. Like we've said before, some shit isn't meant for the office, and it's no one's business but your own."

I nodded in assent because that had always been our agreement, but I felt this situation was different from any other we'd been put in before.

Before James could respond, there was a light knock on the door. Angel walked in, face ashen and without a smile. "Ret," she said softly as I turned.

My stomach dropped as soon as my eyes met hers. "What happened?"

Angel was always our ray of sunshine. The single bright light in the office every day. No matter how crazy shit got, she always kept her cool, sprinkling her happiness everywhere she could.

She stepped into the room, still holding the door handle, and swallowed hard before she blew out a breath. "I just took a call that Alese is being transported to Tampa General. You need to go there now."

I was on my feet, pushing Angel out of the way and ignoring James as he yelled after me. I barely remembered running through the office as everything passed by in a blur.

The palm trees whizzed by like feathers in the wind as I weaved in and out of traffic, heading toward the hospital and breaking every speed limit along the way without giving two fucks about any of it. My hands shook, and no matter how tightly I wrapped them around the steering wheel, nothing stopped the fear from seeping into my bones and simultaneously wrapping around my neck like a noose.

I tried to steady my breathing. "She's fine." I repeated those words to myself as I pulled into the emergency room parking lot, put the car in park, and almost forgot to turn the damn thing off before I sprinted toward the door.

"Alese Winters," I told the nurse, trying to play it cool when I was pretty sure she could see my heart beating right through my shirt.

"Ret!"

I turned and saw Nya running in my direction with her cheeks covered in tears and her eyes practically swollen shut. "Nya." I wrapped her in my arms as she collided with my chest. "What happened?" As I searched her face, I pushed back the hair clinging to her wet cheeks.

"We were..." She sucked in a breath, practically hyperventilating and shaking uncontrollably. "We were walking..." Her voice trembled and her lip quivered as she stared up at me with tears spilling down her face.

"Slow down." I pulled her closer, trying to comfort her even though I'd never been very good at the tender things. "Is Alese okay?"

"A car." She clutched my shirt and held on tight, balling the fabric in her fists. "It hit her in the crosswalk," she whispered so softly, I thought I heard her wrong. "I don't know how it missed me."

I had to remind myself to breathe as my chest seized and my muscles locked. "Is she okay?" I asked again, but this time, my jaw was clenched and my teeth mashed together because I realized the answer to my question might not be something I wanted to hear.

"I don't know."

"Mr. North," a woman said behind me.

Nya and I turned together, clutching each other tightly as if we were the only thing keeping the other upright.

"Yes?" My voice trembled, sounding foreign and unlike myself. I always possessed confidence when I spoke. I always had my shit together.

But then, I'd never loved someone the way I loved Alese. I'd never worried about losing anything in my life before because I spent most of my years alone. Alese changed that. She came along at a time when I wasn't looking for anyone. She kind of fell into my lap when I least expected to find someone, and as they said...the rest was history.

The woman held a clipboard tightly against her chest, clutching it the same way I was holding on to Nya. "Can you follow me please?"

I glanced down, and Nya was staring up at me with wide eyes like I had all the answers and could make everything better. Which I couldn't, but she didn't know that yet.

"Come on, doll. I'm sure she's fine." I told that lie like I was a professional bullshitter because the words slid off my tongue like honey.

Nya stayed attached to me with her arm around my back as we followed the woman in the blue scrubs still holding the clipboard through a bustling hallway to a tiny room.

"Where's Alese?" I asked as we entered the nondescript room with nothing but a few chairs and a small table.

"Please sit." She motioned toward the chairs before closing the door and sitting across from us.

Nya sat next to me with one hand on my leg and the fingers on the other one intertwined with mine. Neither of us spoke. What was there to say at a time like this? We didn't dare speak the words or fears we both felt. Saying them made it true or possible, and neither of us had the ability to face what came next.

"I'm Dr. Hughes. I thought it was best we talk in private before I take you in to see Ms. Winters."

"Doctor, be straight with us. Where's Alese?"

She cleared her throat as she placed the clipboard on the table next to her. "She's comfortable at the moment. You're listed as her emergency contact and next of kin so I can speak openly about her condition, but please know she has a DNR in place."

I jerked back in my chair, and Nya tightened her fingers around mine as she gasped. Alese had not told me about having a Do Not Resuscitate order in place. We'd never talked about things like what we wanted if something should happen to us, but I didn't know she had a plan in place.

"Ms. Winters's body sustained numerous injuries from the impact. Before we knew about her DNR, we resuscitated her when she arrived in the ER. We've been able to stabilize her as much as possible, but she's in grave condition."

"Speak English, Doc." My brain couldn't process all the terms. I still couldn't believe I was sitting here, hearing that Alese was possibly going to die. She already had once, I guessed, but they were able to bring her back.

"Ms. Winters has a punctured lung, a broken leg, and internal bleeding."

I didn't move. I couldn't speak, and breathing became difficult. Nya sobbed at my side, holding my hands so tightly my fingers started to tingle, but none of it mattered.

"We need to do surgery to find and stop the bleeding before we can begin to address her other injuries, but the likelihood she'll survive is slim, Mr. North."

The doctor said everything so matter-of-factly, like she was telling me about her plans for the evening. I was sure she'd done this a thousand times, dropped bad news in laps of other loved ones, but this was something

I'd never experienced. The coldness in the way the news was given had me in as much shock as the realization that Alese could very well die.

"If she survives, her recovery will be long and extensive. She might never be able to walk again, and if she does, it will be well over a year before she would be fully mobile again."

The sadness left me, replaced by anger. Anger at the doctor. Anger at the driver. Anger at the world. "I don't care. I just want my girl back. Do whatever you can to save her life."

She stood, grabbing that goddamn clipboard before she straightened. "I'll bring you back to see her now while we prep for surgery."

"Thank you."

We followed her out of the tiny room, back into the hallway that teemed with life. Nya held on to me, practically climbing up my body as she cried.

The doctor stopped outside a room, motioning for us to go in, but I wasn't ready. I turned to Nya and held her by the shoulders, moving her away from me a little. "Nya, listen to me."

She gazed up at me with her swollen face and red eyes, unable to hold back the tears. She didn't speak, but she nodded that she was listening.

"We have to hold our shit together for Alese. Do you understand? We can't scare her."

She dropped her head, staring at the floor as her tears plopped on the floor near her feet. "I can't go in there, Ret. I can't see her like that."

I gripped her shoulders tighter and closed my eyes for a moment. "Stay out here. Let me talk to my girl first. If she seems okay, I'll come get you."

"Go," she said softly.

I released my grip on her and turned my back. I took a deep breath and tried to remember my training from the military to calm myself down, but it didn't work. I was prepared for battle. Send me into hostile territory armed to the hilt, and I could stay level-headed without my hand shaking even a little. But this... This was new territory and one I wasn't sure I was ready to face.

CHAPTER EIGHTEEN

RET

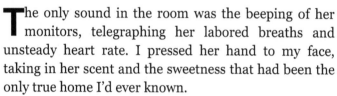

The only sound in the room was the beeping of her monitors, telegraphing her labored breaths and unsteady heart rate. I pressed her hand to my face, taking in her scent and the sweetness that had been the only true home I'd ever known.

Lying in the bed, she seemed so weak and small, but Alese had never been either of those things before, and it didn't feel right. She barely moved as I swept my lips across her skin, closing my eyes and soaking in her softness against me.

She woke up for a moment when I first walked in, staring at me with her big, wide blue eyes before they fluttered closed again. The nurse had told me they had her on a ton of pain killers and drugs to keep her sedated because it was important for her to stay calm.

I tried to keep the fear off my face. I tried to keep my shit together and not let the tears that were threatening to fall overtake me. The last thing I wanted was for her to open her eyes and see me a complete mess. I had always been Alese's rock, and I wasn't about to change now. She needed me to be stronger than I'd ever been, but I wasn't sure how long I could keep up the façade.

I wanted to crawl into bed with her, pull her into my arms, and make her better. It took everything in me to restrain myself from doing just that because I wanted to heal her. I wanted to save her life.

Her hands, arms, and face were covered in scratches and bruises like she'd been in a bar brawl and had come out on the losing end. But I knew the real injuries, the life-threatening ones, hid beneath the surface and were tucked neatly beneath the blankets covering her tattered body.

I placed my mouth next to her ear and set one arm above her head, softly stroking her golden hair as I stared at my girl. "I love you, *piccola*," I whispered without my voice cracking. "Don't give up. I'm not ready to let you go."

But then I realized I'd never be ready for that day. Things like this, shitty events and near-death experiences, made a person realize how precious and fragile life truly was.

"Son." My dad's voice filled the space between the beeps, but I couldn't bring myself to face him.

I couldn't take my eyes off Alese because, any minute now, they'd take her from me. "Pop."

His footsteps were heavy as he crossed the gray linoleum flooring and rested his hand on my shoulder. "Alese," he said softly with a hard squeeze.

"It's not good, Pop."

"Nya filled me in." He took a deep breath, probably on the verge of tears just like I was. The man acted tough, but I knew, underneath, he was a big pile of feelings. He didn't always talk about them, but they lingered, hidden away to maintain his tough-guy persona. "The doctors are outside, and they said they're about to take her down for surgery."

I squeezed my eyes shut, not ready to let her go even though I knew it was her only hope of surviving. How could you say goodbye to someone when you weren't sure you'd ever see them again?

"Gimme a minute."

His hand tightened on my shoulder before his footsteps grew softer, the door closing behind him. I buried my face in her hair, placing my lips near her ear, and inhaled every drop of Alese I could. "Come back to me, Alese. If you can't, I'll understand and I'll love you forever, but fight."

I wanted to hear her say my name. I wanted to hear the laughter I'd grown to love. I wanted to relive the moment we kissed each other goodbye this morning. I wanted everything I couldn't have at that moment.

When the door opened behind me, I knew what it meant. My time was up, and Alese's fight was just beginning. "I love you," I whispered in her ear again. "I love you, Alese."

"Mr. North," the doctor said as she entered the room. "We're ready for Alese now."

I wanted to tell her to fuck off because I wasn't ready to let her go, but I had to man up and I knew this was the only way I'd get my girl back. I kissed her cheek, careful not to hurt her but hard enough that I hoped she felt it too.

"There's a surgical waiting room downstairs, and we'll keep you updated on her progress."

I stared down at Alese as I stood from the chair beside her bed. Her body was so broken, with her injuries clearly evident all over her skin. The road rash, the bruises, the blood that covered almost every inch of her body.

"She's in good hands, and we'll do everything possible to save her life." I knew the doctor's words were meant to calm me and give me hope, but they did neither.

I didn't move. I couldn't make myself walk away. I wanted to stand over her in the operating room, watching as they saved her life. A team of people entered the room and started to prep her bed for the journey downstairs.

"Son," my dad said again, softer this time, the somberness in his voice unmistakable.

I waited for them to wheel her out, watching as she disappeared behind my dad, before I took a step toward the doorway.

I didn't say anything to him as I stood at his side, staring down the corridor in total shock. My pop didn't say anything either; each of us just as lost as the other. The sound of someone sobbing drew my attention away from Alese for a moment, and I found Nya huddled on the floor in tears.

"Nya," I said as my heart seized, not only for myself, but for her too. Alese and Nya had formed such a quick bond, and this would devastate her too. I reached down, pulling Nya to her feet and tucking her against me. I couldn't save Alese, I couldn't protect her, but I could be that person for Nya.

Pop slid his arm around my shoulder and pulled me closer. "Come on, Ret. The guys are on their way."

I followed his motion, moving down the hospital hallway in a haze. Nya gripped my hand tightly, clinging to me. "She'll be okay," I told Nya, but the words were more for me than for her.

Alese had to be okay.

For six long hours, I paced the waiting room, practically wearing a rut in the floor. The guys sat silently, filling the waiting room and refusing to leave. Every time the doors to the restricted area opened, my heart would jump because I thought it was an update on Alese. I'd badgered the poor nurse manning the desk outside at least twenty times for an update, but she always said they were still working on Alese and to be patient.

Patience. Mine had worn out five hours ago. Somehow, I kept my cool, trying to maintain my strength and hopefulness. I'd begged Fran to take Nya home. She'd been through enough trauma in the last few months, and I worried that the added stress would push her over the edge. Nya refused to leave, though, and Fran wasn't going to push her either.

No one wanted to go. No matter how many times I told them they could go home, they refused to leave my side.

"How 'bout something to eat?" Fran asked as her eyes followed me pacing back and forth for the thousandth time.

"I'm good," I told her because the last thing I cared about was eating.

"You need to stay strong for her."

I nodded, but I didn't miss a beat as I continued my steps. If I stopped, I thought too much. If I walked, I stayed focused, picturing Alese well again and in my arms.

"The doc's coming," Pop said, motioning toward the doorway with his chin.

I stalked toward her, barely letting her step foot in the waiting room before I spoke. "Is she okay?"

She pulled the cap from her head and wiped her forehead with the back of her hand. I was on pins and needles, unable to move even in the slightest.

"We were able to stabilize her. She's a fighter, that's for sure. She has a long road to recovery and she's not out of the woods entirely, but we've stopped the bleeding and she's in the recovery room."

I clutched my chest, finally letting out the air I'd been holding in my lungs. I had expected to hear bad news, figured the universe was trying to pay me back for something I'd done in the past.

"Thank God," I groaned, feeling like the weight of the world was finally off my shoulders.

"We'll know more in a day or so."

I stepped forward, wanting to get to Alese as soon as possible. "Can I see her?"

"She's in recovery right now. When she's ready, we'll let you see her, but she may be moved to her room first."

"Thank you," I said and finally smiled.

When the doctor walked out of the room, I turned to face my family. The ladies were in tears, and the guys were shaking their heads and holding their women tightly. Moments like this made us remember how fragile life really was and how quickly everything could change.

CHAPTER NINETEEN

NYA

Two Weeks Later

"**P**lease go to work," Alese begged Ret from the couch. "I have Nya. I'll be fine." She tried to move and winced.

Ret practically leaped across the coffee table and placed his hands under her arms to help her. "I can't leave you here like this."

She'd been home from the hospital a week and hadn't had a minute alone. Even when I was with her, he'd be standing nearby, ready to swoop in and save her in case of some major tragedy.

"Nya will watch me."

His watchful eyes turned to me, and I smiled, shifting nervously on my feet. "I'll take good care of her. I swear."

"The guys don't need me back yet."

Alese rolled her eyes as she tried to adjust her leg on the pillow beneath it. "That's not what Izzy said."

Ret snarled and turned his head. "You two talking about me?"

I was about to run into my bedroom and hide because Alese wasn't going to back down, and I was afraid Ret wasn't going to either.

"Go back to work, Ret. Please. I can only take so much mothering. You're worse than Fran sometimes."

I inched backward, knowing she'd just threw down something Ret didn't want to hear. Fran was divine and one of the sweetest people I'd ever met, but she was a hawk, always circling above everyone and micromanaging.

"You didn't." He stepped forward, shaking his head, and waved his arms. "I can't believe you just said that to me."

"I need some normalcy, baby. Go to work. Let us have a girls' day—unless you want a mani-pedi too."

"Nya."

I swallowed down my laughter and straightened my face because he already looked like he was about to blow his top. "Yeah?"

He pinned me with his stare, his turquoise eyes burning. "You call me if anything happens. I mean anything. Got me?"

"Yes, Sir." I nodded quickly, but I didn't dare crack a smile.

"If shit goes south, you won't get me out of here again until you're fully recovered."

Alese waved her hands toward the door as he stared her down. "We'll be fine. Go."

"Fine," he said, walking toward her and not out like she'd hoped. He leaned forward, brushing his lips across her forehead before gazing into her eyes. "I love you, *piccola*. Don't overdo it today."

"I'll be right here. It's pretty hard to overdo it when I can only move my hands." She smiled up at him before pulling his face down to hers. "Kiss me for real."

Ret didn't hesitate as he pressed his lips against hers, soft at first like he was afraid he could break her. I didn't know if he even realized he'd been treating her with kid gloves since the moment we got home from the hospital, but I was sure, even if I pointed it out, he wouldn't give a damn.

She pushed against his chest when he lingered a little too long, the kiss growing deeper as he tried to sidetrack her. We both knew his game, and although he thought he was the boss, Alese always found a way to set his ass straight.

"Go," she said once again, finally pushing him hard and far enough that his lips drifted away from hers.

He growled, moving slowly as he straightened but kept his eyes locked on her. "I'm going. I'll check in every hour."

"I have no doubt." She shook her head and laughed. "I'm not going to tell you again," she warned after he still hadn't started toward the door.

He grumbled something before snagging his keys off the counter and finally walking toward the door. Alese and I stared at each other, waiting for the familiar click as he closed the door behind him.

We both took a deep breath and sighed, finally alone again without Ret staring at us both.

"Geez, he's so intense sometimes."

Alese giggled, grimacing and holding her stomach as her body moved. "I knew the Fran remark would get his ass in gear."

"That was a low blow."

She shrugged with an unapologetic smile. "It worked."

"Can I get you something?"

"Nothing." She patted the couch next to her. "Come sit."

I hadn't realized I'd been hovering over her just as much as Ret had been the last two weeks. We went in shifts oftentimes. He'd sleep; I'd watch Alese. I'd sleep, and he'd do the same. When we were both awake, the poor woman couldn't get a moment to herself.

I sat on the couch next to her, my ass hanging off the cushion because I didn't want to get too close or hurt her. I'd never seen a couch as big as this, but I still made sure to leave plenty of room between us.

"How are you doing? We haven't talked about what happened yet."

We hadn't talked about the accident at all. After I explained everything to Ret, I didn't speak another word about it. But I had played the sequence of events in my head over and over again, reliving the nightmare of watching Alese's body as she flew through the air and landed on the cement.

"I'm okay." I folded my hands in my lap and twisted my fingers together, dreading going over the day once again.

"I didn't think I'd survive. When that car hit me, all I could think about was Ret..." Her voice trailed off as she reached for my hand. "And you too, of course."

My insides warmed because I never expected her to think about me as she lay dying in the mall parking lot. I wasn't even sure what I'd think about if I were in the same situation.

"You don't have to say that." I squeezed her hand gently, careful not to hurt her because Ret had drummed that into my head over the last week. He treated her like a porcelain doll that could shatter if touched too roughly. "Ret was beside himself, Alese."

"I'm sure he was. I hate that you guys had to go through that."

"No." I slid my hand up her arms, stroking her soft, warm skin and feeling completely at peace. "None of that matters. You're getting better, and we couldn't ask for anything more than that."

"Promise me something," she said, placing her hand over mine as she stared at me.

"Anything."

"Promise me you'll distract Ret a bit. You two need to stop staring at me every second of the day."

I laughed and nodded slowly. "I can promise to try to distract him, and I'll stop staring. But I can't guarantee Ret will do the same."

"We'll find a way." She gave me a devilish smile, and I knew she was cooking up a plan to get a bit of normalcy back into our lives. "We always do."

CHAPTER TWENTY

RET

Alese was right. I needed to go back to work. Not just because they needed me, but for my sanity as well as hers. We'd never been so far up each other's ass as we'd been the last two weeks. But I couldn't imagine leaving her behind until I was confident she was better. I knew Nya was more than capable of taking care of Alese while I was gone, but it didn't help ease my worry after coming so close to losing her.

"Dude," Morgan called. "It's been hell without you, man. I didn't think I'd last another day."

I had barely made it through the front door when he started walking toward me. That was what I loved most about this place. It wasn't just a job; we were a family. A very fucked-up one, but still, we loved each other. None of us would ever admit that shit either.

"Pop bothering you?"

Bear didn't have my ass to be up in while I'd been off. The dude seriously needed to find a new hobby. For the first thirty years of my life, I barely heard from him, but now, he was Dad of the Year and had to know every little thing that was happening in my life. It didn't help that we worked at the same place, but damn, the man could give me a little room to breathe sometimes.

"Fuckin' making me crazy. I have enough shit with my mom, but add Bear to the mix, and it's ridiculous."

I laughed and placed my arm around my stepbrother. The word was still foreign on my tongue, and I wasn't sure I'd ever get used to thinking of Morgan as more than a friend. "I'll take some of the heat off. You can have a little break."

Morgan stepped away and glanced down the hallway, probably seeing if my pop was eavesdropping like he'd done more than once. "He's all up in arms about this case he's working on. He wants me to help, but I'm swamped. Think you can do me that solid?"

"I'll handle him."

"Ret!"

I rolled my eyes, but I knew my dad had heard me. I was actually surprised he wasn't in the waiting room already because he always seemed to know when I was near.

"See." Morgan tilted his head toward the offices. "He's going off the deep end without you."

"I'm on it," I told him, giving a quick chin dip to Angel as I walked by the front desk. She waved, laughing quietly as she talked to someone on the phone.

I made it within three feet of my dad's office when he came barreling out the door and wrapped his arms around me. "Thank God you're here. I've missed you, kid."

"Thanks, Pop," I said as I tried to breathe through his bear hug. "You can put me down now."

He lowered my feet to the floor and slapped me on the shoulder, harder than I expected, and I jolted sideways and glared.

"Sorry. Sorry. I'm just so damn happy to have you back. It's boring without you."

"Need help with a case?" I skipped over the sappy shit, preferring to get right down to business. I didn't have all day and night to chitchat like long lost friends catching up after years of separation.

I'd only been gone a few weeks, but everyone acted like I hadn't walked through the front door in years.

"Yeah. We're about to have a team meeting about it."

The man loved anything that involved the team. Most guys his age dreamed about retirement, but not Pop. He wanted action. He craved adventure, and if it involved watching people banging...it was even better. He loved living on the edge and danger. I wasn't sure he'd ever have a peaceful day the rest of his life. I'd figured Fran would've convinced him to retire by now, but even she didn't have the power to get him to sit at home and watch television all day.

"Lead the way," I said, motioning down the hallway, ready to get the day started.

As I followed behind him, I pulled out my phone and shot off a message to Nya.

Me: Things okay?

Pop glanced over his shoulder and eyed my phone. "Texting Alese?"

"Just checking in on the girls."

"Good idea."

That was when I knew it wasn't a good idea. If Pop thought it was...then it wasn't. When in doubt, do the opposite.

Nya: We're both dead. –Alese.

I stared at the phone and shook my head.

Me: I'll text later.

Nya: Very later.

Well, she told me.

She might have been injured and recovering, but that didn't mean there wouldn't be hell to pay. Alese had a short fuse, and after two weeks of nonstop attention, she was done with it.

James, Thomas, and the rest of the ragtag crew of guys sat around the table, shuffling papers around.

"Look who I found," Pop said, sounding like a total cheeseball, but I knew his heart was in the right place.

"Glad you're back. We could use another set of hands." Thomas gave me a quick nod. "Let's get started."

James gave me a chin lift right before he started to speak. "The Almeda case. Bear, update us real quick for those who may have missed what's going on."

The group seemed to be on edge, but I couldn't quite figure out why. I didn't think being away for a few weeks would be awkward, but there was something I was missing, and I wouldn't stop until I found out.

Me: Dude, why's everyone grumpy as fuck?

Sam glanced at his phone before looking down the table as he picked it up.

Sam: Who the hell knows. I think it has to do with Nya. Ask Frisco. He knows more than me.

Nya?

Me: What's going on with Nya?

Frisco: Some bullshit with that Diego dude.

I breathed a sigh of relief that it had nothing to do with her treacherous parents, but Diego... He was an entirely different animal.

Me: What about him?

Frisco: Another girl has gone missing.

My eyebrows shot up. Not in surprise that he'd found a new victim, but that he did it so quickly without thinking it would set off alarm bells in the BDSM community in Atlanta. Even in big cities, the club community was often tight, and information moved like wildfire. I curled my fingers around my phone and growled, earning me a look from James.

"You up to helping Bear on this one, Ret?" James asked, staring at my hands as I tried my best to crush my phone.

I placed the phone on the table and took a deep breath, trying to calm the fuck down. "I'll be his point person on it."

James nodded, but he kept his eyes on me. "Good. Next order of business is Charmed and Diego Lopez."

I gritted my teeth and pictured the smug bastard with my hands wrapped around his neck, begging for mercy when he didn't deserve any. I'd known Nya wouldn't be his last victim, but I'd make sure there wouldn't be another after this new one. If it was the last thing I did, I'd put his ass behind bars.

"The owner of Charmed contacted me two days ago and said another submissive had gone missing. She had some interaction with Diego but hadn't committed to being with him before she disappeared."

I balled my fist against the table and kept my voice steady when all I wanted to do was yell. "How the fuck did he even get back into the club?"

"He didn't. He lured the girl off site after the owner banned him for life. Another submissive inside the club told her Master what happened, and the information was passed on to us."

"We should've handled him after we found Nya."

Thomas nodded along with James. We all knew we'd dropped the ball on that motherfucker, but it wasn't our case, and we thought the local authorities would follow up on his crimes. But Diego had too much money. He paid off anyone and everyone he could so they'd look the other way, and they did it because they were a slave to the almighty dollar more than they were to human decency.

Thomas stood from his chair and started to pace near the windows at the back of the room. "We can't count on the cooperation of local law enforcement. We'll be calling in some favors with the FBI through Sam and our contacts in the DEA. I'm sure we'll be able to find enough dirt on this man to bring him down so he doesn't have the ability to do this again.

"This is a team project. Once we have enough information and have our contacts in place, we'll be heading to Atlanta to put an end to Diego Lopez. Anyone have an objection?"

No one spoke as they shook their heads. There was nothing that got the team more fired up than a scumbag who hurt women. I had a bigger stake in this than anyone else. I'd seen firsthand the devastation Diego could and did cause.

"Be ready to move by the weekend. We'll be acting quickly on this out of necessity. The man has enough money that he could easily vanish without a trace."

I'd hunt him until the end of time. Eventually, everyone fucked up. I learned that bounty hunting. A person could only stay hidden for so long without a paper trail. In today's day and age, with everything able to be linked electronically, I'd eventually find him. But I wanted to do it before he ruined the life of another girl, or worse, killed someone.

Diego Lopez was going to pay a price, and this time, no amount of money in the bank was going to save him.

CHAPTER TWENTY-ONE

NYA

Ret walked through the door in an even worse mood than when Alese forced him to go to work this morning. He'd barely spoken a word to either of us after checking on Alese and making sure we didn't need anything. He retreated to his office, talking on the phone in whispered tones, and hadn't come out for the last hour.

"You worried about something?" Alese asked as I stared down the hallway toward Ret's office.

"He's grumpy, no?" I dabbed the end of the nail polish brush against the bottle before I went back to painting Alese's toes the most beautiful shade of pink.

"He's moody like a chick sometimes. All men are, but they'll never admit it." Alese closed her eyes and yawned. "Just ignore him. He'll tell us when he's ready."

As I dabbed her last toe, covering the tiny nail somehow without getting any on her skin, I felt a sense of accomplishment. "Why don't you rest, and I'll get dinner together."

She didn't open her eyes as she pulled the blanket closer to her face and made herself more comfortable.

Well, as comfortable as she could be only able to lie in one position because of her incisions. "That sounds like a plan."

I quietly cleaned off the coffee table, careful not to make too much noise so Alese could get some rest. I had an ulterior motive too. I wanted to talk to Ret without Alese around and try to see what was bothering him before we had dinner tonight.

I never did well when people were upset. I was a people pleaser and would do anything to bring a smile to their face, especially Ret's. When Alese finally started to snore, I tiptoed down the hallway toward his office.

I knocked softly and took a deep breath, nervous that he'd bite my head off for disturbing him.

"Come in," he said quickly, but there was no malice in his voice.

Turning the knob, I shook out my nervous energy before walking into his office with a smile on my face and my shoulders pushed back. I'd exude confidence. Something Alese and I had been working on since that day in the dressing room. "Can I get you anything? A drink maybe?"

Ret sat at his desk, sweeping his eyes over me as he propped his chin on the back of his hand, his elbow resting against the wooden surface. "I have some already." His eyes dipped to the half-filled glass sitting next to his arm. "Would you like a glass?"

I hated whiskey. Nothing about the taste or burn as it slid down my throat appealed to me. "I'd love some," I lied because I figured this was my way in.

He turned his chair, grabbing the bottle and glass off a small table behind his desk. "Sit for a bit. I want to talk to you," he said as he turned back around and motioned toward the chair across from him with a dip of his head.

I relaxed into the chair, watching him closely as he filled the glass with more whiskey than I wanted or needed. When he slid it across the desk, I grabbed the crystal glass and placed it on my knee. "Everything okay?"

I figured he wanted to talk about Alese and her recovery—the long road we both knew was coming the day she was released from the hospital. Once her incisions healed and her cast came off, she'd have physical therapy to regain strength and full movement.

"I don't know," he admitted before taking a sip of his whiskey, staring back at me over the rim.

"That doesn't sound good." I lifted the glass to my lips, letting a small amount of whiskey slide over my tongue. Based on the look on his face and the tone of his voice, I figured I'd need a little something to get me through the rest of the conversation.

"I don't want you to freak out."

I moved the glass away from my mouth and stared at him. There was nothing about that phrase that exuded positivity. Saying he didn't want me to freak out did exactly that. "What's wrong? Oh God," I groaned. "Is it Alese? Do you want me to leave?"

Every bad thought I could imagine crossed my mind. Maybe since she'd been released, he realized I was a drain on their relationship. Maybe my welcome here was about to be revoked, and he was plying me with alcohol so I wouldn't flip my shit and have a complete meltdown.

"No. No. It's nothing like that. Drink the whiskey first."

I took another sip, staring at his beautiful face and turquoise eyes, seeing the storm behind their peace. "You're killing me, Smalls."

Ret cracked a smile. "I have to leave town for a few days this weekend. Think you'll be okay with Alese on your own?"

"Of course." Like I'd say no to something like that. I'd do anything for Ret and Alese, and it wasn't like I had to watch her like she was a child. She was starting to be more mobile, barely needing help getting to the bathroom anymore. "She's a lot better than she was a few days ago."

"I feel confident you can handle things. I know she isn't your responsibility, and I..."

I waved my hand in the air, silencing him. "Don't say that. I love Alese. I would do anything for her and for you too, Ret."

His smile returned, matching my own. Saying the words out loud was easier than I imagined. I'd thought them a million times since the day Ret and Alese welcomed me into their home, making me feel part of something special. "We adore you, Nya. I don't know what I would've done without you the last few weeks."

"You would've managed."

Ret was the type of guy that really didn't need help with anything. He was a giver and not a taker, but it was nice to think that he felt I did my part in assisting with her recovery.

"I wouldn't have gone back to work so soon. I wouldn't have slept in weeks either. You do more than you think. You mean a lot to us both."

I hoped I did. I knew the way they moaned, and I wanted more. The last thing I wanted was not to be part of whatever they had, even if it was a small piece of that special something.

"Thank you. I'll take good care of our girl." I paused for a second and glanced down at the glass I'd rested on my leg, wondering if I overstepped my bounds by referring to her as mine. She wasn't. I knew that, but I liked how it sounded sliding off my tongue.

In reality, I was hers. Ret's too. I owed them everything, including my life, my happiness, my love.

"Good. I'll be headed to Atlanta."

My eyes flew to his, growing wide. "Why?"

Atlanta had been my home for years, but you couldn't force me back into that shithole town. The magic I thought it held had worn off quickly once I'd found myself trapped in Diego's mansion.

"A new case has come up." He tried to hide his face behind the glass, but there was something he wasn't telling me.

"And? What aren't you telling me?"

The tension on his face evaporated and was replaced by a small smile. "Am I that easy to read?"

"I've spent a lot of time studying your face, trying to read your emotions so I wasn't caught off guard."

His face tightened. "Are you worried I'm going to be upset with you?"

"I..." I didn't know how to answer that. I wasn't worried he'd hurt me. Ret would never do that, but after being with Diego, I tried to read everybody so I wouldn't be surprised if they lashed out. "No. It's just an old habit I can't seem to shake."

He slowly turned the glass in his hands. "I'll always be straight with you." He paused and rubbed the back of his neck, dipping his eyes toward the desk. "I have to go to Atlanta because of Diego."

I rocked back in my chair, not expecting his name to roll off Ret's tongue. "Why?" I asked, my voice small and soft.

"Another girl has gone missing."

"Shit," I hissed, imagining and knowing firsthand everything she was going through. I covered my mouth as the whiskey started to claw its way out of my stomach.

He dragged his eyes to mine and dropped his hand back to the glass. "We'll save her just like I found you, but this time, we're taking him down forever."

I swallowed down the wicked mix of bile and whiskey and cleared my throat, trying to find the words, but failing. "God, I hope so."

"I could use your help, actually."

"Just don't make me go back there, Ret. I can't step foot in that house again."

He quickly shook his head, and I felt relief. "Never. I just need to know about the first few weeks you were with him. I want to know what I'm going into and where he may be keeping her. Any details you can remember will help us to get everyone out alive."

I sat in silence, running through the events at the start of my captivity and how stupid I was to believe anything good was going to come out of it.

"You want to know now?"

Ret eyed the whiskey in my glass. "Finish your drink first and have another if you need it, but anything you can tell me may help us stop him forever. I'd like to return this girl to her family in one piece just like we did you."

But I wasn't with my family. They were just as crazy as Diego, only on a different scale. Both hid it behind a veil of love and caring, but they all wanted to control me for different reasons.

I lifted the glass to my lips, watching Ret as I guzzled down the contents, wincing as the whiskey burned on the way down my throat. I knew eventually I'd have to spill my guts about my stupidity, and I prayed Ret wouldn't judge me for any of it.

I placed the empty glass on his desk, tipping my head toward the bottle because I wanted more if I was going to spill the story of how I got myself into such a mess to begin with. It wasn't pretty.

He filled the glass again, this time a little more than before. "Nothing you tell me will leave this room. Not even Alese will know what you say. You can trust me, Nya."

I knew I could. He was the person I trusted most in the world. Next to Alese, of course, but she and I had a different relationship entirely.

"The first few days I was with Diego at his place, it was more of a game. I didn't think much of it because we were leaving for New York in a few days, so I thought I'd play along. He said he was testing my ability and my limits and that I was to think of it all as an extended scene." I took another gulp of the whiskey, letting the burn settle deep in my stomach as Ret stared at me. "I thought it was odd because we'd done dozens of scenes at the club, but looking back, I should've known it was all a sick and twisted game."

I was too stupid then. I was too enamored of the man...his beauty and wealth...to question anything he commanded or did because I thought he really cared about me.

"He started with mind games, pushing me further than he did at Charmed, but this time, there was no monitor to step in and save me when shit got bad."

I blew out a breath and tightened my hand into a hard fist. "He'd locked me in a closet, saying he was punishing me and testing my sensory deprivation limits.

He'd leave me in there for hours at a time. When I finally saw light again, I'd be so grateful that I listened to his every command just to keep myself from being locked up again."

"He's a twisted fuck."

I nodded. "We'd discussed my hard limits before we ever hooked up, but as soon as he got me in the house, he made sure to hit every single item I'd made off-limits before."

"Like?"

I couldn't look at Ret anymore. He wasn't staring at me like he was judging me, but I still felt the shame wash over me for my stupidity. "I didn't like darkness and had refused to have my eyes covered during any scene. I think that's why he went there first, locking me up without any light. He knew it terrified me."

Ret twisted his lips, but he remained silent as I took a moment to take another gulp. My vision blurred a little, and the words flowed easier than before as the liquor started to buzz through my system. "When he finally put me in the cage under his bed, I was thankful. How fucked up is that? I was so fucking happy for the bars instead of the dark room. What kind of person is happy about that?"

"It was your fear, Nya. He knew how to manipulate you. Don't ever blame yourself for how you felt. It wasn't your fault."

"Back to the first few days..."

I spent the next hour recounting every moment of torture, agony, and pleasure that Diego gave me, indoctrinating me into his twisted games. Ret sat mostly silent, barely making a facial expression in order to keep me talking. I could tell he wanted to say something, but he didn't as I barely stopped long enough to take a deep breath while I laid it all on the line, and none of it was pretty.

When I finally finished, I dropped my head forward and took a deep breath. "I don't want to say anything more. I'm sure you can imagine what happened after that."

The chair squeaked as his weight shifted, and he rose to his feet. First, his boots came into view and then his eyes as he placed his fingers under my chin and forced me to look at him. "He abused your trust, Nya. Never blame yourself for what he did." My eyes started to tear when I looked up at Ret as he spoke so tenderly to me. "A Dom/sub relationship is about trust, and he made you trust him before he broke his promise. You did nothing wrong. He's to blame, and I'm going to do everything in my power to stop him."

"Just be careful." The thought of something happening to Ret sent a shiver down my spine.

CHAPTER TWENTY-TWO

NYA

"Let's surprise Ret for lunch."

I gawked at Alese as she leaned against the countertop for support, standing next to the small electric scooter Ret had had delivered. "I don't think you're up to it yet."

Ret insisted Alese get a scooter so he didn't have to worry about her falling. Crutches weren't easy for her yet because her incisions were still healing, and it would be weeks before the soreness went away. When he ordered the sucker, I didn't think he meant for us to drop by the office quite so soon.

She scrunched her face and let out a strangled snarl. "It's been almost three weeks. I can't be in this house anymore. I need a little freedom before you two make me half insane."

I knew what it was like to feel trapped all too well, and it was awful. "Fine," I said as I slid off the couch and tucked my toes into my flip-flops. "If Ret gets mad, you have to deal with him."

I could already hear him now. He'd never been one to nag, but ever since Alese got hurt, he'd been a little over the top with his overprotective nature. At times, I knew Alese wanted to lay into him, but she didn't have the energy to argue. Now that she was on the road to recovery, I knew fireworks were inevitable.

She smiled and straightened a little. "If he gets mad, it won't matter because he's leaving in the morning. He can only be grouchy for so long."

I laughed and rubbed my face in the palms of my hands as I shook my head. "It'll be the longest twelve hours ever."

"Psh." She waved her hands. "I'm sure we can find a way to make him happy."

"You've been planning this all morning, haven't you? That's why you had me do your hair and makeup."

She gave me that sweet, innocent look, batting her eyelashes at me like I'd seen her do to Ret to get her way. "Maybe. Does it matter?"

I laughed, knowing her game but loving her just the same. "I suppose it doesn't."

Alese had a plan for everything. I think she'd developed that after being with Ret for so long. I could imagine her free spirit always thinking ahead, plotting her next move to make things go her way when she was younger. Sometimes I could almost see the wheels turning inside her mind.

"Come on. The guys at the office are too much fun, not to mention hot, and the weather's too nice for us to sit inside all day."

"Any of those guys single?" I asked, raising an eyebrow. I didn't know why I blurted that out, but I did. I grimaced as her smile disappeared and her shoulders slumped.

"You leavin' us?"

"Well, I..." I shrugged, not knowing what else to do. "No."

"You can never leave," she said quickly, trying to move in my direction, but stopped as soon as she put any pressure on her cast.

I rushed to her side, grabbing her by the arm, and I grunted. "You know you're not supposed to put pressure on it. You need to slow your roll, missy. If you hurt yourself, Ret will never let you out of his sight again."

She let out a loud huff before shifting all her weight to her good foot and plopping herself onto the scooter seat. "Fine. I'll behave, but we're not staying here today. I need some fresh air, good food, and those hot men."

"Let's do it."

"Hey," she said, grabbing my hand as I stood at her side. She peered up at me with a small, sad smile on her face. "Don't leave us. Not yet. Okay?"

"Yeah," I answered quickly, not even thinking twice about it.

"I know someday you'll want to go, but I'm not ready for that yet."

I stared down at Alese, bruised and still broken, but not letting that stop her from doing anything. My injuries weren't on the outside, visible to everyone, but they were there, lurking under the surface. Being with Ret and Alese was easy. They knew almost everything I'd been through and didn't think any less of me. Having to explain my past to someone else would be damn near impossible and almost paralyzing.

"I don't want to go anywhere." I smiled and touched her face the same way I'd seen Ret do when he wanted to get his point across. "I'm here until you don't want me anymore."

She blinked slowly, moving into my touch. "That day will never come, Nya."

I hoped her words were true. It was easy to say she wanted me around forever and that Ret liked having another woman around the house, even if neither of us was a domestic goddess.

"Let's get out of here before it gets too late."

I didn't ask what we'd be too late for, figuring she wanted to change the subject just as much as I did. I followed her out the front door and down the temporary ramps Ret put down last night, and I did my best to keep everyone happy.

Instead of going out to eat, Alese insisted we grab a few pizzas and sub sandwiches on the way to bring enough food for the entire office. She said something about wanting their energy, but I think it had more to do with the pain involved in getting in and out of the car. The scooter was great, but without an automatic lift in the car, the system for her to get around wasn't foolproof.

She grabbed the subs from my hands and placed them in the basket that hung on the front of her scooter. "This thing kinda rocks," she said, laughing. "I just need to borrow one of Fran's old tracksuits, and I'll be halfway to old age."

I slammed the lid of the trunk, balancing the pizzas in one hand and praying I didn't drop them. "Tracksuit?"

"You don't want to know. Let's just say, Fran wasn't always the hot cougar she is today."

"Okay." I smiled, wondering what she'd been like before Bear.

Alese raced ahead, beeping the horn on her scooter as she got closer to the door. Within moments, Angel, the receptionist, pushed it open and welcomed us both inside.

"The guys are going to love you two for this." She smiled, tossing her long red hair behind her shoulder. "They're always foraging."

I hadn't really paid too much attention to Angel the first few times I'd been to ALFA, but today, I soaked her in. She was drop-dead gorgeous. Not surprising considering I'd met all the spouses at the hospital while Alese recovered. There wasn't a bad-looking one in the bunch. Their husbands were hot too. I'd never seen anything like it before.

Bear, Ret's hot-ass father, came stalking down the hallway, rubbing his belly with his head bopping around. "What do I smell?"

Alese rolled toward him on her shiny new scooter, finally catching his eye. "Hey, Pop. We brought you lunch."

I placed the three large and extremely hot pizza boxes on Angel's desk, thankful to get them out of my hands without dumping them.

Bear stared down at Alese and jerked backward, shaking his head. "You got a scooter?"

She nodded, looking pretty impressed with herself. "Whatcha think?"

"Smokin' hot, babe."

"I just need a little more power, and we can race."

He patted her on the head and smiled. "You've got a long way before that bad boy has any chance of beating my bike, kid, but it's cute you think so."

I chuckled and covered my mouth. I loved Bear. Ret had a dash of his father in him, but he was way more serious. Bear was playful, funny, and was easy on the eyes. For an older man, he had everything going for him.

"Alese?" Ret walked out of his office, heading right for us, but I couldn't tell if he was happy to see us or ready to pop his lid.

"We brought you lunch." She smiled so big, not giving two fucks if he was upset as she lifted his favorite sub from her basket as an offering to keep his ass happy. "See?"

Ret crossed his arms, squaring his shoulders and looking more like a big bad Dom than I'd seen in weeks. He narrowed his eyes as he tilted his head, and for a moment, I readied myself for the ass-chewing we were about to get.

"Don't you think it's a little early for you to be out of the house?"

I gnawed on the inside of my cheek as I moved my eyes between them. I knew it was a bad idea to come here, and I should've done everything possible to keep Alese home.

"Darling, I missed you."

He pursed his lips and was about to say something when Bear stepped between them and grabbed the bag of subs from her basket. "We're happy to see you, kid. It's always good not to lie around too much. Gotta stay strong."

Ret turned his gaze to his father, but he stayed silent.

Bear gave Alese a wink before lifting the pizzas off the desk with his other hand. "Let's take this to the conference room. We could use a little more beauty around this place."

I giggled with Alese and Angel because none of us missed the snarl coming from Ret. His father shut him down, which was good because if he hadn't, I knew Alese would have.

"Lunch," Bear announced, gliding down the hallway with both hands filled.

Like clockwork, the men piled out of their offices, sniffing the air like Bear had done. They didn't speak in words, but short, deep grunts as if it were some secret male language.

"You two are the best," James, one of the owners, said after he walked into the room and spotted Alese and me. He gave us each a quick kiss on the cheek.

I stood at Alese's side as the small army of men pawed at the food, filling paper plates that Angel had brought in just behind Bear. After the men had almost cleaned everything out, I grabbed sandwiches for Alese and me before going back to stand near her.

"Ready for tomorrow?" Alese asked as she unwrapped her sub.

The man at Angel's side, Thomas, I think was his name, rubbed his hands together and smirked. "We're ready to kick some ass."

"Yep. That fucker's going down." Bear took another bite of his sub and had a few pieces of lettuce stuck in his beard. "That's a guarantee."

They exuded fearlessness and strength. If anyone could bring Diego down, it would be them. I picked off some of the toppings on my sandwich, hiding my eyes behind my hair as they started to talk about Diego and how they had everything in place to bring him to justice.

I just hoped they knew what they were getting into, because Diego always covered his ass.

CHAPTER TWENTY-THREE
RET

Sam glanced up from his phone and exhaled. "Everything's finally in place."

"Thank fuck," Morgan said at my side as we sat inside a blacked-out SUV down the street from Diego's, looking like something out of a movie.

Getting some of our contacts on board had been harder than we thought. The FBI and other agencies were overworked and understaffed, but a favor was a favor. We knew eventually they'd come around because we'd helped them out of more than one jam over the years.

That was the thing about working for the government. It was all about who you knew and if you'd scratched their back before. Being former military and a bounty hunter, I had contacts all over the country, from local law enforcement to the most covert black-ops agencies. Couple that with Sam's friends in the FBI and James and Thomas's DEA buddies, and we knew someone was bound to come around.

After some digging into Diego's past, we learned he'd been previously investigated in the disappearance of two females in the last ten years. They were never found, though, and there wasn't enough evidence to charge him. But with the recent crackdown on immigration laws due to the new presidential administration, Immigration and Customs Enforcement could toss him out of the country and send him back to Mexico where he was a wanted man. The police there didn't want him—they were as corrupt as the Atlanta cops—but there was more than one Mexican cartel that placed a bounty on his head.

"Pop and Sam, you two find the girl while the rest of us work on securing Diego."

"I'm all about the rescue." Pop rubbed his hands together. "But..."

"You going to just handcuff him?" Sam asked, interrupting my dad.

"I don't know. We'll see how everything unfolds."

That was a lie. After hearing everything Nya went through, I couldn't just hand Diego over to the authorities without making him pay for what he'd done to her. Not just her, but to every unsuspecting and trusting female he'd gotten his claws into over the years.

The sun hung low in the sky, almost hidden by the trees lining the long street near Diego's place. "I'll go in first." I squeezed my hands into tight fists, stretching the gloves I'd bought just for this occasion.

Sure, this wasn't a covert operation, but I was more than happy to fuck up Diego a little bit before we handed him off to the proper authorities. With the cops on his payroll, I didn't want to leave a trace that I'd been inside. There was nothing worse than crooked cops, depending on supplemental income and suddenly at a loss. I was sure heads would roll, but it sure as hell wasn't going to be any of the guys at ALFA on the hook.

"Let's discuss this as a team," Morgan said as he climbed out of the truck.

The fucker was trying to block me, but it wasn't going to work. I'd already discussed the entire operation with James and Thomas, and they were on board.

James swept his fingers through his hair, waiting for our team to join the others between the SUVs. "Let's go over this one more time. I want zero fuck-ups."

"I'm ready to fuck shit up." Pop cracked his knuckles, hungry for blood.

"Ret will go in first. We'll secure the perimeter before he enters. Once he's inside and verifies the girl's location, we'll enter as backup. Bear and Morgan will retrieve the girl and escort her to safety. The rest of us will be Ret's backup as he takes down Diego."

"Immigration is on the way. They should be here in ten," Sam added.

James gave Sam a quick chin lift and rubbed his hands together. "We better get moving, then. Any last-minute questions or issues?"

"Nope." I shook my head, ready to get moving.

I walked ahead of the group, sneaking around to the back of the property to enter through a rear door I'd seen when I cased the place to rescue Nya.

The lock was easier to pick a second time. Maybe he had a false sense of security with the piles of money he tossed at local law enforcement, but his careless mistake made it easy for me to gain access to the lower level of his home. Nya told me he often spent time in his study, which was located on the second floor near the front of the house.

I took a few steps inside, careful not to make a sound as I moved. The door to the closet Nya told me about had the lock engaged and two dead bolts fastened. What kind of sick fuck would think they actually needed so many locks to keep such a little girl inside? Maybe it was part of a sick, twisted mind game, the sound of each lock closing more terrifying than the last. Maybe it was the sound of them opening to reveal the monster on the other side that got his rocks off.

"Girl's locked inside," I said softly into the microphone so the rest of the team would start to move. "I'm going up."

"We're right behind you."

I moved so quickly, my feet barely touched the floor as I headed up the stairs, straight toward his study. I couldn't stop thinking about the way I found Nya, the sadness and hurt in her eyes as she told me about her time in this very house, and the countless women he'd done the same thing to over the years.

My insides were practically vibrating by the time I pushed the door to his study wide open.

"What the fuck?" Diego jumped to his feet, coming at me with the same burning anger in his eyes as I had raging in mine.

He swung at me, missing as I ducked and jabbed him in the gut. The loud grunt coming from his mouth as he crouched over screamed easy target. The man loved to hurt women, he thrived on their pain, but he couldn't take a small hit without crying out like a little bitch.

My blood boiled as Diego stood in front of me, breathing the same air I did when he didn't deserve to live. No man who did what he did deserved to exist in the same world as the ones he hurt.

Before he came at me again, I lunged forward and thrust my fist upward, connecting with his jaw. His head snapped back, spittle and blood flying from his mouth as he staggered and tried to maintain his footing.

"This is for Nya," I said before striking again, harder than before. He didn't just stagger that time. His body jolted as his feet left the ground, and he fell backward onto the hardwood floor.

I could've stopped then. Just rolled him over and put his hands in cuffs, but I couldn't. The feelings Nya had stirred in me, coupled with my experience as a Dom, made it so I couldn't let that be the end.

I stepped over him, placing my feet on either side of his writhing body, and crouched down. "You like to beat women?" He reached up, trying to push my face away, but I didn't budge. I grabbed his hair, lifting his face closer to mine. "You like to scare them?"

"Fuck you," he spat, blood dribbling down the corners of his mouth.

I laughed and tightened my grip, figuring I'd fuck with his head a little. "I bet the cartel in Mexico is going to love getting their hands on you."

His eyes widened, and he started to swing his arms, trying to break free of my hold. I slapped him, stunning him, but totally loving the wild look in his eyes.

Lowering myself, I sat on his chest, giving him all of my weight and making it hard for him to breathe. "You deserve a slow death, Diego. The cartel may make it too quick for what you deserve."

"The girl's secured," James said from behind me, but I didn't turn around as I glared at the piece of shit below me.

"Can I kill him?" I wanted nothing more than to slowly choke the life out of him. Watching him gasp for his last breaths, knowing they would be his final few, would give me more pleasure than just about anything in life.

"Don't do it. We have too many hands involved now. Let the Mexicans take him out."

I still slid my hands around his neck as he bucked and pleaded with me, with us, to release him. As I tightened my grip, squeezing his neck so hard that his eyes started to bulge and loving every second of watching the sick fuck struggle for air, James placed his hand on my shoulder.

"He's not worth it, man."

I could've argued. I wouldn't feel remorse for ending his life. Trash like Diego didn't deserve any pity or guilt. The world would be a better place without him in it, and if I had to kill him myself...I would.

"Son," Pop said, his heavy footsteps sounding against the hardwood as he came up behind me. "ICE is here."

"Fuck," I hissed, wanting to at least choke Diego to the point that he passed out, but maybe his knowing he was being carted off to the one country he didn't have protection was the way to go. He'd be terrified and maybe feel an ounce of the fear he caused his victims.

I lightened my grip but slammed the back of his head into the floor before I climbed to my feet.

"You'll pay for this," he said in a strangled voice as he rubbed his neck and gasped for air.

The room erupted in laughter because whether he knew it or not, his time for making threats was over and so was his life.

CHAPTER TWENTY-FOUR

NYA

Alese and I had danced around the topic of my being part of their relationship for days. Sometimes I felt like an interloper, like I'd inserted myself into their relationship without being invited. Not just their day-to-day life, but their bed too.

She'd asked me to never leave, but maybe it was because she was still healing from her accident and couldn't get around. The number of pain meds she was on didn't help her make any decisions either.

"Is this awkward for you?" I asked, sitting next to her on the couch, curled under the blanket.

She glanced at me with her eyebrows furrowed, looking confused by my question. I didn't know how I'd feel in her shoes. Before Diego, I'd had boyfriends, but nothing long term and no one I truly loved. I don't know how I'd feel if I were put in her situation.

"What? The three of us?" She rolled her eyes and curled the blanket closer to her chin. "Don't be silly. I love you being here with us."

"Okay."

"The only thing I'm jealous about right now is that you can come and I can't," she told me, letting her head fall to the side to stare at me.

"I'm sorry," I said like it was my fault.

"I was so close last time. So, so close, but I need my damn muscles to cooperate. It feels like it's going to take forever for me to get better."

"It won't," I lied. The doctors said her incisions would heal, but her leg would take much longer. Once the cast was finally removed, she'd need therapy to build up strength.

"Maybe if my incisions would heal. I don't know." She chewed her lips, glancing back at the television. "God, I love this part."

I glanced toward the screen, watching as the characters fell onto the bed, wrapped in each other's arms in a deep kiss. I smiled, sighing at the easiness they had with each other.

"Fuck, seriously. Even this tender shit is turning me on," she groaned and pulled the blanket over her head. "I can't take it."

I pulled the blanket away from her face. "Can I help at all? Do you think if we..."

"If we what?" she asked, a playful smile on her face.

"I don't know. Maybe if you get worked up enough, it'll just happen."

She looked at me almost cross-eyed, like I was speaking another language. "Like a spontaneous orgasm?"

I shrugged and laughed. "Dumb. I know."

She was quiet for a moment, staring at me as I peered back toward the television, suddenly feeling like a complete moron. "It may work. I mean, anything can happen, right?"

"Maybe. Can't hurt, can it?"

"Seriously?" She gaped at me, and I realized what I'd said.

"I mean, it would suck if it didn't work. Maybe we shouldn't."

"Fuck you. We're doing it."

"Now?"

She shook her head and giggled. "When Ret gets back, silly."

"Oh."

"Thank you," she said quickly, reaching down and grabbing my hand under the blanket.

"For what?"

I couldn't imagine what she was thanking me for. I should've been the one thanking her. She could've very easily turned her back on me and not welcomed me into her home and into her life. But that wasn't Alese. She didn't have an ounce of meanness in her body.

"I don't know what I would've done the last few weeks without you."

I felt the same way and couldn't stop the tears from filling my eyes as I stared at her beautiful, warm face. "I love you," I blurted out, saying the words for the first time.

She smiled, squeezing my hand tightly. "I love you too, Nya. Don't ever doubt that you're wanted and loved. Oh my God. Do you know what this means?"

"No," I said softly.

"I'm going to have a sister wife." She smiled.

The tears came faster, falling harder as she spoke. My parents never even said those words of love to me. No one on this planet had uttered such a thing before now. Just Alese, and although Ret didn't say it, I felt the unspoken words in his touch and burning in his eyes.

"Hey." She brushed away the tears from my face with a tender smile. "Can we watch something else? I can't take all this sex and sappy shit. We need some killing or laughs."

I leaned forward, wiping the tears away from my face as I grabbed the remote. There would be no more tears and no more sadness. I was done being that girl. I was part of something bigger, something better. I had two people who loved me, accepted me, and wanted me in their lives.

My phone vibrated next to me, and I practically jumped from the couch. "Fucking hell, that scared me."

"Is it Ret?" she asked, looking over as I pulled the phone in front of me.

"It is."

We both read the screen and exhaled in unison.

Ret: He's captured. It's done.

She was thankful Ret was okay and so was I, but I was happy to know Diego would never hurt another woman again. What I went through and probably dozens of women had gone through before me, no one should ever have to experience.

I was strong enough to withstand his mental games and torture, but others probably weren't as tough.

She pushed her head back into the couch cushion and smiled. "Thank God he's okay."

"Yeah," I said, staring at the screen again because I was a little bit in shock.

I'd never thought Diego would be brought to justice. Men like him, with more money than any human should be able to amass, usually found ways to skate the law because their bank accounts were so big.

But Ret and the guys at ALFA couldn't be bought.

I woke to soft voices mumbling back and forth and blinked a few times, stretching my sore muscles as I yawned. Ret sat on the coffee table, talking to Alese as she sat next to me.

"You're home?" I asked, my voice rough from sleep.

He smiled, leaning his upper body over his legs with his elbows on his knees. "Just got back."

"Everything go okay?"

I'd sat on the couch last night, trying to pay attention to the movie, but couldn't stop thinking about Ret and Diego.

"He's on a plane to Mexico right now. I give him twenty-four hours."

I knew in my heart I shouldn't be happy about someone dying, but if anyone deserved to cease to exist, it was Diego. "That's good."

"It's the best fucking news ever." Alese smiled, pulling herself upright with her hands without so much as a wince.

"Your hands," I said, finally letting my eyes roam Ret's body. His hands were bruised, and his knuckles were swollen.

He glanced down, squeezing his fists tightly. "I'm fine. You should see Diego's face." He smirked. "You ladies do okay without me?"

"Yeah. I think so." My eyes closed for a second, and sleep threatened to pull me back under.

"Nya had a fabulous idea, though."

The sleepy feeling was short-lived as my eyes flew open, knowing exactly what she was talking about.

Ret raised an eyebrow and stared at me. "I can't wait to hear this."

I glanced toward the ceiling, keeping my mouth shut because I was sure Alese could pull off my words better than I could. I'd sound crazy, but somehow, she'd say it in a way that would sound convincing and rational.

"I need to come."

I held back my laughter as Ret smiled and nodded his head. We both knew she could be a handful, and soon, if she didn't get her way or an orgasm, she'd probably be brutal to live with.

"Okay..."

"We're going to try for a spontaneous orgasm."

His eyes darted to me before going back to Alese. "Spontaneous orgasm?"

"Yep." She smiled.

"Want to explain that one to me? Like what... I look at you, and you come?"

She shrugged and laughed. "Not exactly."

Oh God. I wanted to crawl under the blanket and hide because she wasn't pulling off what I told her at all. I wasn't about to enter this conversation to clarify my statement either.

"Nya?" Ret stared at me, but I kept my eyes trained on the blank television behind him, pretending to be in a trance.

"You know how you get me all worked up?"

I breathed a sigh of relief when she started talking because it was becoming impossible to ignore Ret. This was more awkward than any other moment with them, and there were some that should've ranked right up here with this but didn't.

"Yeah." He smirked. "You like when I do that."

"Like sometimes when you only need to blow on my clit and I explode."

"Uh-huh." His smile widened.

"We gotta do that."

"So, lots of foreplay until you don't even need your muscles to push you over the edge."

"You got it." She laughed and folded her arms in front of her. "Just like that."

"I've never heard it called spontaneous orgasm, though."

"It's the best we could come up with in a pinch."

"You love to be pinched," he told her, winking while he moved his two fingers together like he was pinching her nipples.

"Jesus Christ," she groaned.

"What's wrong, baby... Horny?"

"Someone better get me off before I leave wet spots on every damn surface in this house."

I burst out in giggles. I didn't know if it was the crazy expression on her face or the tone of her voice, but I couldn't stop. I tried to swallow it down, but every time I almost got my composure back, I'd look at Alese and lose it all over again.

Alese didn't find it nearly as amusing as I did. "You won't be laughing if he doesn't let you come, ya know?"

My gaze flickered to Ret, and I instantly sobered. "I wasn't laughing at her."

It wasn't like I couldn't come without them, but there was something about being touched by another person that made everything more intense and pleasurable.

Ret stared at me, his face expressionless.

"I swear I wasn't."

The corner of his lip twitched, and I finally took a breath, relaxing a little bit. "It's okay. It was funny. You'll learn that when Alese doesn't get her way, she gets super whiny."

"And bitchy," Alese added.

Ret threw up his hands, still laughing. "Your words, not mine."

"You go three weeks without an orgasm. I bet you'd turn into a complete asshole."

"Babe, let's be honest. I already am."

"Your words, not mine." She laughed.

God, I freaking loved them. I was probably staring at them like an idiot at this point, but I couldn't wipe the smile off my face. I didn't know how I got so lucky to be part of their world. It almost made everything I went through worth it. If it hadn't been for Diego, I never would've found them. Or Ret never would've found me.

"Shall we try this spontaneous orgasm?" Ret cocked an eyebrow, and Alese scurried off the couch faster than I'd seen her move in weeks.

"We aren't leaving the bedroom until it happens."

Ret grabbed her hand and pulled her back down on the couch. "Who needs a bed, *piccola*?" He grinned.

CHAPTER TWENTY-FIVE
RET

Alese squirmed on the couch, squeezing her thighs together and mumbling something I couldn't quite make out behind the gag. The words sounded something like "I'm going to kill you," but I just smiled at my beautiful girl and pinched her nipple a little harder.

She asked for this. She wanted to get so turned on that she could come without having to strain her muscles, chasing the orgasm she rarely let happen naturally.

"Come here," I said to Nya, motioning for her to move closer. "Alese likes to watch. She told me a naughty secret the other day."

Alese's eyes widened, and she shook her head before groaning. Her hands moved against the ropes binding her, probably wishing she could touch herself.

"She did?" Nya asked as she took off her dress and walked toward me.

"She did, my sweet girl. She's a voyeur like you. She loves to watch. Gets off on seeing other people have pleasure."

Alese mumbled into the ball gag and pressed her thighs together again. She was already getting worked up, and we hadn't even done anything.

I held out my hand, and Nya slid her palm against mine. Her eyes were dark with lust. "She's like me."

"How did you feel when you watched us fucking at the club or in the bed?"

Nya let out a shaky breath. Maybe she knew where I was going as I guided her onto my lap. "It was hot. I was so turned on I could barely stand the ache between my legs."

I smiled and nodded. "Exactly. Alese told me not too long ago that she wanted to watch us having sex." Alese moaned, and I pinched her nipple harder, causing her body to twitch. "How would you feel about that?"

Nya's gaze dropped to Alese. "You'd want that?"

Alese nodded, trying to move her hands between her legs, but I swatted them away. "No touching," I told her.

"I know we've never done that before...made love to each other."

"I'm willing to do it to help out a friend. I offer myself up as a sacrifice." Her words came out quickly, and she giggled softly.

"Do you want me, Nya?" My dick was rock hard, straining against my pants and dying to be buried deep inside one of them.

"I do," she whispered and took another step forward, straddling my legs.

I removed my hand from Alese's body and grabbed Nya around the waist. "We'll go slow and take our time. This is about pleasure, but also sealing our connection, making us one."

Nya set her arms on mine, dragging her nails across my skin. "I'd like that."

With one hand, I unzipped my jeans and lifted my ass enough to slide them down my legs, letting my cock spring free in celebration. "Get a condom," I told her, motioning toward the side table where I'd placed one.

She moved quickly, grabbing the condom wrapper and tearing it open with her teeth. She was an eager little one, hungry for my cock as much as I was hungry to be inside her.

I slid the latex over my cock before stroking the shaft and blowing out a shaky breath. "Come here," I told Nya. "Let me touch you."

She climbed onto the couch with my help, guiding her to place her knees on each side of me, using the cushion as support. Alese grunted and struggled against her bindings, drawing Nya's attention.

"Pretend she isn't here," I told Nya, placing my fingers under her chin and bringing her eyes back to mine.

"That's kind of mean, Ret," she said, but there was a hint of a smile.

"She wanted a spontaneous orgasm, didn't she? I don't want there to be any hesitation in what's about to happen. I want her to enjoy every moment and get herself so worked up she barely needs to be touched to come."

Alese sucked in a breath and moaned, but I knew her better than anyone. We'd talked about this. Went over it a dozen times on how to break through the next barrier with Nya. The spontaneous orgasm thing was a nice touch and worked well to get to our ultimate goal. We both wanted Nya here with us. We enjoyed having her around, and she'd become part of us, inseparable and just as important.

I loved her too. A different sort of love from what I had with Alese, but we had years together wrapped up in those feelings.

Nya hadn't moved, just kneeled on the couch cushions, hovering above my body with her perky tits near my face. I slid my arm behind her back, resting the other just above her hip bone at her waist. "Are you okay with this?" I asked again.

She placed her hand on my shoulder, finally connecting herself to me. "Yes," she said breathlessly and nodded. "I want you, Ret. I want Alese too. I want all of this, all of you."

My fingers tightened against her skin as I pulled her closer. I gazed up at her as I leaned forward, gently placing my lips just below her collarbone. Her fingers curled into my skin as she leaned into my touch, wanting this as much as we'd hoped.

Moving slowly, I trailed a path down her chest with my lips, licking and sucking her soft skin as I made my way to her breasts. I slid my hand up, cupping her in my palm and lifting her nipple closer to my mouth. I paused and peered up at her, waiting for a sign to confirm she was still okay with this. She inhaled and smiled as she nodded ever so slightly.

I dragged my tongue down the middle of her breast before closing my lips around her nipple. She dropped her head backward and thrust her chest forward, offering herself to me completely.

I tightened my arm around her back, holding her to me as I sucked her nipple into my mouth, flicking the hardened tip with my tongue. She moaned, making my impossibly hard cock like granite.

Alese moaned as the couch moved, but I ignored her, giving her exactly what she wanted. By the time I touched her again, she would have that spontaneous orgasm she'd cooked up in my absence.

Nya lowered herself over my cock, rocking against the length and driving me crazy with lust. I pulled her nipple between my teeth, applying pressure as I traced the outline of the tip with my tongue. She shivered against me, moving her hips faster.

I flattened my palm against her back and drew her breast deeper into my mouth, trying to focus on her breast and not the fact that she was riding me. I repositioned my hand at her hip, moving it between us and sliding through her wetness.

"You want my cock in you, Nya?"

"Yes," she moaned, not stopping grinding against me.

"I'm going to go slow. Be gentle and let you set the pace. I don't want to hurt you."

"Shut up and fuck me, Ret."

I jerked my head back, and I couldn't stop the slow slide of the smile on my face. This girl suddenly had some teeth, telling me what to do.

When she lifted off me, I instantly missed the warmth of her skin against my cock, but it didn't last long. I ran the tip of my dick through her wetness, wishing I could feel every drop of her need soaking my cock. I fucking hated condoms.

She reached down, taking my cock in her hands, and gaining control. I placed one hand on her hip, peering down at Alese as she watched, unblinking and totally mesmerized. I wrapped my fingers around Alese's nipple, giving it a hard squeeze and she jolted and moaned. She spread her legs, begging to be touched, but I didn't. I wouldn't. Not until she couldn't lay still and was gasping behind the gag in her mouth. Her pussy glistened in the light, her need clearly evident as she squirmed.

Nya lowered herself slowly, enveloping my cock in her warmth with her hands squeezing my shoulders. Although I hated the condom, I loved it too. If it weren't for the thin piece of latex, I'd probably blow my load within seconds of being inside her tight, wet cunt.

She lifted and dropped herself back down, taking my cock deeper as her fingernails bit into my skin. I stared into her eyes, watching as she fucked herself using my cock. I blew out a breath, trying to keep my shit under control as she slowly fucked me silly, driving me close to the edge before I was ready.

Before I could come, I slid my hand between her legs, pressing on her clit with my thumb. Nya moaned, swiveling her hips as her pussy convulsed around my cock. I couldn't take it anymore. Couldn't stop the freight train from plowing into me like I'd broken down on the track, waiting for the devastation. The slowness was something I wasn't used to and didn't expect to affect me as much as it did.

I pressed my thumb harder, circling her clit as my spine tingled and the orgasm slammed into me, stealing the wind from my lungs. Nya bucked, gasping for air as her entire body twitched and quaked against me and her sweet little cunt milked my cock.

Her motion slowed as her head fell forward, covering my face with her soft, brown hair. I sucked in a breath, coming down from a high I hadn't felt in ages. With Alese being injured, I didn't dare touch her and risk hurting her further. But taking care of myself using my hand was nothing compared to the wet warmth of a beautiful pussy.

Alese grunted, wiggling and squirming at our side. I turned to her, smiling as her skin glistened, her flesh covered in a fine sheen of sweat. Her pussy was slick, ready, and needing some attention. I lifted Nya, placing her on the couch next to me before I leaned forward, hovering my lips over Alese's pussy.

She begged me with her eyes, wanting my mouth to devour her flesh and push her over the edge, giving her the orgasm she so badly needed and craved. I brought my lips down, sucking her clit into my mouth and flicked it with my tongue.

Her back bowed, and she screamed behind the gag. I thrust two fingers inside her pussy, delivering the final blow as I sucked her clit harder and sent her right over the edge. Her body rocked, trembling as the orgasm she'd been unable to achieve for weeks finally crashed into her, stealing her breath.

I stayed like that...my face buried between her legs, flicking her clit with my tongue as the aftershocks rippled through her until she went limp, gasping for air.

She closed her eyes as her chest heaved and her body relaxed. I lifted my face, taking in her beauty and realizing I was the luckiest man in the world. Not only did I have the love of my life, but we had Nya too. A beautiful, selfless creature, not broken, but stronger than she even knew.

I undid the gag, wiping away the spit from Alese's cheeks with the back of my hand.

"I could die happy now," Alese said with a smile.

The thought twisted my stomach. We'd come so close to losing her once that even a casual statement like that made me ill, but I didn't want to bring down the mood, and I let the comment slide.

"I got you ladies something while I was gone."

Alese waggled her fingers near my face, needing help up from the totally flat position and probably completely spent. "Help me," she said when I didn't move fast enough. Pulling her gently, I guided her up before I stalked off toward the counter to grab the tiny black velvet pouch.

Before I left for Atlanta, I'd contacted the jeweler who had made the original collar I'd seen on Nya's neck in her graduation photo. I'd asked him for four things. I wanted a proper and extravagant collar for Alese, but I didn't want it looking anything like the one Nya had. I also wanted something to symbolize the connection the three of us built, and it needed to be beautiful and meaningful.

Even on short notice, the jeweler pulled it off and gave me exactly what I wanted. I carried the bag to the couch and kneeled before Nya and Alese. Patting the edge, I motioned for Nya to sit next to Alese because I wanted this moment to be important and memorable.

"Presents," Alese said, her eyes lighting up as soon as she saw the bag in my hand.

Nya hung her legs over the edge and folded her hands in her lap as she peered down at my hands. I couldn't wipe the smile off my face looking at the two of them, sitting on the edge of the couch like two kids on Christmas morning waiting to open their presents.

"I thought long and hard about this." I undid the velvet tie, moving slowly so I could explain everything.

"You're killing me," Alese groaned and dropped her head forward.

"Eyes on me," I said quickly.

Alese snapped her head up immediately, and I placed two boxes in her lap. She squealed and reached for one, but I made a tsk and she stilled. I held out a single box to Nya, and she blushed, staring at me for a moment before snatching the package from my hands.

I held Alese's hand, needing to tell her how I felt. "I've never loved another person the way I love you. You're not only my lover, you're my best friend and partner. I almost lost you."

"But you didn't," she interrupted and bit down on her lip, stopping herself from saying anything more.

"I wanted to get you something special to symbolize our connection and your importance in my life."

"Can I open it?" She smirked and wiggled her fingers underneath my hand.

I laughed and finally released my hold. "There's no person more important in the world to me than you. This is a small gift, symbolizing my love."

Alese tore open the paper and flipped off the lid, revealing the handcrafted, diamond-encrusted choker I had specially made for her.

The light splintered from the stones, and she gasped, covering her mouth. "Oh my God. It's so beautiful."

Reaching up, I removed her old collar before replacing it with the new one. It was the perfect size. Not too loose and yet tight enough to remind her who she belonged to. I didn't know who I was kidding. I belonged to Alese, not the other way around. Even in the bedroom she fucked with my head to get exactly what she wanted, but it was a beautiful game of cat and mouse.

"This is a constant reminder of our connection," I said as I closed the lock on the collar.

Her fingers stroked the cool metal. "I love it, Ret." She lunged forward, the other box falling to the floor, and wrapped her arms around me, hugging me so tight I could barely breathe. "I love you, baby," she whispered in my ear.

My gaze flickered to Nya as she watched us, smiling and tearful. "Nya, open your box, sweetheart."

She was not as fast as Alese as she pulled the paper away from her smaller box. "You didn't have to get me anything," she said as she ran her finger over the lid. "It really wasn't necessary."

Alese released me, moving back to the spot next to Nya and clapping her hands. "This is so exciting."

"Wait," I said, lifting the box off the floor and placing it back on Alese's lap. "This gift is for the three of us."

"Yeah?" Alese looked at me with wide eyes. "All three?"

I nod. "All three. Open yours too."

They moved a little faster now, ripping into the packages, and pulled out their matching bracelets. Nya held it up in front of her eyes. "It's so...so..."

"Baby," Alese said with the biggest smile. "You did good."

I laughed. Alese knew me better than anyone. Shopping for anything, including jewelry, wasn't something I did well or enjoyed. But there was something different about selecting this gift. I wanted the three pieces to be perfect. "The bracelet has three bands woven together—yellow gold, white gold, and rose gold—to signify each of us. Nya, baby."

Nya lifted her eyes to mine. They were filled with tears, but she was smiling. "You've quickly become part of us, inseparable and important. Alese and I couldn't imagine life without you. This bracelet signifies the connection we have and that we're all bound together, tangled with no beginning or end."

"You mean..." She sniffled and wiped a tear away from her cheek. "You want me to stay?"

I placed my hands against her cheeks and stared into her eyes. "We want you to stay forever," I told her.

Nya covered her mouth and burst into tears. I glanced at Alese, wondering if I'd fucked everything up, but Alese touched my hand, letting me know it was all okay.

"You're one of us. I love you, Nya," Alese told her. "I can't imagine life without you anymore. Please say you'll stay."

Nya wiped her face and laughed, causing more tears to fall. "I never..." She laughed and shook her head. "I'm sorry I'm so emotional."

"You be whatever you want to be," I said and patted her knee.

She took three deep breaths, exhaling slowly on each one before stilling. "Not that long ago, I thought I'd spend my life locked in a cage at Diego's mercy. But then you—" Nya touched my face and smiled "—you saved me. You were like something right out of a fairy tale, Ret. Then you and Alese..." She choked back a sob. "You welcomed me into your home, showing me what real love is supposed to look like, and then made me part of something so special and pure. I love you both so, so much." She stopped only long enough to take a breath. "I never want to be anywhere or with anyone else."

I grabbed the bangle from Alese's hands and slid it over her wrist and then did the same for Nya before grabbing mine. Mine was chunkier, more manly compared to theirs, but matching in every other way.

"My girls," I said and pulled them toward me, wrapping my arms around them. "I'm the happiest and luckiest guy in the world."

Alese laughed. "You are one lucky bastard."

EPILOGUE

ALESE

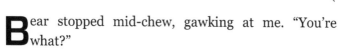

Bear stopped mid-chew, gawking at me. "You're what?"

"We're together and committed," I told him before taking a sip of the wine Fran had just given me.

He looked at Nya and then to Ret as he set down his fork. "You got them both?"

I laughed over the rim of my glass, loving the look on his face. Bear was by far the funniest person I'd ever met. When Ret said he wanted to move to Tampa and that his father was there too, I was hesitant. I knew about Ret's past and his father leaving him and his sister behind after the death of his wife, Ret's mother.

From what I'd heard about Bear, I was petrified to let this man into our lives. He had a criminal record longer than my arm and hung around with bikers. The last thing I expected was to find this fun-loving, goofy, and even sexy man to come barreling into our lives.

Ret nodded with a grin. He knew, just like I did, this would eat Bear up inside. I wasn't worried about breaking the news to him, but Fran was an entirely different story. "Yeah, Pop. They're mine."

My stomach fluttered with those words. I could hear Ret say them over and over again and never tire of them. Bear glanced around again, mouth hanging open, and pushed back from the table.

"Well, fuck," he said, dropping his fork. "If there was any doubt, this proves you're every bit my son."

I laughed harder, covering my mouth so I didn't spit my wine across the table. The man thought of himself as a playboy, but we all knew the truth. He had eyes for only one woman, and she was standing right behind him, not looking the least bit amused.

I sobered, sitting up a little straighter in my chair. "Hey, Fran."

She leaned forward and wrapped her arms around his chest. "You want two women?" she asked, resting her mouth against his ear.

His eyes widened as he stared at me. "No, baby," he coughed and placed his hands over hers in front of him. "I have you. What more could a guy ask for?"

"We can make it a reality," she told him.

He moved his gaze around the table like he needed validation that what she said was indeed what he heard. "What?"

Fran touched his cheek with her mouth and tightened her arms around his neck. "But if you need two, just know I'm not going to be one of them."

He turned quickly and pulled her down into his lap, wrapping his arms around her. "You're all I ever need, Fran. Don't be ridiculous. I can barely handle you sometimes, wildcat."

She raised an eyebrow with no smile on her face as she stared at him. "Mm-hm."

Bear rubbed his beard against her neck until she finally lost it.

"Stop!" Fran wiggled in his lap, laughing. "Baby, be happy for the kids. I'm excited for them."

Fran finally turned her gaze toward me. "Are you happy?"

"Yes," I said.

She looked to Nya. "Are you happy, sweetheart?"

"Yes." Nya nodded.

Fran eyed Ret and shook her head. "I know you're happy. I'm not even going to bother to ask." Turning in Bear's lap, she pushed his plate aside. "I learned something important a long time ago."

"Here we go," Bear muttered.

He was instantly met with Fran's icy glare. "You got something to say?"

"Of course not, love. Talk to the kids," he said, touching her cheek and turning her face away from him.

Nya had her hand over her mouth, trying to hide her laughter, but I didn't bother. Those two had kept me rolling since the day we moved here. Fran was my spirit animal and exactly how I wanted to be as I grew older. She never held back and definitely didn't pull any punches. If she said it, she meant it.

"As I was saying before I was so rudely interrupted..."

Bear rolled his eyes.

"Love isn't something we can control. We don't get to pick who our heart wants, and sometimes it's not as clean as society wants us to believe. I mean, take your father and me." She turned toward Ret, talking straight to him. "I never thought I'd fall in love with a man who couldn't settle and hopped from woman to woman like it was an Olympic sport. People told me we were doomed and he'd never settle down. But here we are, and we're happily in love and completely committed. Right, honey?"

"Of course." He nodded.

"Do whatever makes you happy in life. It can all disappear in a blink of an eye. Live without regret. Love without remorse. And never let anyone make you feel less than you are because they have a stick rammed so far up their ass the damn thing scrambles their brain when they walk."

I blinked and stared. For a second, I thought Fran was going soft on me. She was almost there with her live and love bit, but then in typical Fran fashion, she went to the stick and ruined everything.

"That was beautiful, baby," Bear said and held her tighter, kissing the back of her neck softly.

"Now, I don't care which one of you does this, but someone better start making some babies. I'm not getting any younger, and neither are you."

"Well, I..." I didn't want to tell Fran I had no inclination of ever having a human grow in my body. It wasn't that I was anti kid, but I liked my body, vagina, and life the way they were. I was completely selfish, but I was okay with that and so was Ret.

But Nya...she was another story. She longed for a baby and was open about it.

"We're trying," I said and didn't say anything more. It didn't matter whose body the baby would eventually come out of, he or she would be loved just the same by all three of us.

Bear smacked Ret's shoulder and grinned. "My boy. I envy the task before you." Fran kicked him under the table, and Bear growled. "I meant I don't envy you at all."

On the outside, our relationship probably looked like it was impossible. But on the inside, it was the purest form of love and respect I'd ever had.

This was my life. Parents that weren't mine but loved me like I was their own. A boyfriend and Master who was selfless and loving. And then there was Nya...a best friend, a confidant, and my other half.

A LETTER FROM CHELLE BLISS

Dear Reader,

So... I had planned to create a different story from what you just finished reading. I was chapters in, deep into a horrible event that happened to Alese, when a beta reader gave me hell. She said I couldn't do what I'd just done. That readers, including her, would hate me for it. She made me cut over 4,000 words and change the entire direction of the book. You can thank her for Alese still being alive.

But then I thought...what the hell am I going to do with all these words? Then I figured I'd throw them in as extra because maybe you wanted to crawl inside my brain and see what I had planned for you. You can thank my beta, Renita, for the following chapters not being part of the book anymore.

Enjoy!
Chelle Bliss

DELETED
CHAPTER

NYA

Three months later

The waves rolled over my feet as I stared out at the horizon, watching the sunset like I did almost every night. Ret refused to join me, even when I begged him like I did every night. He grumbled under his breath before he stalked off toward his bedroom and slammed the door.

Losing Alese devastated us both. I might have only loved her for a short time, but the loss was not easier to bear. She brought me back to life at a time when I wasn't sure if I'd ever find joy again. I was just as lost as Ret. His anguish was greater, their love longer and deeper than anything I'd ever felt before.

I didn't know how to console him or what to say to help him through his grief because I hadn't sorted out my own. We had both been in a haze since that night at the hospital. I barely remembered her funeral as it had passed by in a blur.

I'd thought about leaving a few times, figuring Ret wanted to be alone with his grief. He'd asked me to stay, said he needed me here to help him. I hadn't done a damn thing, though. I certainly hadn't helped him in any way.

He was still consumed by sadness and a shell of his former self. Sometimes his anger would get the better of him. He never touched me, but he wasn't the patient man I'd met months ago, and I didn't know how to bring him back or if it was even possible.

"Help me," I said into the wind, talking to Alese like I did every evening as I watched the sunset. "He can't go on like this. I can't go on like this." But just like every night before, there was no reply.

As the sun kissed the horizon, blazing bright and illuminating the sky in a kaleidoscope of colors, I brushed the sand off my legs and headed back toward the house for another quiet night.

God, I missed Alese's laughter. She was like a bright light, filling the house with her giggles and bad food. I'd picked up that torch, burning everything I could get my hands on just to make something seem normal again.

As my feet touched the patio, I turned and let my gaze linger on the endless sea. My stomach growled and I sighed, wishing I didn't have to forage in the fridge for something to cook, only to watch Ret push it around his plate before he stalked off again.

Maybe tonight could be different. I had to try to get him out of his head tonight. The grief was eating him alive. He went to work each day, never with a smile and barely saying goodbye. The guys had stopped coming around, and even his father had started to keep his distance. Although he'd tried for months to help his son heal, even he failed to pull Ret out of his funk.

As I walked through the open sliders that lined the back of the house, I glanced down, spotting Alese's sandals that hadn't moved. Ret hadn't been able to pack away her things and had left everything just where it had been the last time she was home. I couldn't blame him. Moving her possessions, her clothes, even something as simple as her shoes made everything feel so final, and I didn't think either of us was ready for that yet.

I loaded the countertop with every vegetable I could find in the refrigerator and started chopping away like a madwoman. With each chop of the knife, my anger grew, replacing the sadness I hadn't been able to shake.

When the knife slipped and gouged the tip of my finger, I pulled my hand against my body, yelling, "Motherfucker." Blood spilled down my arm, soaking through my T-shirt as I danced around the kitchen and shrieked in pain.

Ret came storming down the hallway, and I turned my back to him, hiding my finger. "What's wrong?"

"Nothing. I just stubbed my toe." A drop of blood fell and landed on the top of my foot. I squeezed my eyes shut and groaned softly.

Damn it.

I'd thought my lie was believable until the goddamn blood. Ret probably would've stalked back toward his bedroom if the cut didn't decide to out me.

Ret placed his hands on my shoulders, turning me to face him even though all I wanted to do was hide. "Jesus. Let me see that." He started to reach for my hand, but I tightened my fist against my shirt. "Come on, Nya. You might need stitches."

"I'm fine, Ret." I stared him down, still clutching my hand to my chest. "Go back to whatever you were doing."

He didn't move, though. He stood in front of me with a stern look firmly planted on his face, his eyes narrowing. "If it's nothing, why do you look like you're about to cry?"

My eyes were filling no matter how much I tried to fight it. "I'm embarrassed, okay?"

I'd never been a good liar. Even in that moment, anyone could see that I was full of shit, but that didn't stop me from sticking to my story.

Ret gripped my waist with his hands before he lifted me in the air. He moved so quickly, I didn't have a chance to react before my ass was on the ice-cold granite countertop.

"What are you doing?" I glared at him as he kept his hands on my sides like I was about to bolt, which I would've if he weren't blocking my way.

He let out a loud, exasperated huff and motioned for me to give him my hand, but I didn't. "I'm not leaving this room until your finger is patched up."

I scrunched my face. Sometimes, like in that moment, the man could be so bullheaded and bossy that I wanted to scream, but then I remembered... I remembered he saved me, and he lost the only woman he'd ever loved. "Don't hurt me, okay?" I whispered, staring into his stormy blue eyes.

He placed his hands on his hips and leveled me with his eyes. "Have I ever hurt you?"

Shit. "No."

Motioning again, he waited with his eyes unmoving as I sat there, kicking my feet against the cabinets and stared back at him. I thrust my hand between us, my fingers still curled into a tight fist with blood trickling between the cracks.

"Stay there," he commanded like my ass had anywhere to hide. He disappeared into the guest bathroom, making a whole lot of noise as he closed a cabinet.

I rolled my eyes as my feet started to move faster because I knew whatever he was about to do would involve pain. The cut already hurt like a bitch, and the last thing in the world I wanted was for him, or anyone for that matter, to touch it.

He placed the first aid kit he'd retrieved from the bathroom on the counter next to me, glancing up as I tried to pretend I wasn't terrified. I closed my eyes because I didn't want to see what he was going to do.

His touch was lighter than I expected as he uncurled my fingers. I held my breath, waiting for the pain to become unbearable as he started to clean the cut.

"Breathe, Nya. I won't hurt you. I promise."

Ret was a man of his word. That much, I knew about him. Since the day he'd rescued me, he'd never lied. But he wasn't a doctor, and my finger wasn't numb.

"It's not that bad," he said after I didn't open my eyes and started getting light-headed. "Look."

Slowly, I opened my eyes, but instead of glancing down at the cut, I looked at Ret. I watched his face change, the hardness of earlier replaced by something almost resembling softness. His hair had grown longer in the last few months, falling over his face and hiding his eyes as he dabbed my finger with a cotton ball.

"You need to keep this clean until it heals a bit."

I was about to say something snarky, but I bit my lip when his eyes met mine.

"The gel I used will relieve some of the pain for a few hours, and we can apply more later." He wrapped a Band-Aid around my finger, pressing gently on the material. "Tomorrow, this is going to be sore, though, but you don't need stitches."

I nodded, staying silent and moving my eyes between him and my finger. He set his hands on my knees, searing me with his touch even if it wasn't sexual in any way. I hadn't touched another person or been touched by anyone since Alese's funeral. Any relationship he and I had before was gone, replaced by a platonic roommate situation.

When he stalked back toward his bedroom, leaving me on the counter with the remnants of what happened, the tears fell harder and easier.

I missed the strong man who pulled me from Diego's cage. I missed the playful laughter of him and Alese. Most of all...I missed my friend.

DELETED CHAPTER

RET

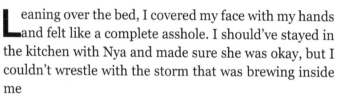

Leaning over the bed, I covered my face with my hands and felt like a complete asshole. I should've stayed in the kitchen with Nya and made sure she was okay, but I couldn't wrestle with the storm that was brewing inside me

For a week, I've tried to pack away Alese's things, telling myself she wasn't coming back. But I couldn't do it. Removing her clothes and even the pair of earrings from the nightstand made everything real, and I wasn't ready for that...not yet.

Two months ago, people stopped asking if I needed help. Every time they did, I practically bit their heads off. There was no right or wrong amount of time for a person to grieve, but I had to pull my head out of my ass soon before I alienated everyone.

I could hear Nya's soft cries coming from the kitchen as I balled my hand into a fist against my leg. The fragrance of her perfume still lingered in the air around me from touching her. I craved the smell, because it was the same perfume Alese wore, although the aroma was on Nya. I wasn't sure if having Alese's scent all over the house was therapeutic or verged on torture.

"Ret," Nya said on the other side of the door before knocking.

I straightened, resting my elbows on my knees and shaking out my fingers to get the bad juju to go away. There wasn't any escaping the feeling, the despair and longing I felt for the woman I loved.

I always had to retain control.

Always.

My entire life was about planning, acting, and being disciplined. From being in the military to bounty hunting, I didn't have time to leave anything to chance. But right now, without Alese, nothing made sense, and I had no discipline.

"Ret," she said again when I didn't reply.

I squeezed my fingers into a ball again before releasing them. I needed to get my shit together for my sake and Nya's. She didn't deserve my mood swings.

"Yeah?"

The door handle turned for a second before stilling. "Can I come in?"

"Come in, Nya." I forced a small smile on my face and somehow maintained the expression.

The door creaked as she pushed it wide open and walked a few feet inside before stopping. "We need to talk," she said, staring at the floor, her eyes hidden behind her hair.

"Come." I patted the mattress next to me, trying to be friendlier than I had been in months.

She walked toward me, her feet moving slowly across the hardwood floor like she wasn't sure she wanted to get too close to me. The bed barely dipped under her small weight as she adjusted herself and folded her hands in her lap.

"What's wrong?"

"I think I should leave," she said, bringing her eyes to mine, filled with tears.

Somehow, I remained still and didn't change the expression on my face. Her words rocked me to the core. Even though Alese was gone, Nya kept me sane. Knowing she was there was enough to keep me from falling over the edge completely. "Why?"

She turned toward me, our knees touching ever so slightly. "I think it's best for both of us if I move out. I'm sure you'd rather be alone than have to deal with me every day."

Nothing about her statement was true, but I hadn't done much in the last three months to make her believe or feel any differently. I took a deep breath and reached between us, cupping her hands in mine, careful not to put pressure on her injured finger. "Nya, the last thing in the world I want is for you to leave."

Her eyes widened. "You don't?"

"I don't." I shook my head slowly. "You're the only thing keeping me from going crazy."

She blinked twice, staring at me with her big brown eyes. "But…"

"I'm serious," I said, interrupting her because she needed to know exactly how I felt. "I haven't burned this house down to the ground because you're around. Days when I want to smash everything inside this room, I don't because you're here. I need you here. I need you in my life to remind me that there's still good."

"I don't know." She grimaced.

I squeezed her hands, running my thumb across the soft skin on top, enjoying the feel of her a little more than I should. "Please don't leave. Not yet."

"It hurts to be here," she whispered.

I closed my eyes for a moment, knowing every bit of that hurt all too well. "I won't stop you from leaving, but please don't go because you think that's what I want."

"I miss her."

"I miss her too. I miss her more than anything I've ever missed before."

Saying the words and expressing how I felt was easier than before. Maybe because I knew Nya felt the same way. She might have only been around for a short time before Alese died, but that didn't mean she didn't feel anything at her death. Nya was the only person in the world who really had any idea about Alese's and my true relationship. People knew about our kink and how we met, but no one had ever had a front row seat to everything like Nya.

"Don't leave now," I begged, squeezing her hands a little tighter. "I can't bear another loss."

I showed weakness, something I'd never been comfortable with before, but I'd do or say anything to make Nya stay.

She furrowed her eyebrows as she gazed at me. "You'd miss me?"

I smiled softly and kept my tone level yet soft. "Of course."

"I..." She swallowed and bowed her head. "I didn't think you wanted me anymore."

Releasing her hand, I placed my fingers against her chin and lifted her eyes to mine. "You're the only reason I wake up anymore, Nya. Without you, I don't know what I'd do or where I'd be." She stared at me, eyes unmoving as I swiped my thumb across her soft skin.

"Alese loved you more than anyone in the world. She would want you to be happy, and so do I. We've been through so much, Ret. So, so much."

I smiled softly, almost sweetly, for the first time in months, wishing I could wipe away both our pain. "You're not sleeping either, are you?"

The shadowy circles under her eyes matched my own. Deep and dark, showing our grief to the world, and no amount of makeup Nya put on could hide it.

She shook her head and closed her eyes. "I get a few hours here and there."

"Me too," I sighed. I couldn't remember the last time I'd felt normal. Sleep had eluded me since the day I'd kissed Alese goodbye.

"Love," I whispered as I sat down on a stool beside Alese's body. I gripped her hand in mine, sweeping my other one down her soft, cool cheek. "Wake up."

I stared at her lifeless body, waiting for some sign of life, but nothing came. The panic that had started to set in gripped my entire frame, rocking my very foundation.

I laid my lips against the top of her hand, kissing her skin softly and searching for her scent, but there was no trace. "You can't leave me. I don't know how to be without you anymore."

The tears came hard and fast, falling down my cheeks and landing on the sheets near her side. My life would never be the same. It couldn't be without her. She was the light in my darkness. From the moment I met Alese, she brought me nothing but joy, showing me the true definition of unconditional love.

"I'm nothing without you," I whispered through my tears and placed my forehead near her stomach, gazing

up at her beautiful, stoic face. "I love you, Alese. I love you so fucking much."

"Son," my pop said before clearing his throat.

I wanted to tell him to go away. I wanted everyone to leave me alone. There was no amount of time that would've been long enough for me to stay at her side. The thought of them taking her away to some cold, dark place for her to be left alone...wasn't something I could bear or fathom. She needed to be with me, in my bed, at my side...alive. But she'd never be again.

"Ret," Nya said softly, pulling me back to the present. "Do you mind if I sleep in here tonight? I'll even sleep in the chair, but I don't want to be alone, and I'm exhausted."

I dropped my fingers from her chin and cupped her hands in mine. "You can sleep in the bed. Alese would have my balls if I made you sleep in a goddamn chair."

Exhausted didn't even begin to describe how I felt anymore. I'd stopped living. I only existed, gliding through my days in a haze of grief and longing for far too long. One thing was for sure...Alese would want me to get my shit together and start living again.

DELETED CHAPTER

NYA

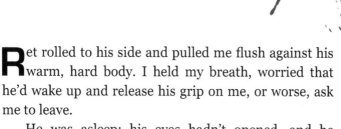

Ret rolled to his side and pulled me flush against his warm, hard body. I held my breath, worried that he'd wake up and release his grip on me, or worse, ask me to leave.

He was asleep; his eyes hadn't opened, and he probably had no idea he'd curled against me. I didn't care if he thought he was holding Alese because it felt good to be touched, to be held, and not to be alone for another night. I turned my face on the pillow and stared at Ret in the darkness, taking in his handsome face at rest and in peace.

I mourned the loss of Alese. She'd become my best friend so quickly, taking me under her wing without so much as a sideways glance or snide remark. But my heart ached for Ret. The dead have no grievances. They have no fear. They have no comprehension of time. The living are the lost. The ones surrounded by darkness, enveloped in the loneliness of living without truly feeling alive.

Ret had transformed before my eyes. He was a strong man, filled with passion and dominance. But everything he was, the control he had, evaporated the moment she died.

I couldn't let him disappear. Alese wouldn't want that for him. She wouldn't want either of us to wallow in despair and stop living. I decided in that moment, while he held me in his arms, his heart beating steady and hard against my side, that I would help Ret to find joy again... to bring him back to life.

It was the least I could do after everything he and Alese did to help me. I'd thought I was dead. As I'd huddled in the cage below Diego's bed, I'd never thought I'd step foot in the outside world again. I'd resigned myself to that reality. The day Ret rescued me, I couldn't comprehend that I was truly free, and I wasn't even sure what that word meant after being removed from society against my will for so long.

"Baby," Ret whispered and tightened his grip as he slept.

I bit my lip as I gazed at him in the moonlight, trying not to cry and interrupt his momentary happiness. There was almost a smile on his face, a dream of someone other than me. So badly I wanted to touch his face, tracing the line of his jaw and the now permanent five-o'clock shadow he'd had for months, but I kept my hands to myself.

I didn't dare wake him. Dreams were an escape from reality. When I was with Diego, I lived for my dreams, begging for sleep to come every night. Those were the only moments of freedom and happiness I had to look forward to, and there was no way I'd steal that away from Ret.

His warm, sweet breath skidded across my face as I lay next to him. I closed my eyes, wiping away everything. The sadness. The loss. I let myself just be as I was wrapped tightly in his arms.

Moments later, Ret moved closer, his lips touching my cheek as they searched for my mouth. Not mine, but Alese's, the woman he loved and was dreaming about. I knew what I was about to do was wrong, but that didn't stop me because I needed this as much as he wanted it.

I turned my face, giving him my mouth, and took what he offered. The caress of his lips against mine was intoxicatingly soft.

***

Hey. It's me...Chelle. So, this is the spot where Renita had a fit and told me I couldn't kill off Alese. I thought long and hard, wondering how you'd feel if she died.

I gave you a reprieve and allowed her to live. It made for a happier story, at least. If you wished I killed her off...talk to Renita.

I hope you loved Guilty Sin!

Love,
Chelle

COMING IN 2018!
Are you ready for more GALLOS?
The Southside of Chicago has never been so dirty.

COMING THIS FALL

See below to learn more about the Southside and keep up to date on the latest news.

COMING THIS JULY
Are you ready for a NEW *GALLO*?

He's always been the player...but he's about to get played.

TINO GALLO
Growing up on the rough Southside of Chicago, I learned early how to play the field. Between my rugged good-looks, rock-hard body, and panty-melting smile, I was used to getting my way.
...But then she walked into my club.

DELILAH MILES
I may have grown up with the finer things in life, but that doesn't mean I take crap from anyone. I'm tough as nails, fiercely independent, and am never afraid to speak my mind.
...But then then he stormed into my life.
*Maneuver is a standalone full-length
prequel novel to the Southside series!*
*Valentino aka Tino is smoking hot, full of swagger, and a total
dirty talker.*
He's not to be missed!

COMING IN JUNE

ACKNOWLEDGEMENTS

I don't even know what to write in this space. I'm sure I could come with a list a mile long, thanking everybody in the world in the creation of Guilty Sin...but I won't.

There are so many people who play some sort of role in helping an author create a new books. From the amazing cover designer, Lori Jackson—you nailed this one, to my fabulous editor, Lisa Hollett—you're a saint, and right down to every readers and supporter.

I can't thank everyone enough for always being there for me. For being a kind ear or sending me a sweet message. I'm truly blessed to have each and every one of you in my life.

It's been a rough two years, but I don't think I could've survived everything with you—my friends and readers—being there to cheer me on and lift my spirits.

Your support and love mean the world to me.

I have some big things planned this year and they're booked I know you're going to LOVE.

So, settle in, buckle up, and be ready!

ABOUT THE AUTHOR

Chelle Bliss is the *USA Today* bestselling author of the **Men of Inked** and **ALFA Investigations** series. She hails from the Midwest, but currently lives near the beach even though she hates sand. She's a full-time writer, time-waster extraordinaire, social media addict, coffee fiend, and ex high school history teacher. She loves spending time with her two cats, alpha boyfriend, and chatting with readers.

JOIN THE MY NEWSLETTER
chellebliss.com/newsletter

www.chellebliss.com

FOLLOW ME
facebook.com/authorchellebliss1
twitter.com/chellebliss1
instagram.com/authorchellebliss

TOP
BOTTOM
SWITCH

CHAPTER ONE

Ret

I've grown bored. It's not something I've ever experienced when it comes to sex. Someone lights my fire for at least a night, but tonight...nothing.

Being a member of The Club has been a great thing. It has allowed me to make a lot of new friends since moving back to Karim, Texas a few years ago. Lately, though, something has been missing. The typical night of fun spent with a submissive doesn't seem to give me the same thrill it did before.

It's my failure, not theirs.

The ladies I spend the night with do everything a Dom could ask. They bend to my will, follow commands, and allow me to push their boundaries. But there's no light. No fire. Nothing to keep my embers simmering, stoking the flames.

"Ret, I don't understand. What's the problem?" Misha asks in a light Russian accent, sliding into the booth across from me with Stella, his submissive, by his side. "I thought you liked Elle."

Turning the glass of scotch in my hand, I grit my teeth and exhale. "I tried with Elle. Twice, I tried. We're not a fit. She's just not my type."

She had everything I wanted on the outside. There was instant attraction, but the more I talked with her, the less appealing she became. Maybe it was her willingness to submit so easily that turned me off.

"I didn't know you had one." Misha smirks before patting his leg for Stella to obey. Without hesitation, she climbs into his lap and melts against his body. I envy their relationship—the trust they have in each other.

"Would you like something to drink, Sir?" The waitress stands by the edge of the table, staring down at me from under her lashes, holding the tray against her exposed hip.

"I'm fine." Annoyed with myself, I wave her away.

Misha motions toward the waitress as she walks away, swinging her hips wildly before daring to sneak a backward glance over her shoulder. "Is she your type?"

"No," I grumble before taking a long, slow slug of my drink, watching Stella and Misha over the rim before movement to my right catches my eye.

"Get your filthy hands off me!" Alese, a notorious Club switch, yanks free of a man's hold and spits in his face just outside our private booth.

He lunges toward her and glares. "Get back here, girl!" He's about to grab her arm when she cracks him across the face.

Preston Stevens, head of Club security, comes from out of nowhere and catches the man's hand before he strikes her. "I wouldn't do that if I were you."

"This bitch," he snarls, spit flying out of his mouth as he glowers at her. "She wanted to play, and then she runs out of the room, screaming like a crazy person."

Preston moves between the two, giving Alese some space. "Are you okay, Alese?"

"I'm fine, Sir." Alese wipes away the tears that have fallen down her cheeks and looks at the floor, letting her golden hair hide her face.

"I'm the one wronged. Why are you asking her if she's okay?" the man asks and takes another step forward, but Preston stops him.

"That newbie just lost his membership," Misha mutters before returning his attention to Stella.

"They better not let him back." I glare at the man and memorize his face. Although I don't mind inflicting pain, I'd never treat a woman like a piece of shit as he just did to Alese.

"May I go, Sir?" Alese asks Preston, crossing her arms in front of her and rubbing her shoulders.

Preston nods to Alese before glaring at the man, daring him to say another word. "Yes, Alese. You may leave."

"Thank you." She scurries off into the darkness and out of my view.

There's always been something intriguing about Alese. We've spoken a few times, but I typically scare her off. It never bothered me. Switches aren't really my thing, especially one like Alese. She can't seem to find her footing in either role, Dominant or submissive.

I've watched her enough to know that she is a submissive, but she hasn't admitted it to herself. Finding the right partner will make her realize her true nature.

"Let's have a chat in my office," Preston says to the newbie and points toward the security office.

"I didn't do anything wrong. If anything, you should be escorting that slut out the front door."

"Sir." Preston clears his throat and looks around the room before grabbing the man by the shirt. "Right now, it's best if you don't say another word."

The asshole mumbles under his breath and knocks Preston's hand away. "We don't need to talk. This club is bullshit. I'm done."

"We're sad to see you go." Preston has a great poker face. When the man stalks off toward the stairwell, Preston walks quickly and motions to another Suit to follow.

"Maybe you should play with Alese," Misha says.

The thought of touching her has made me hard. Maybe it's the fight she has in her that turns me on suddenly, but it has never happened before. When I'm about to reply to Misha, I glance over and snap my mouth shut.

He's whispering in Stella's ear, stroking her neck, but he's staring straight at me. Even though I can't hear what he's saying, I can't look away. His hand traces a path down her chest, following the edges of her V-neck dress. "You like that, girl?" he asks loud enough for me to hear.

Her back arches, and she moves toward his touch. "Yes," she whispers.

Misha smirks and cocks an eyebrow in my direction. I nod and give him the go-ahead. If I'm not going to spend the night with someone, I may as well watch someone else enjoy himself.

"Spread your legs," he tells her, rubbing her nipple through her dress with his thumb. "Don't come until I tell you to." She nods and shimmies down his lap before his other hand disappears below the table. "You're here to please me, girl. You're my plaything tonight."

She nods again as her chest begins to rise and fall faster. Her lips part, but not a sound comes out of her mouth.

CHELLE BLISS

My cock hardens inside my pants, and my breathing becomes uneven. It's not Stella that's turning me on, it's her response to him and their connection.

Stella's a beautiful woman, one of the prettiest in The Club, but completely off-limits to me. The way she responds to Misha—to his touch, to his words—turns me on.

I touch myself, squeezing my cock and praying that my hard-on will subside, but I fail. Between seeing Alese's tear-filled eyes and hearing Stella's tiny moans, I'm so turned on that the strain against my jeans becomes unbearable.

He toys with her nipple, pulling on it, and she sucks in a sharp breath. "You like that, don't you, girl?"

She doesn't speak, but she moves her chest toward his hand. His lips find her neck, licking a path up to her ear. He moans and cups her breast in his palm, tweaking her nipple between his fingers. "You get me so hard. Do you feel how much I want you?" Misha whispers against her ear.

She moans, squeezing her eyes tighter and causing little creases around the edges. I fist my dick harder, trying to find some relief, but I only make it worse.

Misha's arm starts to shake the table as his pace quickens. I can almost smell her arousal from across the booth, and my mouth waters from the scent.

"Lucky bastard," I whisper so quietly that only I can hear over the music in the background.

Stella's body starts to tremble, her creamy skin glistening under the lights. Her breathing changes, and she lets out a small moan.

Misha's hand stops and he whispers in her ear. She nods before his hands start to move again under the table. "Open your eyes, Stella. I want Master Ret to watch you fall apart in my lap."

Her head slowly moves off his shoulder, and her eyes flutter open. I swallow, my mouth suddenly dry when our eyes meet.

Without breaking eye contact, and with one hand still holding my hardened cock, I pick up the scotch and watch intently over the rim. I try to quench my thirst, but it doesn't work.

I don't need a drink.

I need a submissive to end my hunger.

Stella licks her lips, making my situation worse. Setting the glass down on the table, I keep my hand wrapped around it and slide my fingers up and down the wetness.

Her breath falters and she blinks slowly, her eyes rolling back for a moment when her mouth falls open. She's coming on his hand and looking me straight in the eyes.

I smirk, loving the face a woman makes when she comes. There's nothing sexier than watching someone shatter.

When she collapses against him, gasping for air, I use the opportunity to leave. I need to find someone to quench my thirst.

I'd never thought about settling down, finding someone to sit at my feet and take care of. But recently, it's all I keep thinking about. Pushing thirty has me reevaluating my life. I no longer want a plaything. I want a lover, a partner, and the one who completes me.

CHAPTER TWO

Ret

I'm about to head out for the night, giving up on any hope of satisfaction, when I collide with a soft body. She stumbles backward, her high heels teetering when I reach out and grab her arms to steady her.

"Shit!" she screeches and clings to my arms. She's a mess of blond hair and heels that are too high and should be illegal.

"Steady," I mumble and pull her forward. I forget about the hard-on still straining against my jeans.

"Thanks," she says behind her hair as she finds her footing, but she's still clutching my forearms. "What a shit night," she mutters when she releases my arms and brushes the hair away from her face.

"I saw," I tell her when I realize it's Alese. "That guy seemed like a complete prick."

She closes her eyes and exhales. "You have no idea." Her eyes dip down to my crotch before flitting back to my face. "Not a good night for you either?"

I should remind her of protocol. She should be calling me Sir, but right now I think she could use a break, and I'm too sexually frustrated to even care. "No, but not as bad as you, *piccola.*"

Her nose wrinkles. "What's that mean?"

I hold out my hand near her face, waiting for her to give me approval when she nods. "It's Italian for little," I tell her as I brush a strand of hair away from her eyes.

"I'm not little." Her cheeks flush, and she breaks eye contact.

I smirk, not realizing I'm still touching her face. Alese may be around 5'6" without heels and over 5'10" with them, but she still doesn't match my 6'4" frame. "But you are, compared to me." My hand slides across her skin instinctively, cradling her cheek in my hand.

Her tongue darts out, sweeping across her bottom lip. "Thank you," she whispers, keeping her eyes downcast.

"Do I make you uncomfortable?" My thumb moves across her skin, slowly stroking her cheek.

She swallows hard, still not looking me in the eyes. "Yes."

My cock grows, loving the way she responds to my touch and her inability to look me in the eye.

Tonight's display with the newbie member isn't the first time she's had trouble either. Time after time, she would try to give herself to someone but ultimately fail. She has a trust issue. Sometimes she'd try to be a Domme, taking classes, but she never really had the ability to boss anyone around.

"Do you want to have a drink with me, Alese?" It comes out of my mouth without a thought.

Her head snaps back, bringing her gaze to mine. "Now?"

"Yes." I nod and scan the room, seeing two open seats at the bar. "We can sit at the bar if you're more comfortable. I think we both deserve to unwind a little before we leave."

Her eyebrows draw together, and she looks serious. "Just a drink."

"Just a drink," I tell her and nod. "Bar?"

"Um," she mumbles and pulls at her lip, peering around my body and scanning the bar. She shakes her head with a slight frown. "I'd rather sit in a booth, please."

"As you wish." I hold out my arm to let her walk in front of me, but I have ulterior motives. I want to check out her ass, and I prefer not to have my hard dick on full display.

She pauses for a moment, glancing down at my crotch before giving me a crooked smile. "I understand." She winks and takes off toward the booth area, swaying her hips from side to side on her five-inch heels.

She stops in front of the dance floor, scanning the booths. "Where do you want to sit?"

"You pick." I rub my chin and watch her carefully, trying to figure out why she now looks so appealing to me.

"Hmm," she mumbles and purses her lips. Her eyes sweep to the left and then to the right. "I just don't know. Maybe." She moves to her left and heads toward the one at the end, but she stops and turns around. "No, not down there."

"No?"

"I don't want to sit by the bathrooms."

"Okay," I mutter and bite the inside of my lip to stifle my laughter. "To the right."

She stops walking and peers down at the end. "But that's near the VIP area. I don't think I want to sit by them." She chews the nail on her index finger and looks between the two booths. "I don't know. You pick."

Her reaction is completely in tune with her personality. She wants to be in charge, but she can't make a decision. Being a Dominant, whether male or female, a person needs to be able to make a decision and follow through. From the whispers I've heard around The Club, Alese doesn't have the ability to make decisions about little things, let alone ones that deal with sexual dominance.

I place my hand on the small of her back and stare down at her. "May I?"

Her shoulders slump, and her chin dips toward the floor. "Yeah. It's fine."

"Let's go down by the VIP area." My hand presses harder, resting near her bottom, moving her toward the right to the quieter end of The Club.

She doesn't pull away, but she walks in step with me as we head toward the table, allowing me to keep my hand against her skin. After she slides in, I follow, leaving about a foot of space between us—just enough room to make her uncomfortable and test her boundaries. She doesn't try to scoot away, but she fidgets with her hands in her lap and avoids eye contact.

I motion to the waitress and look down at Alese. "Do you want to talk about what happened earlier?"

She bows her head and concentrates on the movements of her hands. "I don't know."

"It'll stay between us. Maybe I can help you work through whatever problem you had with him so it doesn't happen again." I'm lying. I really want to get in her head. Find out what makes her tick and what triggered her to run away from the Dom.

"I need a drink first."

"What can I get ya?" Marta, the waitress, asks and keeps her eyes downward, unlike the girl earlier.

"I'll take a Johnnie Walker Blue, and Alese would like…" I pause and look over at her. "What do you want?"

She shrugs. "Wine?" She says it more like a question than an answer.

"She'll take a glass of Dom Perignon, Marta. Thank you."

"Yes, Sir." She nods and saunters toward the bar behind our booth.

"Thanks," Alese says.

"You've had a bad night. You deserve only the best."

We sit in silence and wait for Marta to return. She sets the drinks down, staring at me under her eyelashes before giving a sideways glance to Alese and pursing her lips.

"Thank you, Marta." She smiles and disappears.

I move the champagne closer to Alese using the backs of my fingers. "Drink up."

She grabs the flute with both hands and lifts it to her mouth. Her fingers tap nervously against the glass while she gulps. She's changed out of her Club clothes and has on a pair of jeans and a spaghetti strap tank top that shows just the right amount of cleavage.

Before I even raise my glass, she sets the empty flute down and slumps forward. I pause, holding mine in front of my lips. "Do you want to tell me what happened now?" My eyes never leave her, locking on to her over the rim of my glass.

"I wanted to play tonight." Her voice is soft as she speaks toward her lap. "We talked for a long time before I finally agreed to go with him."

"Did you discuss your desires and limits before you agreed to play with him?"

She nods and her chin quivers. "I did."

"Okay, so what happened when you went with him?" I want to ask about her list, but I figure it's none of my business since we're not going to be doing a scene together.

She squirms in her seat. "Everything was going fine. We were going to start playing, and things got out of hand."

My eyes narrow, tightening on her face. "Look at me, Alese," I command, waiting for her to comply. When she does, I continue. "I need specifics. Maybe we can figure out what went wrong so you don't have the same mistake in the future."

She swallows and clutches her chest with her arms. "He strapped me spread-eagled to the table." She blows out a shaky breath. "It was cool at first. Then..." She pauses, and tears start to form in her eyes.

Suddenly I feel like an asshole for pushing her to talk. "Alese," I whisper and move closer, putting my arm around her shoulder. "You don't have to continue."

She wipes her face and looks up at me. "I want to finish." Her voice is a bit stronger, but she's still hesitant. "He blindfolds me, which isn't my favorite, especially when I don't know someone." She glances toward the ceiling and squeezes her eyes shut. "I didn't know what he was going to do next."

I stroke her arm, slowly sliding my fingers around her skin to soothe her. "He gagged me," she whispers and drops her chin.

Moving my fingers to her face, I raise her eyes to me. "There's nothing to be embarrassed about. He went against your limits. We're all into kink, and for that, I'll never judge you. I want to help and nothing more." Actually, I want to gag her too and bury my cock about ten inches deep inside her pussy, but I don't tell her that.

She nods and lifts her chin. "I screamed, but no one could hear me with the gag in." She drags her eyes to mine. "I was so scared. I panicked."

"Is that all that happened?"

She touches her throat. "Can I get another drink?" Her lips smack together, and I want to feel them under my fingers.

I've barely touched mine because I've been too busy watching, listening, and fantasizing. "Stay here. I'll get another."

As I walk to the bar, I can't get the image of her spread-eagled and completely helpless out of my mind. I wonder what her screams sounded like—were they high-pitched or more of a grunt? "Another," I tell the bartender and set her glass on the counter.

Reaching down, I adjust my cock, which hasn't gone down since the moment I ran into her. At this rate, I'll still have blue balls when I drive home. Listening to her speak, the panic in her voice, turns me on.

I don't notice when Beebee sets the glass back down in front of me. "Ret, are you okay?" she asks, touching my hand and pulling me out of my thoughts.

"I'm fine," I tell her, waving off her concern before grabbing the glass and heading back to the booth.

"Here, *piccola*."

She immediately takes it and starts to take a large gulp. I touch her hand, pushing the glass away from her mouth. "Slow down." Some of the champagne dribbles down her chin, and I catch it with my fingertips. If she were mine to do with as I wished, I'd have her suck every drop off my fingertips. But instead, I lick the champagne off my own. "Where were we?"

She moves the flute around the table and avoids looking at me. "So he gagged me, which was already on my off-limits list of activities."

"Look me in the eyes when you speak, please," I tell her because I want to see what really terrifies her and what may actually turn her on if she just gives it a chance.

"Sorry." She winces and draws her bottom lip between her teeth. When she releases it, there are tiny teeth marks in her flesh.

I move, adjusting my cock in my pants from the sight of her marked flesh. If she glances down and catches sight of my hard-on, I'll probably be the next person to get slapped in the face.

"So after he tied me up, blindfolded me, and gagged me, he attached nipple clamps. But not just any nipple clamps." She clutches her breasts in her palms and crosses her arms. "He used forceps, but he clicked them one too many times."

"Fuck," I mutter, scrubbing my hand down my face. Those could be powerful weapons when playing with the right person, especially if they enjoyed pain.

"I screamed and tried to stop him from attaching the next one, but I was tied too tightly to the table and my cries were muffled by the gag." She raises the glass and looks up at me, and I nod my approval. When she sets it back down, she licks her lips.

She probably doesn't even realize what she's doing to me. Listening to her tale of torture sounded more like an amazing Friday night to me, and it would give me plenty of mental images to go by when I got home tonight.

"So there I am—blind, unable to speak, bound, and with forceps pinching my nipples so tightly tears started to stream down my face."

"I gotcha." The girl's driving me crazy, painting the perfect mental image.

"Then I feel something cold against my clit," she stammers and closes her eyes. "It's a pump, and I can't wiggle away from it."

My brows furrow, and although I'm turned on, I'm also pissed off. If I saw that man right now, I'd tie him down to a table and use a fuck machine to penetrate him in the ass until he screamed for mercy. The entire time I'd use an electric cattle prod on his balls, shocking him over and over again.

"But I can't get away," she whispers and covers her mouth.

"Where the fuck were the Suits?" They're supposed to be there to stop shit like this from happening to a Club submissive.

"I don't know." She wipes her eyes, using her fingertips near the edges by her thick, catlike eyeliner. "So after he put the pump on me, I thought I was going to pass out. My heart was racing and I couldn't breathe. I started to choke on my own spit." Her hand rests on her neck and she swallows. "I heard something metal clinking together."

"Wait. Was he saying anything during this?"

"Every time I screamed, he'd slap the inside of my thigh and call me a dirty slut." Her legs close, not in the way to lessen her hunger, but to stop a memory. "I'm not a masochist, Ret."

"Understood." I nod and feel a little pang of sadness at her admission. She may not be a masochist, but I'm sure I'd find a way to make some level of pain enjoyable. If it's done right, with more pleasure, the pain fades and helps heighten the sensation.

"I was thrashing and yelling as much as I could, and before he could use the metal thing I heard on me, the door flew open and a Suit appeared."

"Thank fuck," I mumble. Assholes like this "Dom" she went with turn people off to the kink they came here for in the first place.

"I was so scared of him. When the Suit came in and removed my gag and blindfold and asked if I wanted the scene to end, I said yes. When he pushed me further and asked if the man had done anything to me against my will, I lied." Her head drops forward, and her hair cascades in front of her face. "I was too scared of him to tell the truth."

"*Piccola.*" I gently place my arm around her shoulder and stroke her arm. "Come here," I tell her, urging her to move closer. "Cry on me if you must."

Without hesitation, she curls into my side, burying her face near my chest, and cries. Her tiny hands fist my shirt, clutching harder, matching her sobs. My hand strokes her hair, comforting her in her time of need.

As a Dom, I have rules. Every Dom should have them.

I never torture anyone against her will. Hell, I'll push a boundary or two, but only if we have complete trust in one another. Never before, and never without complete certainty that it's something she truly wants. Too many people come to clubs to play and get their kink on, but without a realization of what the lifestyle truly means or the repercussions playing with strangers may cause.

"It's okay," I whisper down at her. "You're safe with me."

She cries for a few more minutes, before wiping her tears on my black shirt. She peers up at me with puffy red eyes, and it adds another layer to my fantasy. She's beautiful, but the tears make her blue eyes almost glow. "Thank you, Ret. You're a good guy."

I smile, but I know those words aren't true. A good guy wouldn't want to do everything the man who had tortured her had done. A good man wouldn't sit here with a semi hard-on as she cried into his shirt. Fuck. A good man wouldn't want to see her cry again and know that he caused her the pain that made her weep. But I wanted all those things. "Would you like me to drive you home?" I ask, to keep up with the good guy theme she's bought into.

She blinks rapidly as her red eyes widen. "You'd do that for me?" Her hand fists my shirt tighter as she gazes up at me.

"I would." I tap my index finger against the tip of her tiny, slender nose. "I want to make sure you get home safely." *What a crock of shit.* I've never driven a girl home from The Club, no matter how rigorous our time together had been. But there's something different about Alese. I want to explore her depths and crawl inside her brain.

"I'm a mess," she says and sits up, wiping the tears that have caused her mascara to streak down her face.

"You're beautiful just the way you are." Because, believe it or not, there's nothing sexier than seeing smeared makeup from crying.

"I am?" She gapes at me with wide eyes. "You think I'm beautiful?" she whispers.

"I do." I smile and squeeze her shoulder tighter, pulling her closer against me. A small smile spreads across her face, and the sadness in her eyes vanishes. Using the back of my hand, I wipe away the few stray tears that cling to her cheeks. "Let me take you home and make sure you're safe. We'll talk another day."

"You want to talk to me again?" The pupils of her eyes dilate as she shifts in her seat.

I have her and I know it. She can't hide the subtle clues that her body throws off. "I do, but only if you're comfortable with me."

"But I..." she starts to say and wrinkles her nose. "I've heard things."

I laugh because I can only imagine the shit that has been said about me. "What have you heard?"

She glances down, unable to look me in the eye. "You never play with someone more than a few times without growing bored of them. You're strict and want complete obedience. Also, you're looking for nothing long term."

"That's not true."

She tilts her head back against my chest and peers up at me. "Which part?"

"That I'm not looking for anything long term." My hand sweeps up and down her arm, the warmth of her skin sending little sparks through my fingertips.

The tiny creases in her forehead deepen, and she pushes herself away from me. She adjusts her body, straightening her back, and looks me straight in the eyes. "Why haven't you found a partner, then?"

"Are you looking for something long term?"

"Yeah."

"Why haven't you found a partner?"

She chews on her bottom lip for a moment. "I haven't found the right match."

"Me too, Alese. I refuse to settle for anything less than perfection."

Her face relaxes and she snorts. "Perfect doesn't exist. You're going to be waiting a while."

I laugh too because she's probably right. Lifting the scotch to my mouth, I watch her eyes as they twinkle from the overhead lighting.

"I keep hoping to find a partner, but there's always something that stops me." She places her hands on the delicate stem of her champagne and turns the glass slowly between her fingertips. "I don't know if I can keep trying after what happened tonight." She presses her lips together and narrows her eyes while she's staring at the glass. "I never thought I'd be that girl."

"What girl is that?" I ask, taking another sip of my drink, letting it sit on my tongue before swallowing.

She leans backward and slouches down in the booth. "I'm going to be the forty-year-old woman who's never been married, with a house full of cats to keep me company."

I move my glass, swirling the ice cubes through the liquid and watching the ripples splash against the sides. "How many cats do you have?" I ask before taking another sip.

"None." She laughs softly and covers her mouth. "I just see it in my future," she mutters behind her palm.

I start to laugh and choke on my scotch. "You're funny."

She shrugs, dropping her hand, and begins to fidget with the glass. "I just don't want to be the stereotypical old maid."

I place my hand on her forearm, rubbing her skin with my thumb. "You won't be. You just need to be more selective about who you play with."

"And what about you?"

"What about me?"

"Why are you still single? You're handsome, Ret." She smiles sweetly, glancing at me out of the corner of her eye.

I smirk at the compliment. "You're quite beautiful, Alese. Stop selling yourself short and playing with just anyone. Be selective."

She scoffs. "I'm not easy to deal with."

I chuckle softly and squeeze her arm. "None of us is." She gives me a toothy grin, and I use the opportunity to rub her arm with my palm. "Let me ask you a question. I've heard you're a switch and that you keep trying your hand at being a Domme. Why?"

She sits up, keeping her arm under my hand, and props her elbow on the table before resting her head in her hand. "I tried for a while to be a submissive. After I got frustrated, I figured maybe I was wrong and really wanted to be the one in control. So I started training, going to workshops here, and learning everything I could. But then when I find someone to let me play with them, it turns into a total mess."

"How so?" I ask, watching her reactions carefully.

"I just never know what to do next. Even after we have a lengthy discussion of their hard and soft limits, I freeze up when we're alone."

"You're not a Domme."

"I'm not?" She gapes at me, her head jerking back slightly.

"You're not a switch either."

"I think I am." Her teeth dig into her bottom lip again, chewing on her tender flesh as her forehead wrinkles.

"I hate to spoil your delusion, but you're submissive through and through, Alese."

She purses her lips and narrows her eyes at me. "Then why can't I find someone who makes me believe it?"

"I can show you."

CHAPTER THREE

Alese

He said the words I wanted to hear. For months, I've been watching him and dreaming about what it would be like to spend a night with Ret.

Whether he knows it or not, he's the most wanted unattached Dom here. His large, 6'4" body, wide shoulders, and muscular legs are just the bonus to his handsome face.

"You think you can turn me?"

His full lips twitch. "I think I can make you realize exactly who you are."

"Hmm," I mutter and tap my finger against my chin as if I have anything to think about.

"But," he says and turns his body to face me. "You need a break after tonight. No rough play or scenes for a while for you, *piccola*."

My chest tightens at the thought. "You think I'm traumatized?"

"I think you've been through a bad experience, and he may have ruined your ability to really trust anyone, especially me, without taking time to build a foundation."

My eyebrows shoot up and my heart begins to race. "So you, like, want to have a relationship?"

He pauses, staring deep into my eyes, and my mouth feels suddenly dry. "I think we need to take some time to explore your boundaries through a power exchange. We'll start with simple things. After I feel you're comfortable and trust me enough, we can take it further."

My throat tightens and I cough. "What are simple things?"

"I won't touch you until you beg me, but we'll see how you follow commands. And when the time is right, and you're crawling on your hands and knees, pleading with tears in your eyes and your cunt dripping for me, only then will I touch you."

My stomach flutters and I squirm against the seat. "Okay," I whisper and lick my lips.

His eyes follow my tongue and his body moves. I glance down, and the light hits his lap in just the right way to give me a perfect view. Ret's turned on, his hard-on evident through his tight-fitting jeans. "Don't worry," he says and pushes his cock down. "I know how to control myself."

I lean forward, gazing at him. "I'm game." I smile and hope he doesn't see my body shaking because my foot is tapping wildly against the floor.

"Let's set some rules." He pushes a few strands of his sandy brown hair that had fallen loose away from his eyes.

"Okay," I say quickly and turn to face him, resting my leg on the booth.

"First, I won't touch you sexually until you ask. Small touches to anywhere other than your pussy or breasts are allowed, especially if done with purpose." I swallow hard and nod before he continues. "I want you to follow my commands while here at The Club and also at home."

My eyes widen slightly and my fingertips tingle. "How?"

"You'll be available to me via phone and text when we're not here. If I send you a command, you need to follow it. If it's something you're not comfortable with, you can tell me and we can talk about it before moving forward."

"Understood." I nod and rest my hand on my knee to stop my leg from shaking anymore.

"You can't have an orgasm unless I allow you."

"But—" My lips purse, and he places a finger against them.

"Don't worry. You'll get to come. Your greedy cunt will need to at some point. But I want to own every orgasm you have."

I clear my throat and glance down at his finger as he pulls away. "I can do that," I say, but I wonder if I can keep the promise.

"We're going to go over your list of limits soon, but not tonight. Right now, it's about the power exchange and finding trust in each other."

I nod slowly and feel my palms begin to sweat. "I like the sound of that."

"I figured you would." He smirks before his body shifts, lifting from the seat to reach into his back pocket.

I take the moment to steal a peek at his crotch, and there's a dull ache that settles between my legs. Somehow, Ret made me forget everything that happened earlier.

He's holding the phone in one hand and watching me. "What's your number so I can contact you after I drop you off?"

I glance up and flush when he catches me staring. "Um—" I say before rattling off my number. "I can drive myself tonight."

He shakes his head and rests his palm against my warm cheek. "You're in my care now. After a night like tonight, you need someone to look out for your well-being. The first part of that is me taking you home. No arguments."

"Okay."

"One more thing." His grip on my face tightens, his fingers digging lightly into the back of my neck. "You'll only address me as a Sir or Master from here on out. No more Ret."

My face moves toward his touch, wanting more contact. "Yes, Sir," I whisper and close my eyes, trying to hide my excitement.

"Let's get you home. Tomorrow you may feel differently about our arrangement."

My eyes flutter open and my belly flips. "I won't," I tell him because I've been itching for a shot at *the* Master Ret for ages.

Much of the car ride home we sit in silence. I want to touch him, but I keep my hands to myself. When he pulls up in front of my door, I'm not sure what to say. "Thanks," I squeak out and reach for the handle.

Ret places his hand on my leg. "Wait."

I turn to face his penetrating gaze. "Yes?"

"I'm giving you one last out before we start. Are you sure you want to do this?"

I nod and smile, glancing down at where his hand is searing my flesh. His finely manicured fingernails rest against my skin. "Yes." My voice is breathy and full of want.

"Go inside and take a warm bath before you go to bed."

"I'm more of a shower person," I reply and wrinkle my nose.

His grip tightens on my thigh. "A bath, I said."

"Yes, Sir," I say without conviction.

"Do as you're told, *piccola*."

The term makes my toes curl. Maybe it's the way he holds my leg, but the combination sends tingles down my spine. "I will."

"Good night," he tells me, reaching in front of me to push open the door.

"Tomorrow, we start. You're mine, 24/7."

I lick my lips, trying to find some wetness besides that which is between my legs. "24/7?"

"You do your normal routine, but when I text, I expect a reply."

I nod before pushing the door open. When I peer down at his hand, he removes it, and I instantly miss his warmth. "Goodnight, Sir."

"Goodnight, Alese."

As I climb out, I almost hate that he uses my name. It sounds beautiful coming from his lips, but not as sweet as *piccola*. I twist the keys in my hands, trying to walk slowly to my house. I worry that this was all just a dream. Looking over my shoulder, I steal a glance at Ret, waiting in his car and watching.

Raising my hand, I give him a small wave and a smile. He lifts his chin and motions with his hand for me to keep walking. When I unlock the front door, he revs the engine and speeds away.

My feelings are a mess as I take a step inside. Part of me is nervous, hesitant about what lies before me. But then there's another part. One filled with so much excitement I want to spin around my living room and scream that I'm his.

Just as I'm about to start twirling, I realize this is only temporary. He's helping me find myself. I frown and collapse onto my couch.

What if I want more?

What if I want this to be longer?

Maybe I can be the woman he wants and he can be the Master I've always needed—someone to guide me through my experiences, bringing my fantasies to life.

I give myself a pep talk and decide I'm going to let myself give in. For once, I'm not going to overthink everything.

For now, I'm his *piccola*.

CHAPTER FOUR

Alese

When my eyes open and the light filters in through my sheer curtains, I cover my face. For a second, I panic before I remember it's Saturday. I don't have to worry about work, grading papers, or answering emails. I can relax all day and maybe catch up on some reading.

I sigh, rolling over, and whimper. My nipples are still tender from where the asshole attached the forceps, the bite of them still on my mind. When I finally fell asleep last night, I dreamed of being trapped with that madman. Every time I closed my eyes, I'd see him.

I bury my face in my pillow and reach for the phone on my nightstand. Using only one eye, I read the screen.

Unknown: Good morning, piccola. When you wake up, snap a photo of your toy chest and send it to me.

Ugh. Rolling over, I hold the pillow against my face and scream. Letting someone peek into my toy box is like giving them a window into my kinky soul. I've never shown it to anyone, not even my ex-boyfriends.

When I finally work up the energy to climb out of bed, I do everything but send the photo. I brush my teeth, start the coffee, add his name to my contacts, and straighten up my bedroom—the entire time thinking about its contents.

With a fresh cup of coffee on my nightstand, I kneel on the floor and stare at the box under my bed. It looks inconspicuous, but I know the dirty things that are inside. Slowly I reach underneath and slide it out in front of me.

"For the love of God," I mutter and stare up at the ceiling. "Why?" I don't know if I expect a reply, but one doesn't come.

The box has grown over the years and become more intricate. The contents kept me sane through all the breakups in my early twenties. Carefully, I lift the lid and set it on the floor to the side.

"I'm a perv." I cackle and rock back on my feet before resting my ass on the ground.

Do I take everything out or just send him a photo as is? When it's all thrown together, it just looks like a jumbled mess of plastic and metal. Taking out a rather large dildo, I feel the weight in my hands and cringe. "Jesus," I whisper. "You've been a great lover, but you're going at the bottom."

Although I don't mind pleasuring myself with it, it's a bit large to show him right away. I don't want him to get any ideas. I push aside the contents, toss the dildo to the bottom and cover it up again.

"That's better," I tell myself, leaning forward to get a better glimpse, and realize it helped nothing. Nipple clamps, vibrators, dildos, and other particulars are in full view.

Lifting my phone, I snap a picture because maybe it won't look as bad on the screen as it does with the naked eye. I don't even have to zoom in to see every kinky lover's dream chest. The photo has done nothing but accentuate the collection. I turn the flash off to darken the photo, and once I feel it's hard to make anything out in great detail, I send it to Ret.

Staring at the toys, I smile to myself because I feel sly, like I got one over on him. That is, until my phone beeps.

Ret: Use a flash and lay it out on the floor.

Fuckkkk. He can't be serious.

Ret: I'm serious.

My mouth hangs open, and I peer over my shoulder, wondering if he can see me. "Bastard," I whisper to myself as I start to remove every toy and implement and lay them out in two rows.

Row one is for insertables—dildos, vibrators, and plugs. Row two is for everything else. I hadn't taken stock of my assortment in a while, and I am shocked by the variety and size.

Most of it I purchased after attending a demo at The Club. I figured if I were going to try my hand at being a Domme sometimes, I'd need the tools for the job. Usually, I ended up using them on myself for pleasure because I couldn't seem to pull the trigger with anyone else.

Covering my face with my hands, I try to figure out how to get out of sending the photos. It won't all fit on one screen, so I'll have to take a number of shots. My hands drop from my face when I come up with the brilliant idea to stand and take one shot from far away, hopefully making it difficult to see.

I snap one, with the flash on, and send it off before checking it. After it switches from *Delivered* to *Read,* I open it too and zoom in.

"Fucking hell," I say to myself and scroll to the left.

Everything is visible—clear as fucking day.

I set the phone down in front of me and sit cross-legged before reaching for my cup of java. I keep my eyes on the screen, waiting for his response as I take a sip.

I'm not really embarrassed by my collection, but I'm worried about what he'll think or use on me. It's both exciting and scary.

Ret: *Thank you*, piccola. *Send me a photo of your hard and soft limit sheet next.*

That, surprisingly, is less worrisome. I've shared it with many people during my time as a Club member. It not only covers what I'm willing to do, but also what I've done.

I click a few buttons and send it off to him without hesitation.

I shake my head and take another sip, letting the vanilla cream sit on my tongue before swallowing.

Ret: *We'll discuss this list together next time we see each other. Today, I want you to put in the purple butt plug, and don't take it out unless you must or I tell you to remove it.*

I purse my lips, twisting them around. Not because I dread the idea of shoving something in my ass—I've done if before, many times. I know that wearing it all day will turn me on. The tiniest movements will send waves of pleasure through me.

Me: *Yes.*

I sigh and pluck the purple one from the assortment and set it to the side. As I start to throw the toys in the box and wonder how many times today I'll have to pleasure myself to maintain my sanity, he sends another text.

Ret: *You're not allowed to touch yourself. No coming until I say so.*

I flick off the screen and groan.

Ret: Be a good girl and follow directions, and I'll make it worth your while.

Again, I turn around and wonder if he can see me. I laugh to myself and shake my head because I'm probably not the first girl he's done this with, and he can see my reactions coming before I do.

I climb up on the bed with the plug and a bottle of lube. "Thank God he didn't pick the pink one," I say, covering the plug in the clear lubricant. The pink one I've always had issues with inserting on my own.

As I rise up off the bed, balancing my body on one arm, I slide the plug against my asshole and ready myself. Slowly, I work it inside, turning myself on from the contact. A small pinch of pain causes me to wince before it's fully seated.

I collapse, letting my ass get used to the fullness and wonder how this happened. How did I let Master Ret in?

My phone beeps and I scurry to the edge to see what he says next.

Ret: Take a photo of it.

I gape at the phone. *He can't be serious.* I remember what I had on my list. Exhibitionism is marked *Yes* with a willingness of 5 which means *Hell Yes*.

Reaching behind, I try to take a good photo without giving him too much of a view. Craning my neck in this manner doesn't seem to work. I roll onto my back, spread my legs and raise them high in the air. Reaching down, I snap a photo and take a quick peek. *Not too shabby.*

I send it off to Ret and wait for my next order. I did tell myself last night that I'd give in to him. For once, I'd put my faith in someone else.

Ret: Good girl, piccola. Meet me at The Club tonight at 8 p.m. Remember—no touching.

Me: Yes.

I shake my ass, letting the plug move around, and I can already feel the wetness between my legs. It's only noon, and I'm dreading the next seven hours of my life.

CHAPTER FIVE

Ret

I spent the entire day sending her short messages, filled with commands to test her comfort and willingness to comply.

An hour before I leave for The Club, I send her a message with a few simple commands.

Me: Leave the plug in, wear a skirt or a dress, no panties, and be on time.

I head out and make a pit stop at my favorite adult store. She's missing something in her collection, and I figure we can have some fun with it tonight—although, it'll probably be more fun for me than her.

When I arrive, I run upstairs and reserve a room in case we get to that point. Standing at the bar, I order a drink and keep my eye on the entrance as I wait. Mak, the owner and my friend, wanders through the area and spots me. We chat for a few minutes, but my attention is elsewhere.

"You all right, Ret?" he asks, following my line of sight.

"Yeah, I'm good," I tell him and drag my eyes to his. "I'm just meeting someone."

He cocks an eyebrow and smirks. "Someone I know?"

"Alese," I answer quickly and wait for him to call me crazy.

"Interesting choice, but possibly the smartest one you've ever made."

"I think my hard-on last night may have restricted some blood flow to my brain, but for the first time in a long time, I'm excited about tonight."

He slaps me on the back and laughs. "Have some fun." His eyes dart toward the door. "She's here," he tells me and motions to the entrance with his chin.

When I turn around to look at her, my heart starts to race. She's dressed in a plaid cheerleader style miniskirt, red tube top, black thigh highs and matching fuck-me pumps. She smiles at me as she speaks to the hostess.

"Keep me posted," Mak says and taps me on the back before leaving me alone.

Every step she takes toward me, I imagine the plug in her ass, rubbing her insides. "Good evening, *piccola*," I say when she comes to a stop in front of me.

She stares downward. "Good evening, Sir."

I touch her chin and raise her eyes to mine. "Please look at me unless I tell you otherwise." We're still trying to find our trust, build a connection, and eye contact is vital at this point. Her eyes flutter to mine and she grins, but she doesn't speak as I drop my hand from her face. "How are you feeling tonight?"

"Horny," she replies with a small smile.

I laugh softly. "I'm sure you are. But as I said before, I won't touch you until you beg me and I feel you're ready."

Her smile fades, and the corner of her mouth twitches as her eyes begin to roam.

"Eyes on me," I remind her. Sometimes, looking someone in the eyes is the most uncomfortable thing for a person to handle. It shows our vulnerability.

"Sorry."

"Would you like a drink before we go sit down?" My plan isn't to get her liquored up and take advantage of her, but she could use one to take the edge off her nerves.

"Yes, please," she stammers.

"A glass of your best champagne," I tell the bartender, but I keep a watchful eye on Alese.

She fidgets at my side, moving back and forth between her feet, and grimaces.

I grab the drinks off the bar and turn to face her. "Let's sit and talk a while."

She nods and follows behind me, her heels clicking on the floor as we move. I wait in the aisle of the VIP section for her to sit first. I want a bit more privacy so I can test her comfort before we go upstairs. I slide in next to her and set down my drink before moving hers closer.

"You only get one drink tonight, so go slow."

She probably thinks she's the only one uncomfortable with a plug in her ass, but my cock is screaming for relief.

"I'd like to discuss your list and then your wants and needs. Are you comfortable with that?" It's a talk we need to have, even if it pushes her comfort level. With her experience, it shouldn't be an issue.

She wraps her hands around the glass, rolling it between her palms. "Okay."

"First, I want to know you've worn the plug. I need you to crawl to the end of this seat and show me."

I know she has, but this is a test. Would she willingly comply with my command, or protest?

She draws her lips into her mouth, her eyes flashing with uncertainty for a moment before she moves. She raises her ass high in the air and crawls as I instructed. She pauses, glancing at me over her shoulder.

"Now spread your legs and raise your skirt," I tell her, reaching down and squeezing my cock in my hand.

She lifts her skirt, giving me the most beautiful view of her ass, and looks back at me with red-stained cheeks.

"Open your cheeks," I tell her, lifting an eyebrow and gritting my teeth to hide the need in my voice.

She complies, reaching around and moving her cheek to the side, giving me the most spectacular view. The purple plug is snugly inside, and her pussy is glistening even in the dim light of the VIP section. She moves, causing the plug to shift and my cock twitches.

"Wider," I say because I want to stare another moment. She puts her head down and spreads herself more. I groan softly and squeeze my dick harder. This is going to be a test of will on my part.

"Perfection," I tell her and lick my lips, itching to touch her, but I keep my hands to myself. "You may sit now." My cock is throbbing, but I release it when she turns around and adjusts into the booth. "Tell me about yourself."

Her eyebrows draw together for a moment before relaxing. "What do you want to know?" Her hands wrap around the glass again, sliding her fingers up and down the wetness that has formed.

"Everything," I tell her through gritted teeth, transfixed by her hand movement.

"There's not much to tell, really. I'm twenty-seven years old. I live alone, and I'm a teacher."

"Ah," I say, clicking my tongue against the roof of my mouth. "It makes sense."

"What does?"

"That you're a teacher. You're used to being in control all the time. It has to be hard to come here and change. I want this to be a place you can come and let everything go. The pressure. The stress."

She nods and bites her lip. "It is different." She laughs softly before lifting the glass to her lips and taking a tiny sip.

"Why are you a member of The Club?"

Everyone has different reasons for joining. Some just want to play with like-minded people. Some are looking for a long-term relationship that centers around kink. Others are looking for a 24/7 master-slave relationship.

She holds the glass in her hand but doesn't set it down. "At first, I joined to enjoy my kink, but it's changed over time. I'm getting older and sick of playing around without my center. I want to find that person I click with—the one who becomes my other half. You know what I mean?"

I nod, because I do.

"I don't want to give up the lifestyle, though, but I want to have something with more meaning. A connection to someone so strong that I can't breathe without it."

I exhale and give her a small smile. "I know exactly what you mean."

"Do you want that?" she asks, glancing up at me.

"I didn't think I'd ever want to settle down, but lately, it's become more appealing to me, *piccola*." She smiles and blinks slowly as I continue to talk. "Do you like being a Domme?"

She grimaces and sets the champagne on the table. "I thought I would. The classes were really interesting, but every time I try, it's an epic failure."

"Did it bother you today when I told you what to do?"

She shook her head and grinned. "It was sexy," she whispers and bats her eyelashes at me, staring at me from under her lashes. "I felt naughty." Her cheeks turn pink and she squirms.

"Good. Are you comfortable with me?" When she nods her agreement, I grab my phone from my back pocket. "Let's talk about your hard and soft limits together and see where it leads."

"Okay." She shifts her body to one side and moans, which earns her a wink.

"Let's start at the top."

For a solid hour, we go line by line through her checklist. The activities she wasn't willing to partake in were beatings, blindfolds, bruises, cages, caning, clothespins, receiving marks, stocks, thumb cuffs, and swallowing semen.

I pause over the line about semen and tap my finger against the screen. "We need to discuss the swallowing semen limit for a moment."

She blinks and nods slowly, but she doesn't reply.

"Why?"

"Well," she says and clears her throat before averting her eyes. "I don't want to swallow a virtual stranger's semen. I mean—" She pauses and brings her eyes to mine. "If I'm in a committed relationship with someone, I don't have a problem with it at all. But I'm not doing it for everybody."

I nod, and although I love it when a woman swallows everything I have to offer, I like that Alese is selective. It makes it special. "I can understand," I tell her and start on her list of things she'd like to explore more.

She likes for people to watch, just like Stella, doesn't mind being slapped in the face, which could be hot. She also likes having her hair pulled, doesn't mind nipple play as long as it doesn't include forceps, she likes being spanked—which I think happens a lot to her anyway.

There are many things she is willing to do that she hasn't had much experience with. She wants to be double penetrated, she wants to get more anal experience, which thrilled me to no end. She has never used a violet wand, but the idea excites her, and she's never had a TENS unit used on her.

I don't know how she's lasted in this club for so long without hitting those items on her list. But there are some Doms who have a specific fetish. I know mine. I love a girl's ass as much as her pussy, and there is something about Electro-Play that has always enthralled me.

"Can we go to a private room?" I ask after we finish the end of her list and have gone over the topics in depth. "I still don't plan on touching you."

She swallows hard, pausing with the champagne glass in front of her lips. "Yes," she stammers out with widened eyes.

"Are you comfortable with me?" I asked her before, but I need the reassurance that nothing has changed between us.

She nods and starts to gulp down the remaining champagne in her glass.

"Same rules apply. No gags, no restraints, no touching."

Her nose wrinkles when she hears my words. "Then, what will we do?" she asks before licking the last drop of champagne from the rim.

It's my turn to grimace. My cock is so hard after picturing scenes together while going through her list. The way her tongue caressed the lip of the glass has me wishing I hadn't promised not to touch her.

"You're going to pleasure yourself, and I'm going to watch."

"Oh," she says and sits up straight. "Okay."

I set my lips in a firm line and raise an eyebrow. "Try that again."

"Yes, Sir."

I smile and slide out of the booth, watching her groan and close her eyes as her bottom moves across the seat. The plug scrapes against the leather, and her body jolts with each movement.

"Don't worry, *piccola*. You'll find relief soon enough," I tell her and snicker with my back turned to her as I reach out for her to take my hand.

I give her fingers a tiny squeeze as we climb the stairway and glance over my shoulder at her to make sure she's not freaking out.

This could be really great or a complete clusterfuck. Based on her responses so far, I'm guessing it'll go off without a hitch and probably with her begging for me to touch her.

When we enter the VIP lounge, I stop and grab her by the shoulders. "Are you still comfortable with the idea of going into a room alone with me?"

Without hesitation, she says, "Yes," and nods her head.

My grip tightens. "I reserved Private Room Two for us. I could leave the door cracked, even though it's against regulation, if it makes you more comfortable."

She shakes her head and looks me straight in the eyes. "I'm fine. I know you're not *him*. Sir—" she starts and pauses. "Sir, the one thing I know is that you have an impeccable reputation. You may not be easy, but no one speaks poorly of you."

I release her shoulders, motioning toward the room next door. "Let's agree that green means you're good, yellow is nervous but we can proceed, and red means stop and we'll discuss things."

Her head bobs and she shakes out her hands. "I can remember that."

It's Club Basics 101. We aren't a couple with the cute little words that set off alarm bells in my head. I want something we can both remember, so this doesn't fall to shit in a hurry.

I hold out my hand and wait for her to place her trust in me. When she slides her palm into mine, I close my fingers around hers and lead her to the room.

She walks in first, eyeing everything and slowly turning in a circle. "Nothing's set up."

I shake my head and smirk, because I have my own plan. "I have a bag of stuff," I tell her, and I reach into the cabinet where I placed it earlier tonight.

Her hands are clutching the bottom of her skirt, and she watches me with curiosity as I unzip the bag. "Brought your own?" she asks and laughs.

I nod and pull out the remote control bullet I purchased for her earlier. It is my present to her and is for her to use when we aren't together. It is the latest, greatest, state-of-the-art bullet on the market. Anytime she's near Wi-Fi, I can control the vibrations and sensations from my phone, even at great distances.

"What's that?" she asks, crouching down on the other side of the table.

It's time to set some ground rules. We aren't friends chatting about toys. As soon as we stepped into this room, we had our roles—she is the submissive and not my buddy.

I stand quickly, grabbing her by the arm and bringing her with me. My hold on her isn't rough, but it conveys a message. "Let's get a few things straight, *piccola*. When we stepped into this room, hell, the moment you entered The Club, you gave yourself to me. We're not friends. You're my submissive. From here on out, you don't speak unless I give you permission to speak. Understand?"

She nods and bites the side of her lip.

"Remove your clothes, fold them, and place them on the chair. Once you're done, climb up on the table and wait for my next command."

I cross my arms in front of my chest, waiting for her to start undressing. When she dips her fingers inside the waistband of her skirt, I kneel down and start to rifle through my bag, grabbing a few things that could make for a fun night—especially for her.

When I carry the toys over to the table, I glance at her and see she's watching me as she undresses. I give her body a once-over and smile. She's simply stunning. Her curves are lush, and her porcelain skin makes it impossible to look away. Her nipples pebble from the coolness of the air as soon as she pulls her tube top over her head.

I lick my lips and wonder if her skin tastes as sweet as it looks. She blinks a few times, folding the tube top in her hands, and looks toward me. Her hand stops moving, and I drag my eyes to hers, realizing I've been caught.

Her cheeks are stained pink, and her chest starts to heave the more I keep my eyes on her. My eyebrow lifts because, even if I'm watching her, she should still follow the orders I've given her. "Leave the thigh highs on and get on the table," I say in a stern tone.

She doesn't look away, keeping her eyes glued to mine as she backs up to the table and climbs on top. Her legs start to move, going back and forth as she grips the edge of the table at her sides. She's nervous and I know it. That's the only reason I'm not going full big, bad Dom on her ass. After her most recent experience, the last thing I want to do is scare her off forever.

"Lie back and prop your heels up on the edge," I tell her and pull a chair in front of her, but I leave plenty of room so that I can't touch her even if I extend my arms.

The back of the table is angled up, so she's reclining and able to see me. Her feet shuffle against the edge before finding a comfortable position. Sitting in the chair like this, I have a perfect view of her body. The purple plug is still nestled tightly in her ass, and her cunt is wet and wanting.

"Spread your legs wider." Slowly her legs start to fall to the sides but stop short of my goal. "More," I command and rub my hands together.

If she were mine and she acted this way, I would've already swatted her with a crop on the inside of her thighs to convey my message without words.

"Grab the black bullet off the table and get ready."

Her head tilts to the side, and her eyes roam over the toys, growing wide. She plucks the bullet from the table and waits for what I have to say next as I remove my phone from my pocket.

"Rub it against your sweet, needy cunt."

She reaches down and rubs it against her opening, moaning a little with each pass over her clit. I press a button, letting the bullet come to life.

"Oh," she moans, surprised by the new sensation.

I start it slow, letting the low hum drive her wild with lust. When she starts to move her hand faster and her legs begin to shake, I tell her, "Put it inside you." The last thing I want is for her to come too early. She hasn't earned the right, and it wouldn't serve any purpose except for her to get off quickly.

We are here to test her control. Finding out if she's truly a switch or if she has everything needed to make an amazing submissive.

She rubs it on the outside of her opening, pushing it inside a little before letting it pop free. Before I can say another word, she pushes it in a little farther and moans.

I close my eyes and take a deep breath. My balls ache, and my cock is straining against the fabric of my jeans, moving in her direction. Swallowing hard, I try to tell myself that I can do this. Even though I'm in control, I feel anything but—hard-ons do that to a man.

I fantasize about my cock dipping inside her instead of the bullet, and my cock grows harder. When she pushes it inside and it disappears, I let out the breath I was holding.

"Push it deeper," I tell her with a shaky voice. I grit my teeth, frustrated that I'm giving away my need by the sound of my voice.

She sticks a finger in her mouth, wrapping her lips around it and covering it with saliva. My heart starts to pound harder, and I'm transfixed by the way she's sucking the single digit.

I adjust in my chair, making my situation worse as my jeans rub against the head of my cock. Her eyes dip, and I can tell she sees the situation she's put me in when a small smile spreads across her lips. When she pops her finger out of her mouth, she licks her lips and sets it on her clit.

"Don't touch it," I say and lift my chin. "Push the bullet deeper and don't stop until it's seated against your G-spot."

She bites her lip, which I've grown used to and find sexy, and reaches forward, dipping her finger inside. When her hand starts to pull back, I change the setting on the bullet to intermittent and kick it up from a one to a four.

Her body twitches as soon as the vibrations change. When her hand finally falls away, I tell her, "Rest your hands at your sides."

She looks toward the ceiling and tries to relax her body, but with each jolt, her bottom rises off the table and she tenses.

"Don't move. Stay still." I'm being repetitive, but in her current state, I'm not sure how much is registering. I increase the power and move the intensity to a six.

Her pussy clenches and her toes curl when the vibrations grow more intense. Wetness starts to seep from her, trickling down her body and landing on her plug. Her fingers start to fidget and her legs tense, starting to close.

I press the *stop* button, and her legs fly open.

"Don't close your legs, or I can do this all night," I lie, because if I had to sit here for hours and stare at her open legs, I'd be liable to touch her when I promised not to tonight.

She moves her ass, scooting farther down the table and giving me a better view. I can smell her need. It's starting to fill the room, driving me mad with lust. I restart the bullet, setting the pulse to every three seconds and the vibration back to six. With each lick of the bullet inside her, her thighs tense and relax.

I palm the phone in my hand, trying to stop myself from grabbing my cock, and lean forward, wanting and needing a better view. Actually, I'm torturing myself.

She looks between her legs, licking her lips, and she watches me as I try to find a comfortable position. Her smirk is unmistakable and sly. When her pussy contracts and her bottom rises, my eyes move on their own to watch her body react.

"Get the clit pump and attach it, but don't click it more than twice." My eyes move to the table, lifting my chin when she pauses.

I've found clit pumps to be fascinating and useful. They engorge the area, making it swollen and sensitive. Some women can come from the pump alone.

With shaky hands, she rests the tube against her clit and does two quick pumps on the gauge. She groans and her eyes roll back from the suction. Her clit fills the bottom portion of the tube, plumping up and turning a bright red. She becomes restless, her fingers dancing at her sides and her pussy convulsing uncontrollably.

"Do not come," I tell her, and her eyes snap to mine. "Relax your muscles." She complies and her legs fall open a little more. "Stay like that." I get up from the chair, my cock pointing straight at her, and unzip my pants. "Don't move, or there will be consequences."

She wants to say something, and her mouth opens before she snaps it shut. Her eyes are pleading with me, wanting me to relieve her of the need that's filling her, driving her mad, but I don't give her the permission she so badly wants.

When I push down my jeans, her eyes widen as my cock springs free. It's red, hard as steel, and aching. Bending over, I move my pants to my ankles and sit back down in the chair.

My hard-on is standing straight up, wanting to be inside of her. I wrap my hands around the shaft and watch her eyes as they follow my strokes. "Another pump," I say, gripping my dick harder.

She tries to find the pump without looking, her fingers shaking as she wraps them around the handle and squeezes.

I smirk as I see her clit crawl up the inside of the tube, growing larger from the pressure. Her hips jump and she gets wetter. She closes her eyes, probably trying to stave off the orgasm that's ready to break free.

"Eyes on me." My fingers touch the tip, stroking around the crown and sending shockwaves straight to my balls. I slide my hand down, resting it at the base of my shaft and squeeze, causing it to grow larger. "You want this inside that greedy cunt, don't you?" I wave it and relax my legs, letting my feet slide against the floor to give her a better view.

She nods and her chest starts to heave, her breathing becoming erratic. With one hand stroking my cock, I use the other to increase the speed of the bullet and move the pulses to come quicker.

Her eyes widen, but they stay locked on mine, staring at me between her legs. Her knees are shaking, and her muscles are tense as she tries to keep herself open. Her blinking slows and her fingernails start to dig into the leather on the table.

Even though she can't come yet, it doesn't mean I'll deprive myself any longer. I won't touch her until she asks, but it won't be tonight. There's no way I could walk out of here without looking like I had a stick up my ass from the massive boner.

As my fingers move, slowing and squeezing toward the tip, her eyes follow. I grit my teeth and grunt, wishing it were her cunt wrapped around me instead of my hand.

"Do you want this inside you?"

"Yes," she says in a breathy voice.

I shake my head, gripping my cock tighter and increasing the speed of my stroke. I'm pleased to know that she wants it, wants me, and feels comfortable enough to watch.

Her beautiful pussy is glistening and wet, stuffed with the bullet. The quicker I stroke, the more her hips start to follow my movement.

"Don't come," I tell her again, reminding her of my earlier command as I get closer to my own climax.

When I can't take it anymore—the scent of her surrounding me, my eyes locked on her—I give myself a few final strokes until my balls tighten and my body begins to shake.

I can't stop it. I don't want to either. As the come starts to pour out of me, dripping down my fingers, I work it into my flesh.

"Fuck!" I moan. My strokes start to falter, the sensation overwhelming me. I break eye contact for a moment and glance at her needy, tight pussy.

She's dripping, her pussy contracting, and her bottom is slightly rising off the table. *She wants me.*

After my body stops shaking, I get up and grab a towel and start to wipe myself clean. If she were mine, I'd make her lick it off—every last drop of me would be inside her. I hold back a sigh, wishing things were different. But they aren't.

For the first time in a long time, I'm excited about playing with someone. My stupid ass had to set the parameters that I wouldn't touch her. "Idiot," I whisper to myself. She's licking her lips, watching as I clean up the last drops of come that dot the tip of my still hard cock.

"Someday, *piccola*. Someday, I'll let you taste me."

Her lips part and her breathing picks up speed. She's writhing now, her clit trying to find relief from the constant pressure.

"Another pump," I say, wanting to be a tad sadistic since I know how badly she wants to come.

She groans softly, wrapping her fingers around the handle and giving it a short, quick squeeze.

"Lay your knees against the table." I want a better view. There's something about the female body that's always fascinated me—even as I grow older, my intrigue only grows.

Slowly, she lowers her knees to the table, causing her pussy and tits to jut out.

"Your poor nipples. They need some decoration." She shakes her head and draws her lip into her mouth as I smile. "Grab the bull rings from the table and put them on."

They are the newbie nipple jewelry. They don't really pack a bite, but they have just enough pressure to make the person wearing them feel pleasure.

"Squeeze your nipples first to make them harder," I say and feel my cock twitch inside my pants.

For fuck's sake.

I shouldn't be getting hard already, but my body reacts to hers.

The tips of her fingers grip her nipples and give them a hard squeeze. Her bottom lifts in response, the new sensation making her needier. She moans, loving the feel of her nipples being touched.

"Put them on." I glance at the bull rings that look like hoop earrings but are open with balls to grip the nipple with just enough pressure to stay attached.

287

She releases her nipples, giving them another squeeze first before reaching for the bull rings. First, she attaches the left and exhales, closing her eyes for a moment. As she attaches the right, her tongue darts out and swipes across her bottom lip.

I fight every urge in my body to blink, not wanting to miss a moment of it. Her nipples stick up, held that way by the rings, erect and hard. "Wet your fingers and run them across the top of your nipples."

The simple pinch of anything on the nipple heightens the feel of even the lightest touch. She swallows before gathering the moisture left on her lips to wet her fingertips. Two fingers hover over her nipples, and she closes her eyes as she lowers them, gliding them across the tips.

She moans, her knees pulling away from the table.

Poor thing. To be so needy and to be helpless to make it stop has to suck, but I'll give her relief soon enough. Although I like her needy, I don't want to drive her so far over the edge that she'll never want to meet me here again.

"Enough," I tell her as her fingertips continue to caress the tips. "Remove the cylinder."

Her clit is huge, almost filling the tube after being left like that for more than ten minutes. Her fingers feel around for the button, keeping her eyes locked on me as she finally releases it and sets it to the side.

Peeking through her hood, her clit is sticking out, completely engorged and begging for attention. She is wetter than she was before—the suction like a mouth wrapping around her clit with no remorse or escape.

I rub my hands together and lean forward to get a better view. "Eyes on me. Touch yourself. You're only allowed to use your fingers to come." Without looking down, I put the bullet on high. No more intermittent pulses, just constant vibrations that lick her G-spot.

She traces a path down her belly, stroking the side of her clit, testing the sensitivity. Her back arches off the table, and she gasps.

"Touch it," I say through gritted teeth, feeling myself teetering on the edge again. "Don't move your hand away until I tell you."

Slowly, she traces tiny circles around her clit, her bottom rising up and down as if trying to get away from the overwhelming stimulation. The bullet vibrates, almost audibly, and the plug shifts with each convulsion of her sweet cunt.

The closer she comes to her orgasm, the smaller the circles her finger makes, eventually moving back and forth at a rapid pace. Her toes curl around the edge of the table, and her legs shake wildly.

"Eyes on me," I remind her.

Her moans grow louder, her body quaking uncontrollably as her back arches. When her breathing stops and she bears down, riding out the orgasm, the bullet moves, barely visible inside her.

She writhes against the table, her body turning from side to side while trying to keep her feet planted on the edge. *Good girl.*

So far I'm pleased with her ability to follow directions without much hesitation. With a little more training and time, she could become the perfect submissive. Sex is only a part of it. The person offering their service has to be willing to trust their partner and give themselves over completely, for any purpose.

When her body relaxes and she gasps for air, I know my work here is done.

CHAPTER SIX

Alese

I barely make it down the stairs to the main floor of The Club. I have one hand in Ret's and the other gripping the railing, holding on for dear life as I try to steady myself and not tumble to the bottom.

He helps me to the same booth we sat in earlier. The evil bastard made me keep the plug and the bullet nestled inside me when we left the room. Like I didn't have a hard enough time walking from the intense orgasm, having my ass filled and my pussy stuffed make everything worse.

When I slide across the seat, the plug digs deeper into me. I squeeze my legs together, trying to relieve the pressure that built up during the walk, but my overly sensitive clit only makes things worse.

"Let's talk about tonight and how you feel," he says, motioning toward our waitress we had earlier.

"I feel good," I tell him, staring straight into his eyes.

"Was it hard for you to follow commands?" he asks and rubs the palms of his hands against his jeans.

I shake my head. "Not really. Usually, I find it hard, but you made me comfortable and so turned on that I was willing to do anything you told me."

"Good." He smiles and glances toward the waitress when she sets our drinks down. "How do you feel about the plug and bullet still being inside of you?"

"Fine," I lie through my teeth and plaster on a fake smile. Literally, I have my jaw clenched when I answer him.

"Liar," he says and laughs before pushing my drink in front of me. "But it shows me your dedication."

He continues to talk, but I tune him out. Not because I'm not interested, but because he's so handsome I can't help but watch his facial expressions and the movement of his lips. They're fuller than those of most men—lush and completely kissable. The slight stubble on his face makes him look older and more domineering.

The same strand of hair that constantly falls in front of his face springs loose and rests against his forehead. I want to reach up and move it, just to touch him, but I resist the urge.

"What do you think?" he asks, pulling me from my appraisal of him.

"Can you repeat the question?" I smile, my cheeks burning with embarrassment.

He raises an eyebrow, and the corner of his lip twitches. "Do you want to meet me here again next weekend?"

Without hesitation, I say, "Yes." And I nod a little too eagerly.

"Good." He smiles and my heart flutters. "But I won't promise not to touch you next time."

I can't stop myself from smiling more. "I'd like that." I pull my bottom lip in between my teeth. If I am being completely honest, I want him to touch me right now.

"But not until you ask for it. Normally, if you were mine, I'd do what I want. But since we're new and you're still not convinced of your submissiveness, I'm going to go easy on you."

My eyes widen, and I'm caught off guard. "You are?"

He nods. "I won't for long, so don't get too used to it."

I lick my lips, his words sending a tingle down my spine. "What does easy mean?"

"If things work out and you agree, I'm going to make you mine. Then I expect complete submission."

My hand goes to my neck, and I can feel my heart racing under my arm. Hearing him say that makes my body ache for his touch. Which is odd, because no one has ever had this effect on me before.

I try to swallow the sudden dryness in my mouth. "I like the sound of that." I take a sip of my newly delivered champagne, relishing the coolness as it slides down my throat, and the sweetness skids across my tongue.

He rubs his chin with one hand and stares at me. "We'll see how this week goes, plus our time together next weekend, and then we'll check if you feel the same."

"This week?" I ask, choking on my drink.

His hand drops to his drink, moving it around the table and swirling it within the glass. "I'll be texting you all week. I expect you to wear the plug during the day while you're at work, but you can take it out once you get home. When the plug comes out, the bullet goes in."

I cough and grip my throat, trying to clear the last bit of champagne that's causing me to choke. "All day?" My voice is strangled as I reply.

"All. Day," he says, punctuating each word for effect. "Understood?"

My shoulders hunch, and I drop my voice to almost a whisper. "But I'm a teacher."

He raises an eyebrow, challenging me. "And your point is?"

Normally, I'd argue the point, hence my switch tendencies. But for some strange reason, I don't with him. What am I talking about? I know why I don't try to get out of it—because I want him.

The time I spent together with him, looking into his eyes and watching him touch himself, was the single most erotic period in my life. No other man has come even remotely close to his ability to turn me on.

"Fine," I mumble and turn the glass between my palms.

He laughs lightly, his face softening, and my belly flips in response. "Be good this week, and I'll make sure you enjoy next weekend."

My heart starts to race at the thought of him touching me. I stare at him, fantasizing about the moment he slides his thick, long shaft inside of me. I must've been lost in thought because my body jolts when he turns the bullet on full blast.

"Oh!" I moan and gasp when my palms flatten against the table.

"Pay attention to me when I speak," he says and turns it off.

Instantly, I miss the sensation and wonder how far to push my luck to get another shot. "Sorry, Sir."

"Better," he says and lifts the glass to his mouth. Again, I watch as his lips touch the glass, wishing I could feel his mouth on me.

"When you're alone this week, you're not allowed to come unless you ask for permission first."

I purse my lips and try not to let my frustration show. When I don't answer right away, the bullet starts again.

I'm happy for a moment, shifting my body and causing the plug to dig deeper in my ass.

"Alese?" he says.

"Yes! Yes!" I scream as my clit rubs against my thigh, and I'm close to coming before the vibrations die.

"You're already breaking the rules."

I glance down and peek through my eyelashes at him. His partially amused smile makes me blush. "I'm sorry." I clear my throat, and even I know it's bullshit as it comes out of my mouth.

"Repeat the last thing I told you." His eyes darken, and I wonder if I should push my luck but decide against it.

"I'm not allowed to come without permission." My voice isn't smooth, and I linger a little too long on the last word.

His hand clamps down on my leg, holding me in place as the bullet starts up—more intense than the last time. I want to squirm, but his hand stops me. *Bastard.*

"Good, *piccola*," he whispers to me, keeping his hand on my knee when the vibrations stop.

My back slumps into the corner of the booth, and I'm just as turned on as I was upstairs. This is going to be a long fucking week.

When we finish our drinks and he exhausts me with conversation, I wonder if I'll run home and instantly dig into my toy chest for my favorite vibrator.

"Don't even think about it," he says as if he read my mind while we stand at the door.

My eyebrows draw together as I peer up at his large frame. "What?" I play the innocent card and shrug my shoulders.

He leans forward, bringing his mouth so close to my ear that his lips are almost touching me. "Do not come. Don't test me, Alese, or you'll be sorry."

A shiver runs down my spine and my body clenches, the bullet and the plug making everything worse. His voice is so deep and sexy that I could almost get off from his words alone.

"Yes, Sir."

He places his hand on the small of my back and walks me to my car. I'm so turned on by his simple touch and his smell, besides everything else, that I wonder if I'll ever be able to fall asleep.

He opens the door, and I slide in. "Text me when you're home safely."

I nod and grip the keys tightly in my hand. "I will."

"Until next time, Alese," he says, closing the door and taking the air from my lungs with him.

I relax into the seat and allow myself to take a few deep, cleansing breaths. "Man, he's intense yet not," I say so only I can hear.

I start to giggle with excitement because, after months of secretly watching Ret, I've had my first taste and I want more.

Before I can move to start the car, I yelp. I grip the steering wheel, my fingers strangling the leather, before the vibrations stop.

Ret: Go home.

I laugh again and start to look around, finding that he has only backed up a few feet and is watching me with his arms crossed and his phone in one hand.

I wave and bite my lip, laughing softly as I start the car and pull away. My eyes are moving between the road and his reflection in my rearview mirror as I come to a stop at the exit.

I've never wanted to give myself to any man more than I want to throw myself at Ret's feet and beg him to become my Master.

I never thought that would happen. But there's something about him that makes me want to give up control. There's something in the way he talks to me that makes me feel wanted. I crave his attention, wondering when the next time will come that he'll text me or give me a command.

I'd never tell him, but the very idea excites me to no end.

CHAPTER SEVEN

Ret

I have to admit something to myself. Something I have been pushing out of my mind for the last week—I want Alese.

Not just to play with her, but I want to make her mine.

I'd just about given up on that possibility. No one seemed to excite me anymore, and no matter how hard I tried in a scene, the sizzle just wasn't there.

Alese was, in a simple word, fun.

I think she keeps me on my toes as much as I do her. She has just enough fight in her to make it almost a game, but a very sexy one.

She listened, for the most part, this week. Leaving the plug in and the bullet as requested. Once I caught her without it, asking for photographic evidence. She wasn't able to send a photo, and I told her she'd be punished for it.

Every night, we'd talk on the phone and discuss our days, and we covered every topic under the sun. I don't know if I've ever gotten to know a woman outside the bedroom as much as I have Alese.

Maybe that's the part I had been missing. Everything was always based around sex, with no other real-life experiences weighing in on the relationship.

The first three nights I let her come, but only on Skype with a perfect view of her pussy. I'd pleasure myself out of her view and watch as she used her finger to get off. The only vibrations she was allowed to feel were those of the bullet, which I controlled and used the entire time she played with herself.

With three days left until we'd see each other, I refused her request to orgasm. I wanted her primed and ready by the time I saw her again.

This was part of my begging master plan.

By the time the weekend rolls around, I am hornier than I think I've ever been. I don't remember walking around, even as a teenager, with a hard-on as much as I do when talking to her.

"Are you ready for tonight?" I ask her when I call about an hour before we are supposed to meet.

"Yes, Sir." Her voice is strong and sure.

"Meet me in the same room at seven. When you enter, remove your clothes and kneel in the middle of the floor with your head down. Leave the bullet and the plug in and fold your hands in your lap. I expect full cooperation, Alese."

"Yes, Sir," she replies, her voice wavering this time.

"Again, I won't touch you until you give me permission, but once you open that door, there's no turning back unless you say red or yellow. Understood?"

I can hear her swallow on the other end of the phone. "I do, Sir."

"I won't go beyond your limits, but I will test your boundaries."

"I expect nothing less, Master."

It's the first time she's called me Master, and my heart leaps in my chest. I smile, thankful I'm alone, and the heaviness in my balls grows. *Fuck*. I'm a perpetual hard-on with this woman.

"I'll see you in an hour, *piccola*. Be ready for the night of your life. I'm going to show you what it really means to be *mine*."

I surprise myself with the statement. It's been forever since I've used the word *mine*. No one has been worthy of the title. Alese did that. She made me want things, bigger than just a play partner. I want what Misha and Stella have, and for the first time, I believe it to be possible.

I walk into The Club just a few minutes after seven, not wanting to arrive before Alese. Mak catches me before I head upstairs.

"I saw Alese," he says with the biggest grin.

"And?" I ask, glancing toward the stairwell.

He raises his eyebrows and smirks. "I don't think I've ever seen her happier. I don't know what you did to that girl, but she almost floated through here."

I laugh. "Orgasm denial."

He nods and slaps my arm. "Works like a charm. Dare I say that you actually look..." He rubs his chin and studies me for a moment. "Happy?" It sounds more like a question than a statement.

"Unfuckingbelievable, but I am," I admit and rub my hands together. "I've been looking forward to this all week."

"I knew you two would hit it off." I tilt my head and purse my lips with the word *bullshit* hanging on the tip of my tongue, when he speaks again, "She just needed a real Dom to show her what she truly is."

"You shouldn't have let her struggle," I tell him and cross my arms in front of me.

"Sometimes you can't tell a person something. They need to find out the truth on their own."

"Uh-huh. *Bullshit,*" I cough into my shoulder. "I better go. She's probably waiting for me."

"No doubt. Have fun," he tells me as I start to walk away.

I wave to him over my shoulder and don't bother to look back. I can feel his smile, and I heard it in his last statement. I climb the stairs, taking them two at a time out of excitement.

When I reach the door to Private Room Two, I stand there and take a few deep breaths, fisting my hands at my sides. I roll my neck to relax, but even though I jacked off earlier, I'm just as hard as I was the moment my eyes opened this morning.

I turn the handle and see Alese, kneeling on the floor in a flawless position. Without being told, she faces the opposite direction with her legs spread, giving me the ideal view of her ass and the plug still nestled inside.

I groan softly and step inside, pushing the door closed with my ass and dropping my bag to the floor. I stare at her for a moment and don't move, hearing nothing but the sound of my heart hammering in my chest. I wipe my hands against my jeans and take a step forward.

"Perfect position, *piccola,*" I tell her, starting off with praise as I walk behind her. Her blond hair is cascading down her back, and it's the only thing visible on her body besides the plug.

She doesn't move and keeps her face cast downward. I kneel in front of her and see that her nipples are already hard, and her skin is pebbled with goose bumps. "Spread your legs wider," I say, but I keep my hands to myself.

She complies, spreading her legs wider, giving me a breathtaking view of her needy, wet pussy. Even with her face down, I can see the smile on her lips.

"Are you ready for tonight?" I already know the answer. We discussed it every night this week. She promised to give herself to me, to let me do what I felt was necessary, and if all works out, maybe I'd make her mine.

"I am," she whispers.

Her knees are red as they rest against the cold, cement floor, and she moves a bit, trying to stay in the position and relieve some of the pressure on her joints. I pop up and grab a crop from the wall.

Standing in front of her, I place my feet shoulder width apart and stare down at her, waiting for her to fidget again.

"Did you come today?" I ask, even though I know the answer. I just want to see if she'll squirm again knowing I have the crop in my hand.

"No, Sir," she answers quickly and doesn't move.

I tap the crop against my leg in plain sight for her to see. "Do you want to come?"

She grimaces and I know she's uncomfortable. No one has probably made her sit in this position, at least, not for very long. "I do," she says but forgets to call me Sir.

I slap the inside of her thigh, causing her to jump. "What did you say?"

"I do, Sir," she says quickly, sucking in a breath right after.

"Stand." I tap the crop against my leg a little harder, enough to make a noise as the leather makes contact. She stands without grace and keeps her eyes downcast as I watch. "Bend over and touch your toes."

For some women, this could be humiliating, but for Alese, it's exhilarating. I've watched her enough to be aware that it turns her on, knowing I'm looking at her. "Move your legs wider."

She moves them two feet apart then bends at the waist to grip her ankles. Her ass rises in the air, the plug moving with her and the bullet cord lying against her pussy, sparkling from her need in the overhead light.

She is teetering, trying to stay in position when I decide she could use a tiny obstacle. Reaching into my pocket, I pull out my phone and start the bullet.

Her body rocks forward, but surprisingly, she doesn't let go or fall over. A small part of me is sad, wanting to see her skin reddened by the crop. I run the leather across her bottom, following the curve of her ass.

She watches me from between her legs, and I tilt my head, letting her know I've caught her before cracking her across the ass. "Eyes down," I tell her as she grits her teeth not to cry out.

Moving the crop to the top center of her back, I trail it down her spine to her ass. "Get up on the table and position yourself on all fours."

I can tell she's relieved not to be in that position any longer because I know it's hell on the back. I've tried it myself and am not a fan. The women who can hold it for long periods deserve serious credit.

She raises her head, moving her knees and palms against the padded table until she finds a comfortable position. Placing the crop at the top of her ass crack, I slowly slide it down until I reach the plug. Moving quickly, I give the plug a few quick strikes and watch her body tense at the contact. "I think you need a bigger plug," I say, bending over to get a better look, and I feel my moderately hard cock turn into something harder than granite. "Wouldn't you agree?"

"Yes, Sir." Her head dips forward, and I know she's both excited and dreading the insertion of something bigger. Her ass is probably perfectly happy with the small plug pushing on just the right spots.

"Do you want to insert it or shall I?" I know this is the only decision I'll allow her to make tonight.

"You, please, Sir" Her voice is airy.

I drag my bag closer to the table and pull out a butt plug. I kneel, keeping my back straight so I'm eye level with her bottom, and slowly work the plug out. She moans softly, trying to hide the pleasure, but I can hear it loud and clear.

Alese is an ass girl. Based on what I saw in the first text photo she sent me, she loved playing with it herself.

When it pops free, I drop it to the floor and grab the lube to cover the new plug. Her ass is constricting at the loss. Before I begin to work the new plug in, I pull out my phone and start the bullet to make the transition more pleasurable for her.

Her ass rises and her stomach dips toward the table like she's trying to get more sensation. When the plug is covered, I touch it against her ass and she tenses. "Relax. It's not much bigger than the one you had in," I lie as I slowly push the tip inside her hole.

She groans and grips the sides of the table tightly. I pull back, giving her ass a chance to relax before pushing it in a little farther. Her groan turns into a moan the more I push it in and pull it out. Moments later, it's fully seated inside of her. I still haven't touched her with my hands and I'm dying to, probably more so than she is for me to touch her.

"Good girl," I say, giving her praise as the plug wiggles as she constricts around it. "Reach between your legs and remove the bullet." Doing it myself may risk skin-on-skin contact, and I won't do that until I know she's completely on board.

She reaches between her legs and pulls on the cord until the bullet slides out and dangles from her fingertips. I grab it quickly and set it on the floor next to the plug.

"Lie on your back." I grab a few more items from my bag and smile at what is about to happen next.

She watches me as I open my hand, showing her two nipple sucks. She bites her lip and blinks but doesn't protest. "I'm going to attach these," I tell her.

She nods, licking her lips as she stares at me. I lick the rim and move my hand above her breast, hovering over her already hardened nipples. "These shouldn't pinch." I place them against her skin.

When I release my fingers and the suction begins, she pulls in a sharp breath and her body twitches. She doesn't grimace or wince as I move to attach the second. Her eyes close and her mouth falls open as the second one takes hold. I flick it with my finger and her body jolts, her eyes flying open.

"Eyes on me, *piccola*." I bend over and grab a Hitachi wand and an extra-long, thick dildo and wonder how long it'll be before she's begging me to touch her. I'm about to find out how long she can go without coming before being driven mad with lust.

"I won't tie you up because you're not comfortable with it and we aren't going to test your boundaries in that way yet, but you need to grip the sides of the table and scoot down, taking the same position as last time you were up there."

She nods slowly and moves her bottom down to the edge.

"Feet too," I tell her and tap the end of the table with the large dildo. Her eyes widen as she sees it before she puts the back of her head against the table and wiggles her fingers, gripping the table harder.

I touch her knees with the wand, pushing them farther apart. She squeezes her eyes shut, and I lean forward and flick the suction cup attached to her right nipple. Her body jerks and her eyes fly open, meeting mine. "No closing your eyes and absolutely no coming."

Without using my hands, it's pretty hard to discipline her. I wish I had three hands at this moment. It would make my life so much easier.

She nods and I rest the dildo on the table, reaching in my bag for something else. I can't gag her, but I want to cut down on the amount of noise I know she's about to make.

"Open," I tell her, holding a piece of leather in front of her mouth. "I won't gag you, but I need you not to be as loud as I know you will be."

She opens her mouth, her eyes growing wider before she clamps down around the leather I'd set on her lips.

Before I pick up the rubbery dildo, I press a button on the plug, one I hadn't shared with her. It comes to life, sending powerful vibrations through her. She moans, her teeth bearing down against the leather strap.

Gripping the dildo in one hand, I rub it against her wetness. I love that about her. She always seems ready and willing for me. I don't know if she's like this all the time, but the thought that it is only for me gives me a secret thrill.

I work it inside her slowly—an inch at a time—and let her greedy pussy adjust to the fullness of the new plug. She groans, lifting her bottom from the table, and I pull the dildo all the way out.

"Do you want to come?" I ask, peering down at her body. She nods and mumbles against the leather strap. "Do not move, or you'll go home unsatisfied."

I fucking hope she can follow this order because if she goes home needy, I sure as fuck do too.

I push against her opening, sliding the first three inches in slowly and past the biggest part of the plug. I flick on the wand with my thumb and use my other hand to rest it against her already enlarged clit.

Her toes move, curling around the table, but the rest of her stays still. Poor thing. I'm not letting her come until I can fuck her, but she doesn't know that.

I can feel her pussy clamping down against the dildo, making my progress a little harder but not impossible.

Lifting the wand off her, I refuse her the orgasm that's no doubt already building inside of her. The wand is the most powerful vibrator on the market. No one could stop the orgasm from coming using it, and it is my favorite weapon when forcing a woman to orgasm multiple times.

When her muscles relax and I can push the dildo deeper inside her, I restart the wand and her muscles tense again immediately. I work the dildo in and out of her, moving faster and then slowing my pace. Every thirty seconds or so, I lift the wand long enough so her nearing climax will slip away. I repeat this over and over again until her chest's heaving and her body's covered in sweat.

I turn the wand up, making the vibrations more powerful and making the orgasm come quicker. But again, I deny it as soon as her body starts to shake. She's moaning and groaning around the strap, tiny dribbles of spit sliding down the sides of her face.

My cock is in a bad way. Hard as stone and straining to break free, but I concentrate on her and don't pay any attention to my needs.

Her bottom starts to move off the table, chasing the wand as I remove it from her clit. In response, I pull the dildo out quickly, leaving her with nothing but a full ass.

"Please," she groans, biting down on the strap with teary eyes. "Please, I need to come."

"You want to come, but you don't need to," I tell her, and I don't feel an ounce of guilt.

"Touch me," she begs.

"Not yet," I tell her and press the dildo against her opening, pushing it inside slowly.

Once it's fully seated, I hold the wand against her clit, and her knees start to shake. Working the dildo in and out, I watch her body as it reacts, craving the stimulation. Again, when I see her breathing start to falter, I move the wand away and deny her again.

"Fuck," she screams. "Please, Sir. Touch me. I need you."

"I'll give you a choice." I hold up the wand and show it to her. "You can have the wand and no dildo, or you can have my cock. Which one do you want?"

She lifts her head and catches a glimpse of my bulge straining to break free. She's wonderfully sexy, spread-eagled with a strap in her mouth, completely mindless with lust. "Your cock, please, Sir."

"Are you offering yourself to me?"

"I need you inside me," she says as more saliva dribbles down her chin.

I smile, pleased with her willingness to accept my cock over the wand—not all women would make the same choice. I reach under the table and pull out the stirrups, wanting to get better access to her tight, warm pussy. "Spit out the strap." I want to hear her moan as I thrust my length inside of her.

Her eyes draw together, and I can see she's piecing together that I could've given her the stirrups to use earlier, which would've made it easier on her, but that wasn't the point to this evening.

I unzip my pants, pushing them down before kicking them to the side. Digging around in my bag, I grab a condom from the box and tear it open with my teeth. My need is so strong, my hands are almost shaking. I can feel it, but it's not visible—at least, I hope it's not. Rolling the condom down my shaft becomes a chore; the damn thing barely fits. After a moment of struggle with her eyes watching my every movement, it's finally in place.

I step forward, standing between her legs, and I touch her knees with my bare hand. It's the first flesh-on-flesh contact I've had with her in a sexual way. "Are you sure?" I ask because... I don't know. I've never asked someone more than once, but I'm having way too much fun with Alese to do anything to fuck it up.

"Please fuck me," she begs, and her eyes plead with me to hurry it the fuck up.

I fist my cock, stroking it as I take a step closer. "I want you to be mine, Alese. Can you do that? Can you leave your switch behind?" I poke her opening with the tip of my dick and she gasps. "Do you want to become my submissive, my partner?"

Her eyes widen, and her mouth falls open. I can see her throat bob as she swallows. "Yes. I want to be yours," she replies with so much conviction that I believe every word.

"Brace yourself," I tell her. "You're in for one hell of a ride."

Mine. I push inside of her in one quick, unforgiving thrust.

Mine. I pull back and spread her knees wider before gripping the tops of her hips in my hands, holding her body so it can't escape the impact.

"Are you mine?" I ask her, slamming into her again.

Her pussy clenches around my cock, sucking me deeper. "Yes, Master," she moans as tears start to stream down her face.

Master.

A week ago, I never would've thought I'd be here right now, claiming someone as my own. If anyone would've said it would be Alese that I'd choose as my partner, I would've told them they were fucking mad.

Somehow, it happened, though. I am buried balls deep inside her sweet, warm cunt, and I know I am home.

EPILOGUE

Alese
Six months later

My eyes are downcast as I sit next to Ret, with his hand resting on my thigh. I'm to be seen and not heard until I'm given permission to speak.

"How are things going with your sub?" Misha asks like I'm an object and can't hear.

Ret's hand tightens in warning because he felt my body tense. "I couldn't be happier. Alese has come along faster than I would've expected."

Faster than expected. What the fuck does that mean?

I glance up with my eyelashes and bite the inside of my cheek to hide my scowl.

Misha laughs, his hand slapping against the table. "Somehow, you turned someone who couldn't make a decision about what she wanted to be into the docile creature at your side."

"She wasn't undecided. She just hadn't found the man to help her accept her true nature."

Stella moves slightly, tapping my toe with hers, and I can almost read her thoughts.

We've become friends because our Masters are friends. She's been a lifesaver. When I have a question

I don't want to ask Ret, which happens often, I turn to Stella for the help.

"Well, she's like an entirely different person," Misha says.

My fingernails dig into the leather seat because I'm still me. Men seem to overstate their importance in changing us. Stella told me that men just want their egos stroked and to feel important, and I can see how that is true in Misha's case, maybe. But Ret, he's an entirely different creature.

The silent type. The strong man who doesn't need to say much to convey his message. A little touch is all it takes to let me know how he feels or what he needs.

By his grip on my leg, he can read my body language, and he is giving me a silent warning not to respond.

"So how's work, Ret? Working on an exciting case?"

"It's been busy, but some opportunities have opened elsewhere. I may be moving soon," Ret replies, and it sends my stomach into a tailspin.

We talked about his possible move last week. I never really knew what Ret did until we started on this journey together. I found out he was a bounty hunter and traveled the world in search of criminals. The thought of him risking his life makes my heart ache.

"Where to?" Misha asks.

"I have a few possibilities." Ret's being cagey with his answer, and his hand lightens on my thigh before his thumb starts to stroke my skin, calming me.

"We'll miss you if you leave. What about Alese?"

"We haven't decided if she'll follow."

My body tenses with his response. I did decide, though. I just haven't shared the news with him. He asked me if I wanted to go with him, and in that moment,

I wanted to say yes, but he told me to think about it. I know it's a big decision, but there's nothing really here for me without him.

I would still have my job, but I could be a teacher anywhere. The one thing I wouldn't have is Ret. He's not replaceable. I tried for years to find my other half, the one who got me, and now that I've finally found him...I won't lose him.

"Sorry to cut this short, Misha, but I need to speak with Alese for a while."

"I'm sure you're going to do a lot of talking." Misha laughs.

Ret's hand tightens on my thigh as he pulls me with him out of the booth. I follow behind him, my eyes still staring at the floor and my stomach doing backflips.

I know exactly where we're going when we start to climb the steps. We're not going to talk at all. We're headed to the private rooms, but instead of going to our usual room, he takes me through a different door.

"Sit on the bed." Ret stands at the entrance to the room, holding the door open for me.

I don't speak when I walk past him. I sit and fold my hands in my lap, staring at his feet as he walks in my direction.

"Alese," he says and kneels on the floor in front of me. "Look at me." His hands cover mine.

I drag my eyes to his.

"We need to talk about me leaving town."

I nod slowly, but I don't speak.

"Do you want to come with me?"

I nod again.

"Speak to me."

"Yes, Master Ret. I want to go with you."

"You sure you want to give up your job and life here in Texas to follow me?"

"I'm completely sure. There's nothing here for me without you."

His hand finds my cheek and strokes it so tenderly I can feel tears threatening to form. "It's a big step, *piccola*."

"I know," I say in a quiet voice. "But I know what I want, and I want you, Master Ret."

His thumb glides across my bottom lip, and my heart skips a beat. "I love you, Alese."

It goes from skipping to a dead stop. "You love me?" My mouth hangs open, and the tears I'd been able to control start to well in my eyes.

"I do," he says, smiling at me with such tenderness that my heart starts again, but it's now beating in an erratic rhythm.

"I love you too," I whisper and blink, letting a tear fall down my cheek.

He swipes it away with the pad of his thumb. "You've made me so happy."

"You've changed my life," I say as more tears begin to follow the path of the first.

"Let's celebrate," he says as he stands and places his hands on his hips.

"Um," I mumble and wonder what the man has up his sleeves. Using the back of my hand, I wipe away the tears.

"Undress and kneel," he commands me.

And as if we didn't just profess our love for each other, I stand, removing my clothes slowly while I watch him. The look of lust in his eyes is unmistakable.

When I kneel, I rest my hands in my lap and wait. He

wanders away, and I watch out of the corner of my eye to see what he has planned.

He undresses, placing his clothes on a chair across the room. When he steps in front of me, his massive hard-on in my face, I wait for his command.

"Climb up on the bed and lie down," he says without touching me.

My eyebrows draw together as I crawl onto the bed with my back to him.

"Do you know what I'm going to do to you?" he asks as he climbs onto the bed and covers my body with his.

I shake my head and brace myself.

"I'm going to make love to you, Alese."

I gasp before his mouth covers mine, sucking the air from my lungs. Ret makes love to me. He doesn't toy with me, holding my orgasms just out of reach. Instead, he's gentle, loving, and slow.

And I know that I've made the right decision. I'm no longer alone. My biggest fear of becoming a reclusive cat lady is no longer on the table. I have my other half.

On the outside, to people not in the life, I must look weak. But loving a man, no matter who he is, takes the strongest person in the world. Giving myself to him completely and trusting that he'll do what's right is my biggest leap of faith.

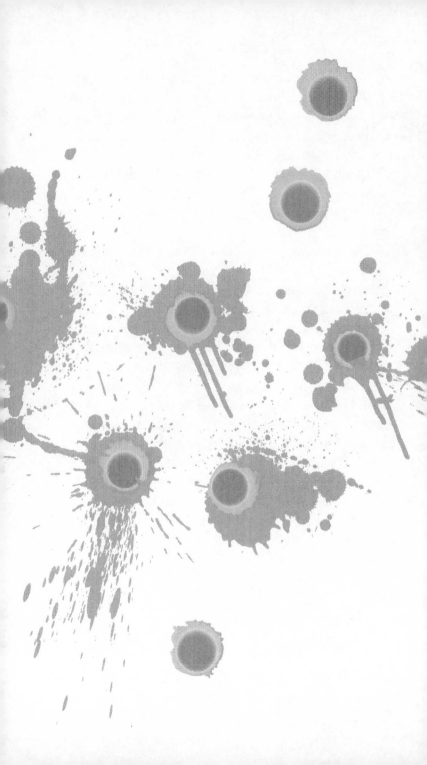

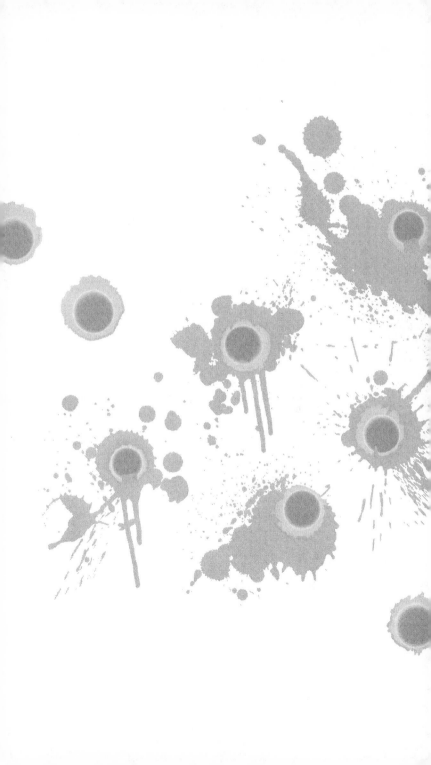

Made in the USA
Columbia, SC
29 January 2022